LÉON AND LOUISE

A Novel

ALEX CAPUS

Translated by
John Brownjohn

This edition has been translated with the financial assistance of Pro Helvetia, the Arts Council of Switzerland

prohelvetia

First published in German as *Léon und Louise* by Alex Capus
© 2011 Carl Hanser Verlag München

First published in 2012 by
HAUS PUBLISHING LTD.
70 Cadogan Place, London SW1X 9AH
www.hauspublishing.com

Translation copyright © 2011 John Brownjohn

ISBN 978 1 908323 13 2

Typeset in Garamond by MacGuru Ltd
info@macguru.org.uk

*Your parents' nudity doesn't bear
overly close inspection*
ÉRIK ORSENNA

For Aaron

1

We were sitting in the cathedral of Notre Dame, waiting for the priest. Multicoloured sunlight slanted down through the rose window on to the open, flower-bedecked coffin on the red carpet in front of the high altar. A Capuchin monk was on his knees before the Pietà in the ambulatory, a stonemason perched on some scaffolding in a side aisle. The abrasive noises he was making with his trowel went echoing around the 800-year-old pile. That apart, peace reigned. It was nine o'clock in the morning; the tourists were still having breakfast in their hotels.

We mourners were not numerous. The dead man had lived for so long, most of his friends and acquaintances had predeceased him. Seated in the front pew were his two sons, his daughter and daughters-in-law, and his twelve grandchildren, of whom six were still unmarried, four married, and two divorced. Right on the outside sat the four great-grandchildren – they would eventually number twenty-three – who had been born before 16 April 1986. In the gloom behind us, stretching away to the exit, were fifty-eight empty rows – a sea of unoccupied pews that would doubtless have accommodated all of our ancestors back to the twelfth century.

We were an absurdly small congregation for such an enormous church. That we were sitting there at all was a final joke on the part of my grandfather, who had been a forensic chemist at the Quai des Orfèvres and was highly contemptuous of the priesthood. Were he ever to die, he announced in his latter years, he wanted a funeral service in Notre Dame. When it was objected that the location of the house of God should be a matter of indifference to an unbeliever, and that the local church around the corner would be more appropriate for a modest family like ours, he replied, 'No, no, *mes enfants,* get me Notre Dame. It's a few hundred metres further and will cost a bit, but you'll manage it. Incidentally, I'd like a Latin mass, not a French one. The old liturgy, please, with plenty of incense, long recitatives and some Gregorian chant.' Then he smirked beneath his moustache at the thought that his descendants would chafe their knees raw on hard hassocks for two-and-a-half hours. His joke appealed to him so much that he incorporated it in his repertoire of stock phrases. 'Unless I've made a trip to Notre Dame by then,' he would say, or, 'Happy Easter, *au revoir* in Notre Dame!' From being one of his stock phrases, my grandfather's joke eventually became a prophecy, and when his hour actually struck we all realized what had to be done.

So there he now lay, waxen-nosed and with eyebrows raised in an expression of surprise, on the very spot where Napoleon Bonaparte had been crowned Emperor of the French, while we sat in the pews which his brothers, sisters and generals had occupied 182 years before us. Time went by and still the priest didn't appear. The rays of sunlight were no longer falling on the coffin, but on the black and white chequerboard flagstones to its right. The sacristan emerged from the gloom, lit a few candles, and withdrew again. The children shuffled around on the pews, the men kneaded their necks, the women straightened their backs. My cousin Nicolas produced his puppets from an overcoat pocket and treated the children to a performance whose highlight came when the stubble-chinned thief hit pointy-capped Guignol on the head with his club.

Then, far behind us, a little side door beside the main entrance opened with a faint creak. We turned to look. Streaming in through the widening gap came the light of a warm spring morning and the sounds of the Rue de la Cité. A small grey figure wearing a bright red foulard slipped into the nave.

'Who's that?'

'Is she one of us?'

'Is she part of the family?'

'Or could it be…?'

'You think?'

'Never!'

'Didn't you pass her on the stairs one time?'

'Yes, but it was pretty dark.'

'Stop staring.'

'Where's the priest got to?'

'Does anyone know who she is?'

'Is it…?'

'Maybe…'

'Would you all be quiet!'

I could tell at a glance that the woman wasn't a member of the family. Those short, brisk strides and the hard high heels that sounded like hands clapping as they hit the flagstones? That little black hat with the black veil and the proudly jutting chin beneath it? That deft sign of the cross and that graceful little genuflection beside the stoup? She couldn't be a Le Gall. Not by birth, at least.

Little black hats and deft signs of the cross just aren't us. We Le Galls are tall, phlegmatic folk of Norman stock who take long, deliberate strides. Above all, our family is a family of men. Women belong to it too, of course – women we have married – but whenever a child is born to us he tends to be a boy. I myself have four sons but no daughter; my father has three sons and one daughter; and his father – the Léon Le Gall who lay in the coffin that morning – also sired three boys and a girl. We have strong hands, wide foreheads and broad shoulders, wear no jewellery other than a wristwatch and wedding ring, and have a predilection for plain clothes devoid of frills and furbelows. We couldn't tell you, without checking, the colour of the shirt we're wearing. We seldom have headaches or stomach-upsets, and even when we do succumb to them we sheepishly conceal the fact because our notion of manliness precludes the possibility that our heads or our stomachs – especially not our stomachs – are soft and susceptible to pain.

First and foremost, though, the backs of our heads – our occiputs – are conspicuously flat, a peculiarity much derided by the women we marry. If informed of a birth in the family, the first question we ask relates not to the baby's weight, stature or hair colour, but to the back of its head. 'What's it like, flat? Is it a genuine Le Gall?' And when one of us is carried to the grave, we console ourselves with the thought that a Le Gall's head never lolls around on its final journey but lies nice and flat on the floor of the coffin.

I share the morbid sense of humour and cheerful melancholy common to my brothers, father and grandfathers. I like being a Le Gall. Many of us have a weakness for drink and tobacco, but we have a good prospect of longevity and, like many families, we firmly believe that, although we're nothing special, we're unique notwithstanding.

This illusion cannot be substantiated and is wholly

unfounded. To the best of my knowledge, no Le Gall has ever achieved anything worthy of remembrance by the world at large. This is attributable first to our lack of any outstanding talents, secondly to indolence, thirdly to the fact that as adolescents most of us develop an arrogant contempt for the initiation rites of a conventional education, and fourthly to the strong aversion to Church, police and intellectual authority that is almost invariably handed down from father to son.

This is why our academic careers end usually after secondary school but at latest after our third or fourth term at university. It is only every few decades that a Le Gall manages to complete his studies properly and reconcile himself to secular or religious authority. He then becomes a lawyer, doctor or cleric and earns the family's respect, albeit coupled with a touch of mistrust.

A certain amount of posthumous fame does, however, attach to my great-great-uncle Serge Le Gall, who was expelled from school for taking opium and became a warder at Caen Penitentiary shortly after the Franco-Prussian War. He went down in the annals because he tried to end a prison riot peacefully and without the usual bloodbath, an endeavour for which one of the convicts thanked him by splitting his skull with an axe. Another forebear distinguished himself by designing a stamp for the Vietnamese postal service, and my father laid oil pipelines in the Algerian Sahara as a young man. For the rest, however, we Le Galls earn our bread as scuba instructors, lorry drivers or civil servants. We sell palm trees in Brittany and German motorcycles to the Nigerian traffic police, and one of my cousins is a private detective who hunts down runaway debtors for the Société Générale.

But if most of us cope with life quite well, we owe this mainly to our wives. My sisters-in-law, aunts and paternal grandmothers are all strong, efficient, warm-hearted women who exercise a discreet but undisputed matriarchy. Many of them are more successful and earn more than their menfolk. They handle the tax returns and do battle with school authorities, and their husbands repay them by being gentle and dependable.

We tend to be peace-loving spouses, I believe. We don't tell lies and do our best not to drink to a physically pernicious extent, we steer clear of other women and are DIY enthusiasts, and we're definitely fonder of children than most. At family get-togethers it's customary for the men to look after the babies and infants while the women sun themselves on the beach or go shopping. Our wives appreciate the fact that expensive cars aren't essential to our happiness and that we've no need to fly to Barbados to play golf, and they take an indulgent view of our compulsion to frequent flea markets and come home laden with peculiar objects. Total strangers' photo albums, mechanical apple-peelers, worn-out slide projectors for which slides of the correct format have long been unobtainable, genuine naval telescopes that display everything upside down, surgical saws, rusty revolvers, worm-eaten gramophones and electric guitars with every other fret missing – we blithely tote such curious oddments home and spend months cleaning, polishing and trying to repair them before giving them away, taking them back to the flea market, or dumping them in the dustbin. We do this to restore our vegetative system. Dogs eat grass, well-educated young ladies listen to Chopin, university professors watch football, and we mess around with old junk. At night, when the children are asleep, a remarkable number of us produce modest oil paintings. And one of us, as I know at first-hand, secretly writes poems. Not very good ones, alas.

The front row of pews in Notre Dame was vibrating with suppressed excitement. Could the new arrival really be Mademoiselle Janvier? Had she really dared to turn up? The womenfolk looked rigidly to the front again and stiffened their backs as if the coffin and the eternal light over the high altar were their sole focus of attention. But we men, who knew our women, realized that they were tensely listening to the staccato click of the little footsteps that made their way sideways into the central aisle. They then performed a ninety-degree turn and, without the least hesitation, without any *ritardando* or *accelerando*, pressed on with the regular beat of a metronome. Those of us who were peering out of the corner of our eye could then see a little woman, light-footed as a young girl, climb the two red-carpeted steps to the foot of the coffin, rest her right hand on the side, and silently move along it to the head, where she at last came to a halt and remained for several seconds, almost like a soldier standing at attention. She raised her veil and bent over. Spreading her arms and supporting herself on the sides of the coffin, she kissed my grandfather on the forehead and rested her cheek against his waxen visage as if intending to stay there for a while. She did so with her face in full view, not protectively averted in the direction of the altar. This enabled us to see that her eyes were closed and that her red, carefully made-up lips were curved in a smile that grew steadily broader until they parted to emit an inaudible chuckle.

She released the dead man at last and resumed her erect stance. Taking her handbag from the crook of her arm, she opened it and quickly removed a circular, dully glinting object the size of a fist. This, as we were to discover soon afterwards, was an old bicycle bell with a hemispherical top whose chrome plating was threaded with hairline cracks and had peeled off in places. Having closed the handbag and replaced it in the crook of her arm, she rang the bell twice. Rri-rring. Rri-rring. While the sound went echoing down the nave, she deposited the bell in the coffin, then turned and looked us in the eye, one after another. Beginning on the far left, where the youngest children were seated beside their fathers, she surveyed the entire row, her eyes lingering for perhaps a second on each individual. When she got to the far right she gave us a triumphant smile and set off. Heels clicking, she hurried past the family and down the central aisle to the exit.

2

My grandfather was seventeen when he first met Louise Janvier. I like to picture him as a very young man in the spring of 1918, when he strapped a reinforced cardboard suitcase to the luggage rack of his bicycle and left the parental home for ever.

What I know about him as a young man doesn't amount to very much. A surviving family photograph of the period shows a sturdy lad with a high forehead and unruly fair hair eyeing the photographer with an inquisitive air and his head on one side. I also know from his own accounts, which he delivered laconically and with feigned reluctance as an old man, that he often skipped secondary school because he preferred to roam the beaches of Cherbourg with his friends Patrice and Joël.

It was on a stormy Sunday in January 1918, when no sensible person would have ventured within sight of the sea, that the trio discovered, amid flurries of snow, the wreck of a little sailing dinghy washed up on the furze-covered embankment. It was holed amidships and slightly scorched overall. The boys dragged the boat behind the nearest bush. In the weeks that followed, since the legal owner never got in touch with them, they personally and with great enthusiasm repaired and sanded and painted it until it looked brand-new and was unrecognizable. From then on they spent every spare hour out in the Channel, fishing, dozing and smoking dried seaweed in tobacco pipes carved from corn cobs. And when something interesting was bobbing in the water – a plank, a hurricane lamp from a sunken vessel or a lifebelt – they went off with it. Warships sometimes steamed past so close that their little craft skipped up and down like a calf turned out to graze on the first day of spring. They often remained at sea all day long, rounded the cape and sailed westwards until the Channel Islands appeared on the horizon, not returning to land until dusk had fallen. At weekends they spent the night in a fisherman's hut whose owner hadn't had time to board up his little rear window properly on the day he was mobilized.

Léon Louis Le Gall's father – my great-grandfather, in other words – knew nothing about his son's sailing dinghy, but he was somewhat concerned to note his habit of gallivanting on the beach. A chain-smoking, prematurely aged Latin master, he had chosen to study the language at an early age purely to cause his own father as much vexation he could. He subsequently paid for this pleasure by spending decades in the teaching profession, becoming mean, hidebound and bitter in consequence.

In order to justify his Latin to himself and continue to feel alive, he had acquired an encyclopaedic knowledge of the relics of Roman civilization in Brittany and cultivated this hobby with a passion in grotesque contrast to the limited nature of the subject. Agonizingly monotonous and wreathed in cigarette smoke, his endless classroom lectures on potsherds, thermal baths and military roads were not only legendary but dreaded throughout the school. His pupils compensated by watching his cigarette, waiting for him to write on the blackboard with it and puff at the piece of chalk instead.

That his asthma had exempted him from military service on the day general mobilization was proclaimed he regarded as a blessing on the one hand and a disgrace on the other, because he found himself the only man in a common room full of women. He had flown into a terrible rage when informed by these female colleagues that his only son had hardly been seen in school for weeks, and his lectures at the kitchen table, designed to convince the boy of the value of a classical education, had been interminable. Léon, who merely sneered at the value of a classical education, tried in his turn to explain why his presence on the beach was now indispensable: because the Germans had recently taken to disguising their submarines with wooden superstructures, coloured paintwork, makeshift sails and fake fishing nets.

His father thereupon demanded to know where, pray, was the causal connection between German submarines and Léon's absence from school.

The disguised German U-boats, Léon explained patiently, would sneak up on French trawlers undetected and sink them without mercy, thereby worsening the French nation's food supply situation.

'Well?' said his father, trying to stifle a cough. Any form of agitation could bring on an asthma attack.

Extremely valuable jetsam – teak, brass, steel, sailcloth, oil by the barrel – was washed up every day.

'Well?' said his father.

These precious raw materials, said Léon, had to be salvaged before the sea washed them away again.

While their argument headed inexorably for its dramatic climax, father and son continued to sit there in the seemingly relaxed and nonchalant pose characteristic of all Le Galls. They had stretched out their legs beneath the kitchen table and were leaning back so far that their buttocks had almost lost contact with the seats of their chairs. Being tall and heavily built, they were both extremely sensitive to gravity and knew that the horizontal position approximates most closely to a state of weightlessness because each part of the body has to support itself alone and is unencumbered by the rest, whereas sitting or standing stacks them one on top of another. They were angry, and their voices, almost indistinguishable now that Léon's had broken, were shaking with barely suppressed fury.

'You'll go back to school tomorrow,' said Le Gall senior, struggling to quell a cough that was ascending his throat from the depths of his chest.

The national war economy was heavily dependent on raw materials, Léon countered.

'You'll go back to school tomorrow,' said his father.

Léon urged him to think of the national war economy. He was worried to note his father's laboured breathing.

'The national war economy can kiss my ass,' his father gasped. Conversation was thereafter interrupted by a paroxysm of coughing that lasted a minute.

Besides, Léon added, beachcombing was a nice source of pocket money.

'In the first place,' his father wheezed, 'it's illegal, and secondly, the school's truancy rules apply to everyone, you and your friends included. I don't like you taking liberties.'

Léon asked what his father had against liberty, and whether he had ever reflected that any law deserving of obedience should be subject to interpretation.

'You take liberties just for the sake of it, growled his father. 'Well?'

'It's essential to any rule that it applies to everyone regardless of who they are, and particularly to those who think they're smarter than everyone else.'

'But it's an undeniable fact that some people *are* smarter than others,' Léon cautiously objected.

'In the first place, that's irrelevant,' said his father. 'Secondly, you haven't so far – to the best of my knowledge – aroused suspicions of any outstanding intellectual capacity in class. You'll go back to school tomorrow.'

'No, I won't,' said Léon.

'You'll go back to school tomorrow!' yelled his father.

'I'm never going back to school!' Léon yelled back.

'As long as you're living under my roof, you'll do as I say!'

'You can't give me orders!'

After this positively classic altercation, the dispute developed into a scuffle in which the two of them rolled around on the kitchen floor like schoolboys and bloodshed was avoided only because my great-grandmother swiftly and courageously intervened.

'Enough of this,' she said, hauling the pair to their feet by the ears, one of them in tears and the other on the verge of asphyxia. 'You, *chéri,* will now take your *laudanum* and go to bed – I'll be up in two minutes. And you, Léon, since the national war economy means so much to you, will go to the mayor's office first thing tomorrow and report for labour service.'

It emerged next morning that the national war economy really could find a use for Léon Le Gall, the Cherbourg schoolboy – but not on the beach as he had hoped. On the contrary, the mayor threatened him with three months' imprisonment if he ever again acquired jetsam contrary to the law. He also questioned him closely about any other knowledge and talents he had that might be relevant to the war economy.

It turned out that, although well-built, Léon was disinclined to expend any muscular energy. He didn't want to be a farmhand or an assembly-line worker, nor did he care to be a blacksmith's or carpenter's dogsbody. The same went for his intellectual energies. He wasn't actually dim, but he'd displayed no preference for any particular subject at school and hadn't distinguished himself in any, so he had no firm plans or wishes regarding his future occupation. He would gladly, of course, have taken his sailing dinghy out into the Channel on voyages of espionage and destabilized the enemy's currency by circulating forged reichsmarks on the German coast. This being no realistic professional prospect, however, he merely shrugged when the mayor questioned him about his plans.

His interest in the national war economy had completely evaporated by now. To make matters worse, the mayor had a neck like a turkey and a blue-veined nose. Being endowed with a strong aesthetic sense like most young people, Léon failed to understand how anyone could take a person with such a neck and nose seriously. Glumly, the mayor went through the list of situations vacant sent him by the Ministry of War.

'Let's see. Ah, here. Can you drive a tractor?'

'No, monsieur.'

'And here. Arc welder required. Can you weld?'

'No, monsieur.'

'I see. I assume you can't grind lenses either?'

'No, monsieur.'

'Or wind armatures for electric motors? Drive a tram? Turn gun barrels on a lathe?' The mayor chuckled. This business was beginning to amuse him.

'No, monsieur.'

'Are you by any chance a specialist in internal medicine? An expert on mercantile law? An electrical engineer? An architectural draughtsman? A saddler or cartwright?'

'No, monsieur.'

'I thought as much. You don't know anything about tanning leather or double-entry bookkeeping either, eh? And Swahili – do you speak Swahili? Can you tap-dance? Do Morse? Calculate the tensile strength of suspension bridge cables?'

'Yes, monsieur.'

'What? Swahili? Suspension bridge cables?'

'No, Morse, monsieur. I can do Morse.'

Le Petit Inventeur, a young people's magazine to which Léon subscribed, had in fact reproduced the Morse alphabet a few weeks earlier. On a whim, he had spent a rainy afternoon learning it by heart.

'Is that true, youngster? You aren't pulling my leg?'

'No, monsieur.'

'Then this would be something in your line! The station at Saint-Luc-sur-Marne is looking for an assistant Morse telegraphist to replace the regular employee. Making out waybills, reporting arrivals and departures, helping to sell tickets if necessary. Think you could do that?'

'Yes, monsieur.'

'Male, minimum age sixteen. Homosexuals, persons suffering from venereal diseases and Communists need not apply. You aren't, I suppose, a Communist?'

'No, monsieur.'

'Then Morse me something. Morse me – let's see – ah yes: "Out of the deep have I called unto Thee, O Lord." Well, go on. Do it on the desk top!'

Léon drew a deep breath, glanced up at the ceiling and proceeded to drum on the desk with the middle finger of his right hand. Dash, dash, dash, dot-dot-dash, dash...

'That'll do,' said the mayor, who didn't know the Morse code and was incapable of assessing Léon's digital dexterity.

'I can Morse, monsieur. Where is Saint-Luc-sur-Marne, please?'

'On the Marne, you blockhead. Don't worry, the front line is somewhere else now. It's an urgent request, you can start right away. You'll even get paid. A hundred and twenty francs a month.'

⁂

This was how it came about that, one spring morning in 1918, Léon Le Gall strapped his cardboard suitcase to the luggage rack of his bicycle, kissed his mother tenderly, hugged his father after a moment's hesitation, mounted his bike, and pedalled off. He accelerated as if he had to take to the air at the end of the Rue des Fossées like Louis Blériot, who had lately flown across the Channel in his home-made aeroplane with its ash struts and bicycle wheels. He sped past the shabby but bravely respectable lower middle-class homes in which his friends Patrice and Joël were just dunking yesterday's sawdusty wartime bread in their coffee, past the bakery that had supplied nearly every morsel of bread he'd eaten in his life, and past the secondary school in which his father would continue to earn his living for another fourteen years, three months and two weeks. He rode past the big harbour in which an American grain tanker was lying peacefully cheek by jowl with some British and French warships, crossed the bridge and turned right into the Avenue de Paris, blithely heedless of the fact that he might never see any of this again. Passing the warehouses, cranes and dry docks, he rode out of the town and into the endless meadows and pastureland of Normandy. After ten minutes his route was barred by a herd of cows and he had to stop. From then on he rode more slowly.

It had rained during the night, so the road was pleasantly damp and free from dust. The steaming meadows were dotted with grazing cattle and apple trees in blossom. Léon rode towards the sun. He had a gentle west wind at his back and made rapid progress. After an hour he removed his jacket and strapped it to his suitcase. He overtook a cart drawn by a mule. Then he met a peasant woman pushing a handcart and passed a lorry standing beside the road with its engine smoking. He saw no horses; he had read in the *Petit Inventeur* that nearly all the horses in France were in use at the front.

At noon he ate the ham sandwich his mother had packed for him and drank some water from a village fountain. In the afternoon he lay down under an apple tree. Squinting up at its pink and white blossom and pale-green leaves, he noticed that it hadn't been pruned for years.

That evening he reached Caen, where he was to spend the night at his Aunt Simone's. She was the youngest sister of the Serge Le Gall whose skull a prison inmate had split with an axe. It was a few years since Léon had last seen her; he remembered the full breasts beneath her blouse, her laughter, her big, red, womanly mouth, and the fact that her kite had soared higher than anyone else's on the beach. Shortly after that, though, her husband and her two sons had gone off to war. Since then, mad with grief and worry, Aunt Simone had been writing three letters a day to Verdun.

———

17

'So there you are,' she said, ushering him inside. The house smelt of mothballs and dead flies. Her hair was unkempt and her lips were cracked and bloodless. She was holding a rosary in her right hand.

Léon kissed her on both cheeks and passed on messages from his parents.

'There's some bread and cheese on the kitchen table,' she said. 'And a bottle of cider, if you want.'

He handed her the toasted almonds his mother had given him as a gift for his hostess.

'Thanks. Now go to the kitchen and eat. You'll be sleeping with me tonight, the bed's big enough.'

Léon's eyes widened.

'You can't have the boys' room, I had to let that and our bedroom to some refugees from the north, and I sold the sofa in the parlour because I needed room for the bed.'

Léon opened his mouth to say something.

'Don't make fuss, the bed's wide enough,' she said running her fingers through her lifeless hair. 'It's been a long day. I'm tired – I don't have the energy to argue with you.'

Without another word she went into the parlour and got under the bedclothes, petticoats, blouse, knickers, stockings and all, then turned to face the wall and lay still.

Léon retired to the kitchen. He ate some bread and cheese, stared out of the window at the street, and drank the whole bottle of cider. Not until he heard Aunt Simone snoring did he cross the passage to the parlour and stretch out beside her, breathing in the sweet-and-sour scent of her female sweat and waiting for the cider's magical potency to transport him into another world.

When he opened his eyes the next morning, Aunt Simone

was still lying beside him in the same position, but she wasn't snoring any longer. He sensed that she was only pretending to be asleep and couldn't wait for him to leave the house. Taking his shoes in one hand and his suitcase in the other, he stole quietly outside.

ॐ

It was a sunny, windless morning. Léon took the coast road via Houlgate and Honfleur. It being low tide, he hefted his bicycle over the wall and pushed it down to the shore, where he rode along the tideline for many kilometres on wet, hard sand. The sand was yellow, the sea green shading to blue near the horizon. The few children who were playing on the beach wore red bathing costumes. Sometimes, old men in black jackets could be seen standing on the sand, prodding tangled knots of seaweed with their walking sticks.

Because his father and the mayor of Cherbourg were far away and couldn't possibly see him, Léon kept half an eye open for jetsam. He found a long, not overly frayed length of rope, some bottles, a window frame complete with catch and stay, and a half-empty can of paraffin.

He got to Deauville at midday and, in the evening, to Rouen, where he was to overnight at Aunt Sophie's; first, however, his father had urgently insisted that he visit the cathedral because it was one of the finest examples of Gothic architecture. Léon considered giving both his aunt and the example of Gothic architecture a miss and spending the night somewhere under the stars. Then he reflected that, although the June days were long, the nights were still cold and damp, and that Aunt Sophie couldn't have a husband or sons at Verdun because she was a lifelong spinster; she was also renowned for her apple tarts. When he reached her house she was standing in the front garden in her starched white apron, waving to him.

Léon discovered when getting up on the third day that his muscles were abominably sore. Climbing stairs was agony and the first hour on the bike plain torture; after that it got better. The wind had gone round to the north and it started to drizzle. Long convoys of army lorries came his way. The glum-faced soldiers seated beneath their canvas hoods were smoking cigarettes and clamping their rifles between their knees. At midday he passed a gutted farm. The blackened beams were festooned with green vetch and birch saplings were growing in the pigsties. A smell of mouldy charcoal came drifting out of the empty window embrasures. Stuck in the dungheap was a rusty pitchfork without a handle. This Léon appropriated and added to the other finds on his luggage rack.

He felt sure he was nearing his destination now; Saint-Luc-sur-Marne's church tower ought to come into view beyond the next hill or the one after that. A village with a church really was situated beyond the next rise, but it wasn't Saint-Luc. Léon rode through the village and up the next hill, beyond which lay another village with another hill beyond that. He bent low over his handlebars, tried to ignore his aches and pains, and imagined himself to be a human machine on wheels – one that didn't care how many more hills lay beyond the next one.

It was late in the afternoon when the hills finally petered out. Ahead of Léon stretched an endless plain bisected by an avenue of plane trees as straight as an arrow. Riding on the level was a relief, especially as it seemed to him that the trees shielded him a little from the side wind. Then, coming from behind him, he heard a noise; a rapid, regular succession of squeaks that grew steadily louder. He turned to look.

What he saw was a young woman on an old and rather rusty gentleman's bicycle. She was seated on the saddle, erect but relaxed, and quickly drawing nearer. The squeaks were evidently caused by the right-hand pedal, which fouled the chain guard every time it went round. She continued to come quickly closer and would soon overtake him. To prevent her from doing so he stood up on his pedals, but after a few seconds she drew level, gave him a wave, called '*Bonjour!*' and overtook him as easily as if he'd been stationary at the roadside.

Léon stared after her as the squeaks grew fainter and her figure steadily dwindled in size until it had traversed the broad plain and finally disappeared at the point where the double row of plane trees met the horizon. An odd-looking girl, she'd been. Freckles and dark, luxuriant hair bobbed at the back from one earlobe to the other. Roughly his own age. Maybe a little younger or older, it was hard to tell. A generous mouth and a dainty chin. A nice smile. Little white teeth with a funny gap between the upper incisors. The eyes – green? A red and white polka-dot blouse that would have added ten years to her age if her blue school skirt hadn't knocked them off again. Nice legs, as far as he'd been able to judge in such a short time. And she'd ridden damned fast.

Léon felt tired no longer, his legs did their duty once more. A sensational girl, that! He strove to keep her image before his eyes and was surprised to fail so soon. He could visualize the red and white polka-dot blouse, the pumping legs, the well-worn lace-up shoes, and the smile, which, incidentally, had been not just nice but blissfully, breathtakingly, heart-stoppingly attractive in its combination of friendliness and intelligence, bashfulness and mockery. But the separate elements refused, however hard he tried, to form a totality. All he saw were colours and shapes; her overall appearance eluded him.

He could still distinctly hear the squeak of the pedal against the chain guard, also her cheerful '*Bonjour!*'. Then it occurred to him that he hadn't returned her greeting. Angrily, he thumped the handlebars with his right hand, making the bicycle swerve and almost falling off. '*Bonjour, mademoiselle!*' he said, softly and experimentally. Then louder and more firmly: '*Bonjour!*'. Then again, with a touch more manly self-assurance: '*Bonjour!*'

Léon renewed the resolution he'd made before his departure, which was to start a new life in Saint-Luc-sur-Marne. From now on, and with immediate effect, he would no longer drink his coffee at home but take it in the bistro and always leave a fifteen per cent tip on the counter, and he would no longer read *Le Petit Inventeur* but *Figaro* and *Le Parisien,* and he would saunter along the pavement, not run. And when a young woman said hello to him, he wouldn't gawp at her with his mouth open, but favour her with a short, sharp glance, then casually reciprocate.

Leaden fatigue had taken possession of his legs once more. Now he cursed the boundless plain. At least the previous hilly terrain had offered an alternation of hope and disappointment; now there was just the unquestionable certainty that he still had far to go. So as not to have to see how far, he rested his forearms on the handlebars, let his head hang down between his shoulders, watched the rise and fall of his feet, and kept an eye on the ditch to ensure he didn't career off the road.

So he failed to notice that, far ahead of him, the overcast had parted and a quiverful of shafts of sunlight was slanting down on the green wheat fields, and that a speck had appeared on the skyline between the plane trees. It wore a red and white polka-dot blouse and grew rapidly bigger. Léon didn't notice, either, that the girl was this time riding without hands. Almost level with him by the time he heard the familiar squeak, she showed him her teeth with the cute little gap in the middle, waved to him, and rode past. '*Bonjour!*' Léon called after her, exasperated at being too late yet again. All he needed now, given that she was behind him once more, was for her to overtake him yet again. Determined to avoid this humiliation, he bent over the handle-bars and strove to speed up. After only a few hundred metres he peered anxiously over his shoulder to see if she had reappeared on the horizon, but he soon straightened up and forced himself to ride more slowly. After all, it was highly unlikely that this meteoric creature would travel the same stretch three times within a few minutes, and if she did, he would anyway lose the race – which to her wasn't one in any case. He braked to a halt and laid his bicycle down on the gravel verge, then leapt over the ditch and stretched out on the grass. Now she was welcome to come. Lounging there chewing a blade of grass like someone who had felt like having a little breather, he would tap the peak of his cap with a forefinger and call out '*Bonjour!*' loud and clear.

Having eaten the last of the three cheese sandwiches Aunt Sophie had given him, Léon took off his shoes and massaged his aching feet. Now and then he peered along the deserted road in both directions. A gust of wind spattered him with drizzle, but it soon stopped. A midnight blue lorry drove past with 'L'Espoir' on the side in gold lettering. Not long afterwards a dog came trotting across the fields. It suddenly dawned on Léon what an ass he was making of himself with his blade of grass and his ostentatious air of relaxation. If the girl passed by again, she would see through his act at a glance. He spat out the grass and put on his shoes again. Then he vaulted over the ditch on to the road and got back on his bicycle.

3

Saint-Luc-sur-Marne station was situated amid wheat and potato fields half a kilometre outside the town, on a branch line of the Chemins de Fer du Nord. The station building was built of red brick, the goods shed of weather-worn spruce. Léon was given a black uniform that had sergeant's stripes on the arm and fitted him – surprisingly enough – like a glove. He was the sole subordinate of his sole superior, Antoine Barthélemy, the stationmaster. A thin, mild-mannered little man who smoked a pipe and sported a moustache *à la* Vercingetorix, Barthélemy performed his duties in a taciturn and conscientious manner. Day after day, he spent many hours drawing little geometrical patterns on his notepad as he patiently anticipated the moment when he could go back upstairs to his official residence above the booking hall. There he was wistfully awaited around the clock by Josianne, his wife of several decades, who had rosy cheeks and plump hips, laughed heartily at the drop of a hat, and was an excellent cook.

There wasn't a great deal to do at Saint-Luc-sur-Marne station. In accordance with the timetable, three local trains travelling in each direction stopped there every morning and afternoon. The expresses sped past at high speed, trailing a slip-stream that took your breath away if you were standing on the platform. The Calais-Paris night train went by at 2.27 a.m., its darkened sleeping cars sometimes punctuated by an illuminated window because some wealthy passenger couldn't get to sleep in his nice, soft bunk.

To Léon Le Gall's own surprise, he proved more or less equal to his job as assistant Morse telegraphist from the first day on. His duties began at eight in the morning and ended at eight in the evening, with a one-hour break at lunchtime. He got Sundays off. One of his tasks was to go out on to the platform when a train came in and wave a little red flag at the driver. In the mornings he had to exchange the mailbag and the bag containing the Paris newspapers for the empty bags of the previous day. If a farmer handed in a crate of leeks or spring onions for delivery as freight, he had to weigh the goods and make out a waybill. And if the Morse machine was ticking he had to tear off the paper strip and transfer the messages to a telegram form. They were always official messages because the Morse machine was used exclusively by the railway.

Léon's assertion that he could Morse had, of course, been a brazen lie. He had passed the practical test on the mayor's desk because the mayor knew even less about the subject than he did himself. Fortunately, however, Saint-Luc-sur-Marne station was a remote place that received four or five telegrams a day at most; so Léon had all the time in the world to decipher them with the aid of *Le Petit Inventeur,* which he had been provident enough to pack.

It was somewhat more awkward when he himself had a message to send, which happened every two days or so. Before settling down at the Morse machine he would closet himself in the lavatory with paper and pencil and translate the Roman letters into dots and dashes. That was all right as long as the telegrams consisted of a few words only, but on his third Monday in the job his boss handed him the monthly report and told him to send it, verbatim and in full, to regional headquarters in Rheims.

'By post?' asked Léon. leafing through the four quite closely-written pages.

'No, telegraphically,' said Barthélemy. 'It's regulations.'

'Why?'

'No idea, it's just regulations. Always has been.'

Léon nodded, debating what to do. On the dot of half-past nine, when his boss went upstairs to his Josianne to have some coffee as usual, he picked up the telephone, asked to be put through to regional headquarters in Rheims, and proceeded to dictate the report as if this had been customary for decades. When the telephonist complained about the unwonted extra work, he explained that the Morse machine had been struck by lightning last night and put out of action.

Léon's room was on the upper floor of the goods shed, far away from the stationmaster's flat. He had his own bed, a table and chair, a washstand with a mirror, and a window overlooking the platform. He was undisturbed there and could do as he pleased. Most of the time he didn't do much, just lay on his bed with his hands clasped behind his head and stared at the grain of the beams above him.

The stationmaster's wife, whom he was privileged to call Madame Josianne, brought him his meals at midday and in the evening. She showered him with maternal solicitude and verbal endearments, called him her sweetheart, cherub, duckling and treasure, enquired after the state of his digestion, the quality of his sleep and his mental welfare, offered to cut his hair, knit him some woollen socks, hear his confession and wash his underclothes.

Apart from that no one troubled him, and this he much appreciated. When a train went by he would go to the window, count the carriages, goods wagons and cattle wagons, and try to guess what they were carrying. On one occasion he went back to his room with a newspaper a passenger had left behind on a bench, but after a few minutes he tired of the reports about Clemenceau's latest cabinet reshuffle, butter rationing, troop movements on the Chemin des Dames and the Banque de France's bullion sales. He couldn't muster any real interest in the national war economy either, now that Cherbourg beach was so far away, and he gradually admitted to himself that, strictly speaking, the only thing in the world that really interested him was the girl in the red and white polka-dot blouse.

Although he hadn't seen her again since the day he arrived, he couldn't help thinking of her the whole time. What might her name be? Jeanne? Marianne? Dominique? Françoise? Sophie? He softly and experimentally said each name aloud and wrote it with his finger on the floral rug beside his bed.

Léon felt happy in his new abode. He didn't miss his old life. Why should he have felt homesick? He could get on his bike and pedal back to Cherbourg any time he wanted. His parents would always, to the end of their days, welcome him with open arms in their eternally unchanging little house in the Rue des Fossées, and Cherbourg beach would still be there when he got back, exactly the same as when he left it, and he would put to sea in the sailing dinghy with Patrice and Joël as if no time had intervened, and after three days everyone in Cherbourg would have forgotten that he'd been away at all. And so, although he sometimes felt lonely, he was in no rush to go home. For the moment, he might just as well remain in Saint-Luc and try out his new, self-determined existence.

———

The only unpleasant feature of his room was the way the goods shed's beams and timber walls creaked and groaned. It was enough to give one the creeps. They whimpered by day when the sun warmed them up; they moaned at night when they cooled down again; they snapped and crackled at dawn when the air was at its coldest; and they creaked at sunrise when they warmed up again. At times it sounded as if someone were climbing the stairs to Léon's room; at others as if someone were creeping across the roof space or scratching the wall of the adjoining room with a screwdriver. Although he knew perfectly well that there was no one there, he couldn't help listening and never got to sleep before midnight.

So he took to going for long bicycle rides through the surrounding countryside after supper and not returning until long after nightfall, when he was good and tired. But because the sea was far away and there was nothing to see for kilometres around but pancake-flat wheat and potato fields threaded with impenetrable hazel hedges and brackish drainage channels, his excursions became steadily shorter and ended ever sooner in the little town.

In the early summer of 1918, Saint-Luc-sur-Marne comprised a couple of hundred buildings arranged in concentric rings around the Place de la République. In the innermost ring stood a pretentiously classicistic town hall, a primary school in the same architectural style, and one or two middle-class residences. There were also a covered market, the *Brasserie des Artistes,* the *Café du Commerce,* and a Romanesque church outside which, despite the priest's fierce opposition, a public urinal had been built by order of the maliciously anticlerical mayor. In the central ring were the post office, two bakeries, a hairdressing salon and a grocer's, as well as a butcher's, an ironmonger's and a clothes shop entitled *Aux Galeries Place Vendôme* from which the little town's female citizens and the local farmers' wives bought what they considered to be Parisian chic. Located among the humbler homes in the outermost ring were the smiths and joiners and the retail outlets of the agricultural association, also a saddlery, the memorial to the dead of 1870, the undertaker's, a machine shop, and the fire station.

So far, Saint-Luc-sur-Marne had survived the hostilities unscathed. The front had come unpleasantly close during the first year of the war and again in the third, and almost within eyeshot there were expanses of ruins that had once been thriving villages, but Saint-Luc itself had been spared the horrors of war. The worst the town had had to endure was the requisitioning of its fire engine by a battalion commander in transit, as well as occasional incursions by hordes of soldiers on leave from the front and doggedly determined to spend all their pay in a single night.

Other than that, the people of Saint-Luc had grown accustomed to the curious fact that the war raged only where it was actually being waged, while only just around the corner buttercups bloomed, market women offered their wares for sale, and mothers plaited coloured ribbons into their daughters' hair.

As a new arrival Léon had assumed that the *Café du Commerce* was the tradesmen's regular haunt, whereas the *Brasserie des Artistes* was the rendezvous of the local artists and intellectuals. Needless to say, it was the other way round. In Saint-Luc, as elsewhere in the world, the most successful lawyers, shopkeepers and craftsmen felt that their lives suffered from a certain lack of aesthetic and intellectual stimulation in the evenings, when they had counted their day's takings and locked them up securely in the safe, so they liked to spend their meagre leisure hours in the *Brasserie des Artistes,* which they held to be an artists' rendezvous because of the nicotine-stained Toulouse-Lautrec prints on its walls. It was in fact a long time since this supposed artists' rendezvous had been frequented by any artists because, outnumbered by their culturally aspiring fellow citizens, they had fled across the square and into the *Café du Commerce.* There Saint-Luc's bohemians now sat night after night at a safe distance from the bourgeoisie, just as bored as the latter and afflicted by the undeniable fact that an artist's life, too, is nowhere near as amusing and eventful as it ought to be by rights.

The bohemians of Saint-Luc consisted of two schoolmasters with literary pretensions, each of whom thought himself by far the other's artistic superior, the church organist, who suffered from chronic melancholia, a bachelor watercolourist, the lisping stonemason, and a handful of old-established drunks, windbags and pensioners. Defiantly cheerful, they all sat together at their regular table near the cylindrical stove whose flue ran straight across the taproom and disappeared through the kitchen wall, drinking Pernod and exhaling garlic fumes, while barely a hundred kilometres away complete age-groups of young men were being shot, gassed and blown to pieces.

To be fair to the windbags, it wasn't their fault that they were doing so well out of the war. The streets were paved with gold now that the government was keeping soldiers and their families sweet with generous pay, allowances and pensions. It was true that money couldn't always buy everything you had a fancy for, but there was plenty of bread, bacon and cheese. The wine at the *Commerce* might be slightly watered down on occasion, but it was cheap and not too sour and didn't give you a headache.

It had naturally come to the ears of the regulars long ago that old Barthélemy at the station had acquired someone to assist him in his far from onerous duties, so Léon didn't have to introduce himself the first time he came through the glass door in his railwayman's uniform. '*A vos ordres, mon général!*' the senior windbag had called, giving him a sedentary salute, and one of the schoolmasters, having joined Léon at the counter, questioned him closely, on behalf of the local community, about his previous existence, present circumstances and future plans.

The regulars were relieved to note in the course of the ensuing evenings that Léon didn't shoot his mouth off or pick fights, but stood quietly at the counter, drank a glass or two of Bordeaux, and – as befitted a youth of his age – politely withdrew after half an hour.

Léon was in the *Commerce* every night. He exchanged a few words, sometimes with the landlord and sometimes with his daughter, who stood behind the counter every Monday, Wednesday and Friday. She was a tall, serious girl who looked rather dreamy but kept an eagle eye on every customer's tab, no matter how big the drinking session. Léon, who was aware that she sometimes threw him sidelong, searching glances, tried to conceal from her that his own focus of attention was the door.

Because he wasn't there for the sake of the red wine, of course, but mainly in the hope that the girl in the red and white polka-dot blouse would sooner or later walk in. She'd had no luggage on the rack of her bike, so she had to be living in the locality – if not in Saint-Luc itself, then in one of the surrounding villages. The town was small. After a few days, hardly a face was unfamiliar to him. He knew the priest and the three gendarmes and the sacristan and the street urchins and the flower girls by sight, but he never rediscovered the pretty cyclist, neither in the churchyard nor the laundry nor the flower shop, nor on the benches in the Place de la République, nor under the plane trees flanking the canal, nor at the entrance to the brick works on the other side of the railway line. He had once sprinted after a female cyclist until she dismounted and turned out to be the wife of the baker in the Rue des Moines. On another occasion he had heard some rhythmical squeaks but failed to locate their source before they grew fainter and died away altogether.

Léon was often on the point of asking the landlord of the *Commerce* or his daughter about the girl in the red and white polka-dot blouse, but he refrained from doing so because he realized that in a small place no good could come of a strange youth enquiring after a local girl. One night, though, just after he had paid, the café door burst open and someone made a swift, light-footed entrance. It was the girl in the red and white polka-dot blouse, except that this time she was wearing a blue pullover, not a blouse. She closed the door behind her with a well-gauged shove and strode purposefully up to the counter, greeting the regulars left and right as she went. She halted only an arm's-length from Léon and asked the landlord for two packets of Turmac cigarettes. While he was taking them from the shelf she fished out the coins and put them in the money bowl. Then she cleared her throat and, with the fingertips of her right hand, brushed a strand of hair behind her ear. It wouldn't stay put and promptly escaped once more.

'*Bonsoir, mademoiselle,*' said Léon.

She turned towards him as if she'd only just noticed him. Looking into her eyes, he seemed to detect, in their green depths, the makings of a great friendship.

'I know you,' she said, 'but where from?' Her voice was even more enchanting than his memory of it.

'Cycling,' he replied. 'You overtook me. Twice.'

'Oh yes.' She laughed. 'It was a while back, wasn't it?'

'Five weeks and three days.'

'You looked tired, I remember. You had some funny odds and ends strapped to the back of your bike.'

'A can of paraffin and a window frame,' he said. 'And a pitchfork without a handle.'

'Do you always cart things like that around with you?'

'Sometimes, if I come across them. By the way, I'm glad your right eye's better.'

'What was the matter with my right eye?'

'It was rather bloodshot. Maybe a midge had flown into it. Or a fly.'

The girl laughed. 'It was a May-bug the size of a hen's egg. You remembered that?'

'And your bicycle squeaked.'

'It still does,' she said, lighting a cigarette. She held it between her thumb and forefinger like a street urchin. 'What about you? Do you prop up the bar here every night?'

Oh, thought Léon. So she knows I come here every night. Oh-oh… That probably means she's already noticed my existence. More than once, too. Oh-oh-oh… And now she comes in and acts as if she doesn't recognize me. Oh-oh-oh-oh…

'Yes, mademoiselle. You'll find me here any night of the week.'

'Why?'

'Because I don't know where else to go.'

'A big boy like you? Strange,' she said. She put the packets of cigarettes in her pocket and turned to go. 'I always thought railwaymen were active types – itchy-footed, even. I must be wrong.'

'I was just going,' he said. 'May I walk with you for a bit?'

'Where to?'

'Wherever you like.'

'Better not. My way home takes me down a dark side street. You'd probably claim we're soulmates or something. Either that, or try to read my future from my palm.'

And she was gone.

4

An unaccustomed silence had descended on the *Café du Commerce* while the girl and Léon were talking together. The landlord had assiduously dried the same wine glass, the regulars had blown smoke rings at the ceiling and used the glowing ends of their cigarettes to bulldoze the ash in the ashtrays into little mounds. Now that the girl had disappeared beyond the glass door they came to life and started talking – at first only haltingly and hesitantly, but in joyful anticipation of the moment when Léon would also disappear and enable them to discuss every facet of the little scene they'd just witnessed. Sure enough, before long Léon buttoned his uniform tunic and waved goodbye to the landlord. Unable to restrain his urge to communicate any longer, however, the latter caught hold of Léon's sleeve, insisted that he have a glass of Bordeaux for the road, and told him all he knew about the girl in the red and white polka-dot blouse.

❧

Little Louise – she wasn't conspicuously short, but people called her that to distinguish her from fat Louise, the sexton's wife – had been taken in by the inhabitants of Saint-Luc like a stray cat two years earlier. Many people claimed she was an orphan who hailed from one of those villages on the Somme of which not one brick had been left on another after the Germans' spring offensive in 1915. Nobody knew anything for sure; when anyone asked Louise about her origins in the early weeks, she silenced them with such feline ferocity that they never dared raise the subject again. She spoke French with a clarity and lack of accent that defied geographical attribution but made it seem likely that she came of good family and had gone to good schools.

Like Léon, Louise had come to the town under the auspices of the direction of labour programme. She worked as an office girl at the town hall, where she ran errands, made coffee and watered the pot plants. She had learned on her own initiative to use the typewriter that had hitherto languished untouched in the mayor's outer office. Little Louise was a bright, lively girl who proved adroit at all she did. The pot plants flourished as never before, the coffee tasted excellent, and she was soon typing immaculate letters.

The mayor, who was very satisfied with her, was surprised to notice after a few weeks that he was, despite himself, becoming extremely susceptible to her unaffected, tomboyish charms. Being conscious of the thirty-year age difference between them, however, he imposed the utmost restraint on himself in his dealings with his office girl and treated her with feigned detachment or aloof courtesy. He did, however, yield to the temptation to make her a present of his old bicycle, which had been standing unused in his barn for years. This Louise used for her official errands, which she carried out in a prompt and reliable manner.

Early in the mornings she rode it to the post office and emptied the mailbox; at half-past nine she fetched the croissants, and just before midday, if unexpected business awaited him in the office, she summoned the mayor from the *Café des Artistes,* where he habitually partook of his apéritif. In the afternoons she was out on her bike again. She delivered judicial demands for payment, official instructions and small-ish sums of money, together with mayoral orders to the beadle, the road-mender and the chimneysweep. But the hardest thing was the invitations she had to convey, on the mayor's behalf, to the families of soldiers killed in action. Thoroughly noncom-mittal, these invitations simply contained a request to their unwitting recipients to present themselves at the town hall at a certain hour on such and such a day. In the early months of the war the persons concerned read them with a shrug and obedi-ently set off for the mayor's office, where they stood in front of his desk, unsuspectingly kneading their caps, and enquired what could be important enough to summon them away from their work. Reading aloud from a sheet of paper, the mayor thereupon informed them in resonant tones that their son, husband, father, grandson or nephew had died a hero's death at such and such a place on the field of honour in the service of the Fatherland, a sacrifice for which the Minister of War in person and he himself, the mayor, expressed their profound condolences and the gratitude of the entire nation.

The mayor sought to mitigate the ensuing scenes of despair, to which he was defencelessly exposed, by consoling the incon-solable with allusions to heroism, patriotism and rewards in the world to come. These they couldn't help construing as a slur on their grief because, if they couldn't have their nearest and dearest back, they wanted at least to mourn his passing.

It could even happen that the mayor had to endure three such scenes in his office in a single day. He started to anaesthetize himself with copious quantities of pastis and couldn't sleep at night despite this, his digestion went haywire and his head became heavy, and grief and nameless dread made itself at home in his office, which had hitherto been a place of dignified self-satisfaction. So great was his distress that he more than once came close to walking into the church and entreating the priest for pastoral assistance, even though the cleric had been his arch-enemy ever since the urinal affair.

Such was the situation in the spring of 1915, when little Louise arrived in Saint-Luc and started running errands. She soon grasped the connection between the mayor's invitations and the rustically maladroit scenes in his office. On perhaps twenty or thirty occasions she saw the city father sweating and shaking behind his desk, struggling for words and composure but never managing to shake off his woodenly official manner; and when she knew for certain that nothing would ever change, no matter how long the war lasted, she decided to act. 'Please excuse me, *monsieur le maire*,' she said the next time she had an invitation to deliver.

'What is it?' asked the mayor, smoothing his eyebrows with his thumb and forefinger and treating himself to a glance at the delectably swanlike curve of her neck.

'Is this another of these invitations?'

'What else, *ma petite* Louise, what else?'

'Who it is this time?'

'It's Lucien, only son of the widow Junod,' said the mayor. 'Nineteen years old, the girls called him Lulu. Killed on February 7th at Ville-sur-Cousances. Did you know him?'

'No.'

'He was home on leave only this Christmas, I saw him at midnight Mass. He had a nice voice.'

Louise took the envelope and went outside. Mounting her bicycle, she rode at full speed across the Place de la République and headed straight for the widow Junod's house on the western outskirts of town. She rang the bell and handed over the envelope. When the widow had torn it open with her forefinger and was staring at it helplessly, Louise said:

'You don't *have* to go there.'

Then she took her by the elbow and led her into the house, sat down beside her on the sofa, and told her that her Lulu wouldn't be coming back because he'd been killed in action.

Louise sat silently on the sofa while the woman threw herself on the floor, screaming, and tore out whole tufts of her hair. Having later submitted to being pummelled by the widow's fists and clasped around the neck by her, she let her cry her eyes out with an abandon she might have been too inhibited to display in the presence of a friend or relation. Louise passed her two handkerchiefs in succession and, when she had calmed down a little, lit one of her sugar-dusted cigarettes, pillowed the widow Junod's head on a cushion, and went into the kitchen to make her some tea. When she returned with a steaming cup, she said:

'Well, I'll be off now. Don't worry about the invitation, Madame Junod. I'll tell the mayor you won't be coming.'

A few minutes later, when she informed the mayor of how she'd handled the matter, he looked stern and said something about taking liberties and breaches of official secrecy, but he was of course extremely relieved and profoundly grateful to have been spared the inevitable scene for once. And when two more invitations cropped up the following day, he didn't send Louise off with an admonition of any kind; on the contrary, he gave her the unsolicited information she needed in order to fulfil her new mission.

'This one's name was Sebastien,' he said, gazing up at the ceiling so as not to have to look down her cleavage. 'He was the youngest son of Farmer Petitpierre. A decent lad. He had a hare lip and was good with horses.'

'And the other?'

'Delacroix, the notary. Fifty years old and childless, both parents dead. There's only his wife. Now go, *ma petite* Louise. Well, off you go.'

From then on the bereaved no longer had to present themselves at the town hall. Louise simply delivered the invitations to their homes; then they knew what was what and could fully surrender to the first great onset of grief while she sat on the sofa like a mute but sympathetic angel of death. The next day or the day after that, they were usually calm enough to send for Louise because they wanted to know details. Louise would then pay them a second visit and tell them everything that had been officially ascertained: exactly when and where and in what circumstances David or Cedric or Philippe had lost his life, whether he had suffered or died a merciful death, and finally, the most urgent question of all: whether his body had found eternal rest beneath the sod or lay strewn across the mud somewhere, blown to pieces, decaying, and lying around for the ravens to devour.

Although Louise seldom had anything consoling to report, she refrained from false embellishment and always told the truth as far as she knew it, realizing that truth alone can stand the test of time. She took her task very seriously, and the inhabitants of Saint-Luc repaid her with warm affection. Becoming accustomed to the ominous squeak of her gentleman's bicycle, they all listened for it and were glad when it grew fainter instead of ceasing abruptly outside their homes.

Many people revered Louise like a saint, but she didn't like this. In order to destroy the halo they tried to impose on her, she smoked her sugared cigarettes, bathed half-naked in the Channel on Sundays, and acquired an arsenal of coarse expletives that contrasted strangely with her slender figure, girlish voice and educated French.

The worst thing was, news of a soldier's death often got to Saint-Luc long before the ministerial notification – for instance when a comrade home on leave reported at the kitchen table that Jacquet, the schoolmaster, was lying at the bottom of a muddy shell-hole with his skull shattered, whereupon the news spread like wildfire from house to house until it reached every kitchen table in the town save the one to which Jacquet, the schoolmaster, would never return; for the spreading of rumours was a punishable offence and notification of a death had to be conveyed to the bereaved through official channels alone, to preclude any distressing errors and mix-ups. This was how it came about that Jacquet's widow, who still had no idea she was one, bought a big joint of beef at the market in joyful expectation of her husband's home leave. Meanwhile, the other women timidly and sympathetically watched her out of the corner of their eye, and then, so as not to arouse suspicion, greeted her as casually as they could manage.

Once Louise had taken over the job, however, this problem too was solved. 'Go and tell little Louise right away,' any soldier coming home with bad news would be told from now on. When Louise's squeaking bicycle pulled up outside her front door, a previously unsuspecting widow knew at once that it would be a long time before she bought a joint of beef big enough for two.

Léon Le Gall walked home in a very pensive mood the night the landlord told him all this. It was not only the first warm night of the year but one of those nights on which you could see the sheet lightning generated by the front line beyond Saint-Quentin; and occasionally, when the wind was blowing from the north-west, you could also hear distant peals of thunder. Léon unbuttoned his jacket and took off his cap. He watched the vagaries of his own shadow, which lay at his feet, short and crisply defined, whenever he walked under a lamp-post, then gradually lengthened and was bleached by the intensifying glow of the next lamp-post until it lay at his feet and grew brighter and paler once more. He removed his jacket and slung it over his shoulder. It was far too warm for the time of year, and he now wondered why it had never occurred to him in the last five weeks and three days, when going for his evening stroll, to take off his official garb with its ludicrous sergeant's stripes.

The station building at the far end of the avenue of plane trees was in darkness. No light was on upstairs either. Léon pictured old Barthélemy, blissfully snuggled up against the comforting warmth of his Josianne, slumbering his way towards another working day beneath a thick duvet. He walked across the station yard to the goods shed, then climbed the creaking stairs. His silent room hummed with the echoes of his memories of the day just past.

He reflected that, next morning and on all the mornings that followed, he would be greeting incoming trains with his little red flag. He thought of his jiggery-pokery with the Morse transmitter, of his fear of the creaking beams, and of his taciturn evenings at the bar of the *Café du Commerce,* and he came to the conclusion that what he had hitherto done in life could not be called good. It wasn't bad either, because he hadn't so far done any damage worth mentioning and had never harmed anyone or done much that he would have been ashamed to admit to his parents; but it was also true that none of his daily doings was truly important, fine or good, and he certainly had no reason to be proud of anything.

❦

Léon didn't know how long he'd been asleep when the sound of voices woke him. It was coming from outside the window, which he'd left open because the night was so warm, and it was accompanied by a peculiar stench – a mixture of disgusting smells whose source he couldn't identify. He got out of bed and looked down at the platform. There in the dim light of the gas lamps stood a long train made up of goods wagons and cattle wagons, and old Barthélemy and Madame Josianne were bustling along the platform from one to the next. Léon descended the stairs in his bare feet, stripped to the waist.

The train was so long, it seemed to have no beginning or end. Many of the wagons were closed and many open, but issuing from them all was that frightful stench of putrefaction and excrement, together with the voices of men groaning and screaming and begging for water.

'What are you doing here, boy?' said Madame Josianne, who was doling out water to the soldiers in a big pitcher. They were sitting or lying on bare wooden planks strewn with straw, their faces glistening with sweat in the light of the gas lamps. Their uniforms were filthy, their bandages soaked in blood.

'Madame Josianne…'

'Go back to bed, my pet, this is nothing for you.'

'But what's going on here?'

'Just a hospital train, my angel, just a hospital train. It's taking the poor fellows south to hospitals in Dax, Bordeaux, Lourdes and Pau, so they soon get better.'

'Can I help?'

'That's kind of you, my treasure, but now go. Go on!'

'I could fetch some water.'

'No need. We're used to it, your chief and I. You young people shouldn't see such sights.'

'But Madame Josianne…'

'Go to your room at once, my pet. At once! And shut the window, you hear?'

Léon tried to protest and looked round for Barthélemy in search of support, but as soon as the stationmaster heard his Josianne raise her voice he came hurrying up. He eyed Léon sternly and pursed his lips so that the bristles of his moustache stood out horizontal, then pointed to the goods shed and hissed:

'Do as madame says! Dismissed!'

So Léon gave up and went back to his room, but he left the window open in defiance of Josianne's instructions. Stationing himself in the shadows behind the curtain, he watched what was happening on the platform. When the train pulled out he flopped down on his bed and, because the whole incident had tired him out, fell asleep even before the nocturnal breeze had carried the last remnants of the stench away.

❧

It so happened that just before work began the next morning, as Léon was on his way from the goods shed to the station building, little Louise came riding along the avenue with her bike squeaking urgently. Reaching the station, she applied the back-pedal brake so hard that gravel crunched beneath her wheels and a cloud of dust went drifting across the forecourt. She left her bicycle in the bike shelter and ran up the three steps to the booking hall. Léon would have liked to follow her, but it was his unpostponable duty to get his red flag from the office and be standing on the platform by the time the 8.07 a.m. passenger train arrived.

When the train pulled in, Louise was the only passenger to emerge from the booking hall. Léon was relieved to note that she was holding a ticket in her hand but carrying no luggage, so she couldn't be going away for long. All that annoyed him was that she waved to him just as he, for his part, had to wave his red flag at the incoming locomotive.

'*Salut,* Léon!' she called as she trotted along beside the train and opened the door of a third-class carriage. Oh, he thought, so she knows my first name. Had he introduced himself last night at the *Café du Commerce*? No, he hadn't. He ought to have, of course. It would have been only polite, but he hadn't, so she must have learned his name some other way – possibly even have made a point of finding it out? Oh-oh. And she hadn't forgotten his name overnight; on the contrary, she had memorized it. And now she had uttered his name with her mouth, lips and little white teeth – with the breath of her body. Oh-oh-oh.

'*Salut,* Louise!' he called when he'd recovered his composure and she was about to jump aboard the still moving train. He stood enshrouded in the locomotive's hissing spurts of steam and waited the regulation minute after which, pursuant to the timetable, he had to signal the driver to continue on his way. The train moved off and Léon, craning his neck, ran to the door behind which Louise had disappeared. But because the platform was too low and the windows were too high, he couldn't see the passengers sitting on the far side of the compartment. Then the train pulled out and Louise was gone.

Léon stared after the red rear light until it was out of sight beyond the brick works, and he kept a lingering eye on the locomotive's plume of smoke. Then he repaired with his red flag to the office, where Madame Josianne had left him some coffee and two *tartines*.

When he went out into the forecourt at lunchtime his eye lighted on Louise's bicycle in the shelter. Looking around to make sure he was unobserved, he went over and examined it. An ordinary old gentleman's bike that had once been black, it had rusty gear sprockets, a worn-out chain and solid tyres with no tread left on them. The gear change was broken and the chain guard bent. Gingerly, he rested his hands on the cracked, bleached leather grips on the handlebars, squeezed them hard and then held both palms to his nose to catch a whiff of Louise's scent, but all he could smell was leather and his own hands.

Crouching down, he examined the chain guard and discovered that it really was the cause of the squeak. He tried to straighten the bent section with both thumbs, but failed because of the sprocket behind it. He fetched two screwdrivers and a hammer from the workshop, removed the metal guard, and hammered it flat against the goods shed's timber wall. Then he oiled the rusty chain, screwed the guard on again, and made one experimental circuit of the station yard.

❧

When Léon embarked on his usual after-supper bike ride into town, he was wearing his slacks, his white shirt, and the grey cardigan his mother had knitted him during her sleepless nights before his departure. Having ridden across the station yard in the afterglow of the sunny day, he set off up the avenue – and saw someone standing beside the fifth plane tree along on the right-hand side of the road.

She was leaning against the tree in her blue school skirt and her red and white polka-dot blouse. Her left hand was imprisoned in the crook of her arm, her right hand held a lighted cigarette. She had raised her right eyebrow far enough to furrow her smooth forehead; the other loomed low over her left eye. Could this piercing stare really be meant for him?

'Evening, Louise. Waiting for me, were you?'

'I never wait for anyone, let alone your kind.' She took a long pull at her cigarette. 'Any of my precious time you steal will be deducted from the end of your life.'

'I can spare a minute or two,' said Léon.

'My bike doesn't squeak any more,' she said.

'Glad to hear it.'

'I don't remember asking you to repair it.'

'Something had to be done,' he said. 'The local farmers were complaining.'

'Why?'

'It was upsetting their cows.'

'Really?'

'Yes, turning their milk sour in the udder.'

'And that's why the local farmers asked the assistant telegraphist at Saint-Luc station for help?'

'I couldn't refuse.'

'The local farmers will be grateful.'

***

'I guess so.'

'What about me?'

'What about you?'

'Do I have to be grateful too?'

'No, why should you be?'

'I owe you, though, is that it?'

'Not for a little thing like that.'

'What do you want in exchange – to show me the stars at night?'

'I'm no astronomer.'

'To show me your stamp collection?'

'I don't own a stamp collection.'

'What *do* you want, then?'

'All I did was bend the thing straight.'

'And for that you want to squeeze my bottom?'

'No, but I could always bend it out of shape again.'

'That would suit me fine.'

'You miss the squeak?'

'People will. They won't be able to hear me coming any more. They'll get a shock when I turn up without warning.'

'I'll screw a bell to your handlebars, then they'll be able to hear you. All right if I walk with you for a bit?'

'No.'

'Which way are you going?'

'I know where *you're* going: the *Commerce*.'

'Yes.'

'The way you do every evening.'

'Exactly.'

'Every inch the stick-in-the-mud railwayman, aren't you?'

'Where did you go in the train today?'

'None of your business. You're going to the *Commerce*,

anyway. I have to go that way too. Leave your bike here. I'll walk with you for a bit.'

࿊

Louise was waiting for Léon at the fifth plane tree the following evening, likewise the next evening and the one after that. They took over an hour to cover the few hundred metres into town because they walked so slowly and paused so often, crossing the road for no reason or even retracing their steps. They never stopped talking. They talked about everything and nothing: about the mayor's cigars and the postman, who was reputed to be his bastard half-brother, about the station and Léon's knowledge of modern telecommunications, about old Barthélemy and his infatuation with Madame Josianne, about the vicious watchdog outside the locksmith's, which frightened passing schoolchildren, and about the delicious chocolate éclairs in the Catholic bakery. They talked about the widow Junot, whose visits to her sister in Compiègne always coincided exactly with the days on which the *curé* went on his pastoral missions to Compiègne. They talked about the quarry behind the station in which fossilized neolithic sharks' teeth could be found, about the black Madonna in the church and the little wood beside the *route nationale* in which the cherries should soon be ripe, and about Colette's novels, all of which Louise had read but Léon hadn't.

From the third evening onwards Louise described her work as an angel of death while Léon looked up at the treetops, listening in silence. Later he told her about Cherbourg, the Channel, the islands and his brightly painted sailing boat while Louise likewise listened in silence, gazing at his face intently.

But once, when he tried to ask about her background, she cut him short. 'No questions,' she said. 'I won't ask you any and you won't either.'

'All right,' said Léon.

While they were talking together like this, he would bury his hands in his trouser pockets and play football with some little pebbles. Louise, gesticulating as she smoked one cigarette after another, would walk backwards in front of him to see if he understood and approved of what she was saying. Léon not only understood but approved of everything she said, simply because it was Louise that was saying it. He found her laughter entrancing because it was her laughter, and he loved her encouraging, searching gaze because it was her green eyes that seemed to be asking, again and again, 'Tell me, is it you? Is it really you?' And he found her errant strand of hair captivating because it was her strand of hair, and he couldn't help laughing when she mimicked the mayor lighting his cigar because the mimicry was hers.

It hadn't escaped them, even during their first walk together, that the citizens of the little town were watching their every step from behind their curtains. That was why they kept well in sight in the street and spoke especially loudly and distinctly, so that anyone who wished could hear what they were talking about. Once outside the *Café du Commerce*, they always stopped and said goodbye without a kiss or a handshake.

'*Au revoir*, Louise.'

'*Au revoir*, Léon.'

'See you tomorrow.'

'See you tomorrow.'

Then she disappeared around the corner and he went into the café and ordered a glass of Bordeaux.

5

At Whitsun 1918 Léon had a whole two days off for the first time. Contrary to his usual routine, he woke early in the morning and watched as his window exchanged the darkness of night for the pale light of dawn and the glow of sunrise. Having washed in the fountain behind the goods shed, he got back into bed. He listened to the twittering of the blackbirds and the creaking of the beams and waited until it was eight o'clock at last – time for him to go to the office and have his *café au lait* under the effusively affectionate aegis of Madame Josianne.

After breakfast he rode his bicycle into town. A storm had swept across the countryside during the night, tousling the maize fields, ripping the last of last year's withered leaves from the plane trees, and filling the canals and ditches with rainwater. Léon made a circuit of the Sunday-silent town, with its gleaming roofs, wet streets and gurgling drains. A gentle summer breeze wafted the scent of flowering jasmine from the gardens into the streets, and the sun proceeded to dry everything before the inhabitants emerged from their houses, blinking, and went to Mass.

Léon got off his bike in the Place de la République, propped it against an advertising pillar and sat down on a bench that had almost dried off. He didn't have long to wait. A few pigeons cautiously approached him, heads bobbing, before reluctantly strutting off when they found he had no bread-crumbs to scatter. An old man in a claret-coloured dressing gown and brown-and-yellow checked slippers shuffled past with a baguette under his arm and disappeared down the alleyway between the town hall and the savings bank. A cloud drifted over the sun and exposed it again. Then, behind Léon's back, the morning silence was broken by a bicycle bell – rri-rring, rri-rring! – and a moment later Louise was standing in front of him.

'I've now got a bell on my bike,' she said. 'Do I owe you something for it?'

'Of course not.'

'I didn't ask you for one, but thanks all the same. When did you do it?'

'Last night, after the café.'

'You happened to have a bell and a screwdriver with you?'

'And a box spanner that fitted.'

Louise leant her bicycle against the advertising pillar, sat down on the bench beside him and lit a cigarette.

'You've got some funny odds and ends on your luggage rack again. What are they?'

'Four blankets and a saucepan,' said Léon. 'And a bag of bread and cheese.'

'Found them all on the beach?'

'I'm going on a trip to the seaside. There today, back tomorrow.'

'Just like that?'

'I want to see the sea again. Eighty kilometres. I'll be there in five hours.'

'And then?'

'I'll go for a walk along the cliffs, collect some more bits and pieces on the beach, and look for a dry spot to sleep.'

'And you need four blankets for that?'

'Two would be enough.'

'You mean me to come too?'

'It'd be nice.'

'If I did, you'd try to get into my knickers.'

'Wrong,' he said.

'What do you take me for, an idiot? Any man tries to get into a girl's knickers if he's alone with her among the sand dunes.'

'That's true,' Léon conceded. 'I won't, though.'

'No?'

'No. What someone wants and what they do are two different things.'

Léon got up and went over to his bicycle. 'Besides,' he said, 'there aren't any sand dunes at Le Tréport.'

'No?' Louise laughed.

'Just cliffs. And a shingle beach. I won't, honestly. Not as long as you don't.'

'Word of honour?'

'I promise.'

'How long do your promises normally last?'

'A lifetime. I'm being serious.'

Louise frowned and pursed her lips, then breathed out through her nose. 'Hang on, I'll go and get some more cigarettes.'

They rode out of town and headed west towards the sea along the wide, dead straight, deserted highroad that led through the charming pastureland of Haute Normandie, which has so generously supplied its inhabitants with the necessities of life since time immemorial. The sun was high, the horizon distant, and they sped past pale-green fields of wartime wheat, as sparse and patchy as an adolescent's beard because they'd been sown by inexperienced women and children. Later, in the hilly terrain far away from the villages, birch saplings were already growing on steep fields that hadn't been ploughed for years.

Louise rode fast, but Léon, being rested and in good shape, easily kept up with her. They looked straight ahead at the road, legs pumping rhythmically up and down, not talking much because their thoughts were focused entirely on the ride and making good progress and getting to their destination. They were happy. Louise pretended not to notice when Léon occasionally glanced at her out of the corner of his eye. Once they held hands while going full tilt and coasted for a bit like that, side by side. Then Louise rang her bell from sheer happiness.

They reached their destination at half-past two that afternoon, quite suddenly and earlier than expected. The sea hadn't announced its presence; the air was no saltier, the sky no wider, the vegetation no sparser, the soil no sandier. The Normandy countryside, with its rich arable land and lush meadows, simply broke off and continued a hundred metres down at the foot of chalk cliffs washed by the grey surf of the English Channel. They rode past the Canadian military hospital that had established itself in a sea of white tents on the cliffs, then along the river and into Le Tréport.

The place had once been a fishing village. Ever since the railway had linked it with the capital, however, the inhabitants' main source of income had been the Parisian holidaymakers who had built themselves fine villas with sea views at the foot of the cliffs. Léon and Louise left their bicycles on the Quai François and walked round the harbour. They watched the fishermen mending their nets, repairing sails, coiling ropes and sweeping their decks with gnarled hands and half-smoked cigarettes in the corners of their mouths. They also eyed the holidaymakers with their pink bootees and gleaming spats, their white sailor suits and translucent linen skirts, their panama hats, skilfully peroxided plaits and ostentatiously Parisian accents. Léon suddenly felt Louise take his arm – something she'd never done before.

'Look at those stuck-up mam'selles with their parasols,' she said. If you ever catch me with a parasol like that, you must shoot me.'

'No.'

'That's an order.'

'No.'

'I've no one else to ask.'

'All right.'

After that they walked on in silence, side by side like a long familiar couple with nothing left to prove. While sitting on their bikes and pedalling they had been free and unconstrained because their destination still lay in the future and the present wasn't what mattered. Now there was no obstacle and no escape left; now it was the present that counted. But even now, as they walked round the harbour, they were neither guarded nor uneasy, just incapable of putting their feelings into words.

Where Léon was concerned, the warmth of Louise's hand on his arm was enough to render him perfectly happy. It was the first time in his life he had been privileged to walk so close to a girl. That he could, if he bent his head sideways only a little, breathe in the scent of her sun-warmed hair was almost more than he could bear.

They walked along the mole to the lighthouse that marked the harbour entrance, sat on the wall and watched the steamers and sailing boats going in and out. When the sun was nearing the sea they made their way back to the little town, walked up the Rue de Paris and visited the Eglise Saint-Jacques, the town's landmark.

Just on the right of the entrance was a Madonna they stood in front of for a long time. It was a crudely modelled plaster figure with a flat face, Dutch doll red cheeks and black, boot button eyes. The Virgin's robe of gold-embroidered blue velvet was entirely covered with slips of paper rolled up or folded several times. These were attached to the garment with pins, but other slips of paper were wedged between her fingers, pinned to her kerchief, or lying on her halo and her feet. Slips of every size and hue could even be seen between her lips and in her ears.

'What are those pieces of paper?' Louise asked.

'They're from seamen's wives asking the Mother of God to keep their husbands safe,' said Léon. 'I've seen them back home. They draw their men's fishing boat on a slip of paper and hope it'll come safe home under the Holy Virgin's protection. Others fold up a lock of their consumptive child's hair in a piece of paper and ask the Virgin to cure it. These days, you'll also see soldiers' photos.'

'Shall we look at some?'

'It's bad luck to do that. The ships would sink, the children die, the soldiers be blown to bits by a shell. And your fingers would rot off if you even touched one.'

'We'd better not, then. Shall we go?'

'Just a minute.' Léon took a notebook and a pencil from his breast pocket.

'You're going to write one?' Louise laughed. 'Like a seaman's wife?'

Léon tore the page out of the notebook, rolled it into a cylinder, and stuck it in the Madonna's right armpit. 'Let's go, it'll soon be low tide. I'll get us some mussels from the rocks for supper.'

Léon bought two baguettes, some carrots, leeks, onions, thyme, and a bottle of Muscadet from a grocer's shop in the Rue de Paris. Then they fetched their bicycles and wheeled them down to the casino in the light of the setting sun. From there a wide boardwalk of oak planks led across the shingle beach and past a long row of whitewashed bathing huts. Behind them stood proud seaside villas with encircling verandas and white curtains that silently, airily billowed and subsided, billowed and subsided, as if they were breathing.

Léon had noticed from the lighthouse that, far beyond the villas at the southern end of the beach, quite a lot of driftwood had collected. This he planned to use as firewood. It was growing chilly now. The last of the bathers had gone home to rinse the sea salt off their bodies and titivate themselves for dinner. Léon and Louise found a dry, sheltered spot between two big boulders at the foot of the chalk cliffs. They scraped away the pebbles until the sand was exposed, then spread out a blanket and Léon lit a fire of dry seaweed and driftwood. Meanwhile, Louise sat on the blanket hugging her knees and gazing out at the orange and lilac sea as if it were the most dramatic spectacle imaginable.

'Let's get the mussels,' Léon said, rolling up his trouserlegs and taking the saucepan from his bicycle. 'There should be some out there in the pools among the rocks, where those gulls are strutting around. The tourists never collect them, they prefer to buy them in a shop.'

The gulls emitted angry screams and reluctantly spread their wings. They took a couple of hops and rose into the air after two or three wingbeats, were caught by the updraught and sailed up the cliff face to the green meadows above, only to dive back at once with their sharp beaks menacingly directed downwards, then go into a glide just before impact and soar into the air again.

There were plenty of mussels in the rock pools, so the saucepan was soon full. Producing two knives from his pocket, Léon showed Louise how to scrape the algae and beards off the shells. Then they returned to their spot between the boulders. He flopped down on the blanket with a sigh. It had been a perfect day; his cup of joy was overflowing. But Louise remained standing. She paced irresolutely to and fro for a bit and lit a cigarette.

'Come here and make yourself comfortable,' he said. 'I won't do anything to you.'

'Be thankful I don't do anything to *you*.'

'Are you cold?'

'No.'

'Like to do anything before it gets dark? Shall we go for a walk along the cliffs?'

'I'm hungry.'

'Supper won't be long.'

'Shall I buy something?'

'We've got everything,' said Léon. All I have to do is slice the carrots, onions and leeks and boil them for a few minutes.'

'Should I get something sweet for dessert? A couple of chocolate éclairs?'

'It's half-past nine,' said Léon. 'I'd be surprised if the pâtisserie is still open.'

'I'll try.'

She was back within half an hour. Meantime, the earth had rotated nightwards. The first stars were twinkling in the sky, the moon had not yet risen. Some dark clouds were drifting so low over the bay that the flashes from the lighthouse grazed their undersides.

Léon removed the saucepan from the fire. He could hear shingle crunching under Louise's feet behind him.

'Supper's ready. Did you get the éclairs?'

She didn't answer.

He stirred the saucepan, fished out a piece of eelgrass and an empty shell. Then he felt Louise come up behind him and rest her hands on his shoulders. Her hair tickled his neck, her breath fanned his right cheek.

'You tricked me.' Her right hand released his shoulder, slid beneath his armpit and pinched his nose. 'You did it deliberately – you played me like a fish.'

'Your fingers will rot off in the night.'

'Is it true, what it says on that slip of paper?'

'Absolutely. For ever and ever,'

Léon freed his nose from her grip, turned round and gazed into her green eyes, which were shining in the firelight. And then they kissed.

6

Léon couldn't have known that, at the moment when he was woken by a steamer's foghorn, half a million exhausted German soldiers were lacing up their boots in readiness for a final assault on Paris. If he had, he might have lain still at Louise's side and not budged from the beach; then everything would have turned out differently. The air was cool and damp, the sky pale and misty. The tide had come in and gone out again, the shingle was glistening wet, the blanket fluff beaded with drops of dew. The spars of a sunken ship were jutting above the surface beyond the breakers.

Léon looked up at the white chalk cliffs in which gulls were roosting in their nests and warming their beaks in their plumage, then higher up at the thin fringe of turf at the very top, above which leaden grey rain clouds were drifting in the wind. It would remain cold and damp on the beach until the warming sun appeared there towards midday. The longer he looked up, the more vivid his sensation that the clouds were not scudding past above his head, but that he himself and the beach and the cliffs were gliding along beneath the clouds.

He propped himself on his elbows and studied the outlines of Louise's slight form, which was rising and falling in time to the surf. Her dark, tousled hair resembled cat's fur. He left her side and got up to fetch wood and kindle the fire again. When the fire was well alight he walked along the tideline, looking for things the sea might have washed ashore during the night. At the eastern end of the beach he found a red and white float, on the way back a plank two metres long and four scallops. He put them all down beside the fire. Then, because Louise was still asleep, he went down to the sea and stripped to his underpants.

The water was cold. He waded out, dived under a breaker, and swam a few strokes. He tasted salt on his lips, felt his eyes sting in the familiar way, and turned over on his back, submerging his ears and letting himself be gently rocked by the waves. And all this while, at the same moment on the Chemin des Dames, the cloying bananalike scent of phosgene gas was creeping along the trenches for the first time in many months and turning into hydrochloric acid in the soldiers' lungs. Tens of thousands of young men were literally coughing up their lungs while the survivors, unless artillery shells had blown them to bits, were fleeing in the direction of Paris with their eyes starting out of their heads and burnt, poisoned skin falling in strips from their faces and hands.

Léon rocked on the waves, enjoying the sense of weightlessness, and gazed up at the sky, which was still wreathed in dark clouds. After a while he heard a whistle. It was Louise, who had sat up and was waving to him. He let the next wave carry him back to the shore, pulled on his shirt and trousers over his wet body and sat down beside her near the fire. Louise cut last night's bread into slices and toasted them over the flames.

'You snored a bit in the night,' she said.

'And you whispered my name in your sleep,' he said.

'You're a bad liar,' she said. 'Some coffee would be nice now.'

'It's starting to rain.'

'That's not rain,' she said, 'just a cloud flying too low.'

'The cloud'll make us wet if we stay here.'

Louise rolled up the blankets while Léon scoured the sauce-pan with sand. Then they pushed their bicycles back into the town. In the harbour there was a bistro that had already opened. It was called the *Café du Commerce* like Léon's regular haunt. Four unshaven men in crumpled linen suits were standing at the counter sipping their coffees and studiously avoiding each other's eye. Léon and Louise sat down at a table beside the window and ordered *cafés au lait* and croissants.

'Oh, we've got into bad company.' Louise indicated the counter with her half-eaten croissant. 'Take a look at those chumps.'

'Those chumps can hear you.'

'Who cares? The louder we speak, the less they'll think we're talking about them. Typical Parisian chumps, they are. Parisian chumps of the first order, all four of them.'

'An expert on the subject, are you?'

'The one with the blue sunglasses, who's hiding his face under his hat, thinks he's at least as famous as Caruso or Zola, when his name's Fournier or something similar. And the one with the moustache, who's reading the financial paper and frowning – he thinks he's Rockefeller because he owns three shares in a railway company.'

'And the other two?'

'They're just high-class chumps who never say hello or talk to people in case they grasp what bores they are.'

'People do get bored,' Léon retorted. 'I do sometimes, don't you?'

'That's different. When you or I get bored it's in the hope that something'll change sometime. They get bored because they're always hoping that everything will stay the same.'

'To me they all look like perfectly normal family men. They've slunk out of the house on the pretext of going to the baker's. Now they're treating themselves to fifteen minutes' peace and quiet before going back to their villas and rejoining their nagging wives and petulant children.'

'You think so?'

'The one in the blue sunglasses spent all night quarrelling with his wife because she doesn't love him any more and he could happily have dispensed with that information. And the one with the newspaper is dreading the interminable afternoons on the beach, when he's expected to play with his children and hasn't a clue how to go about it.'

'Shall we go to the fishermen's café?' asked Louise.

'We aren't fishermen.'

'That doesn't matter.'

'Not to us, maybe, but to the fishermen. They'll think we're Parisian chumps, just because we aren't fishermen.' Léon drew the curtain aside and looked out of the window. 'The wet cloud's gone.'

'Let's go, then,' said Louise. 'Let's go home, Léon. We've seen the sea now.'

ge

Permeated by sun, wind and rain showers, fresh sea air and a night without much sleep, Léon and Louise set out for home. Their route took them back along the same roads, across the same hills and through the same villages as they had seen the day before. They drank water from the same village fountain and bought bread from the same bakery. Their bicycles hummed along dependably, and before long the sun reappeared. All was as it had been the previous day, yet all was imbued with magic. The sky was wider, the air fresher and the future brighter. Léon felt he was truly awake for the first time ever – as if he had come into the world tired and the whole of his life hitherto had wearily traipsed along until this weekend, when he'd woken up at last. There was a life before Le Tréport and a life after Le Tréport.

At midday they had some soup at an inn, then snoozed in a barn beside the road. And although all that had so far happened is pure legend, what began that midday, while they were asleep in the barn, is the account my grandfather often liked to give many decades later of how, at the end of May 1918, he became embroiled in the Great War for the first and only time. He always told his story with charming restraint. It was believable and accurate in every detail, even after countless repetitions, save for one little fib which every member of the family saw through. This was that, for reasons of propriety, Louise wasn't a girl but a workmate named Louis.

When Léon and Louise – or Louis – woke up after an hour's nap in the barn, they heard, through its tiled roof, a distant rumble which they mistook for a thunderstorm. Hastily climbing down from the hay loft, they pushed their bicycles outside and rode off, their hair and clothes full of straw, in the hope of putting as much distance as possible between themselves and the approaching storm and getting to Saint-Luc before it descended on them.

As it turned out, the thunder was not an atmospheric phenomenon but German artillery fire. The rumble developed into a series of crisp detonations. Then the air was rent by hisses, whirrs and howls, and the first columns of debris erupted beyond a small wood. Panic-stricken, they pedalled madly along the highroad while more columns of debris went up behind, ahead and beside them. They rode past a fresh, smoking shell-hole with the roots of a fallen apple tree jutting skywards from its lip. The air was filled with acrid smoke. They were completely disoriented. Since danger seemed to threaten them on all sides, any thought of turning round and going back was out of the question.

Faster and faster they rode through the exploding country-side, Louise in the lead and Léon in her wake, and when the distance between them increased and she looked back enquiringly, he waved her on. 'Keep going, keep going!' he shouted. When she hesitated and seemed to be waiting for him, he lost his temper and yelled, 'Keep going, damn it!' So she resolutely stood up in the saddle and pedalled off.

Louise had just disappeared over a rise in the ground when a cloud of smoke and debris spurted into the air at that very spot. Léon uttered a yell and pedalled madly uphill. He had almost reached the brow of the hill when the road exploded a stone's-throw ahead of him. Debris flew tree-high into the air and a pall of brown smoke billowed outwards. At that moment an aeroplane appeared. It sprayed the road with machine-gun fire, then banked away just as Léon, travelling at full speed with two bullets in his stomach, rode blindly into the crater, where he lost a molar, consciousness, and, in the next few hours, a great deal of blood.

7

At half-past five on 17 September 1928, when Léon Le Gall hung up his laboratory apron in the locker, took out his hat and coat, and set off for home as usual, he never guessed that his life would take a decisive turn in the next few minutes. As he had a thousand times before, he walked along the Seine by way of the Quai des Orfèvres, conducting his usual survey of the second-hand booksellers' stalls as he passed them, then crossed the bridge to the Left Bank and the Place Saint-Michel.

This time, however, he did not for once walk on up the boulevard into the Quartier Latin and turn down the Rue des Écoles, where he lived with his wife Yvonne and their four-year-old son Michel on the third floor of No. 14, immediately opposite the Collège de France and the École Polytechnique, a new, airy, three-bedroom flat with parquet floors and moulded ceilings. This time he deviated from his usual route home by going down into the Place Saint-Michel Métro station and travelling two stops in the Porte d'Orléans direction so as to get some *tartes aux fraises* from Yvonne's favourite pâtisserie. It was the end of the working day in all the French capital's banks, offices and department stores, and the streets and the Métro were populated by thousands of men who looked indistinguishable in their dark or grey suits, white shirts and discreet ties. Many wore hats and most of them sported moustaches, some carried canes and many wore spats, and each was on his way from his very own desk to his very own kitchen table, whence, after his very own supper, he would retire to his very own wing chair and thereafter to his very own bed, where, if he was lucky, his very own wife would keep him warm throughout the night until, after shaving, he would drink coffee from his very own cup and set off once more for his very own desk.

Léon had long ceased to marvel at the banal absurdity of this daily mass migration. For the first few years after he succumbed to the city's gravitational pull, he had continued to suffer from nostalgia and found it hard to stomach the Parisians' barking voices and aggressive self-infatuation, the roar of the traffic and the stench of the coal-fired central heating systems. He had constantly felt surprised to have become one of the hordes who trod the pavements day after day and flaunted their new suits, either sticking out their elbows or hugging the walls, many for a few months only but others for as long as thirty or forty years, some in the belief that the world had been waiting for them alone, others in the hope that the world would notice them yet, and still others bitterly aware that the world has never waited for anyone in the course of its existence.

To Léon, who had then felt cut off from the world and imprisoned in his own thoughts, it had been a mystery how all the other fellows could slurp soup with gusto and aspire to succeed in absurd professions, tell silly jokes and flirt with peroxide blondes, without feeling in the least bit hemmed in or cut off from the world. But then his first son Michel saw the light and loudly brought it to his notice that of course a man has to slurp soup, so a desire to succeed in absurd professions is not unreasonable in itself, and that this exertion is easier to endure if you occasionally tell a silly joke or flirt with a peroxide blonde. Besides, Léon simply hadn't the time to feel cut off from the world and imprisoned in his own thoughts, which meant that a substantial number of philosophical questions pretty soon underwent a dramatic loss of urgency.

Instead, he learned to appreciate the tenderness of an unaffected smile and the unaccustomed delights of an undisturbed night's sleep, and after his first walk with wife and child and pram in the gossamer sunlight of the Jardin des Plantes he was so reconciled to life in the metropolis that he only rarely felt homesick for Cherbourg beach and longed only at quiet moments to relaunch the old sailing dinghy with his friends Patrice and Joël and take it out into the Channel.

But Léon still thought of Louise every day. He was now twenty-eight years old. It was ten years since he had ridden into a shell-hole halfway between Le Tréport and Saint-Luc-sur-Marne. He had never managed to discover how long he lay there in debris and mud and his own blood, sodden by hours of rain, sometimes unconscious from the pain and sometimes roused by its intensity, before a khaki lorry adorned with a red cross came lumbering up at dusk and stopped on the edge of the crater. Two medical orderlies, who spoke a peculiar French and turned out to be Canadians, hoisted him out of the mud with practised hands, applied a pressure dressing to his stomach, and bedded him down in the back of the lorry with twelve wounded soldiers.

'Wait,' cried Léon, grabbing one of the orderlies by the sleeve. There's someone else lying out there.'

'Where?' asked the man.

'On the road. Over that hill.'

'That's the way we came. There's no one there.'

'A girl,' gasped Léon, who was finding it hard to speak.

'You don't say? Blonde or brunette? I like redheads, myself. Is she a redhead?'

'With a bicycle.'

'Nice legs? And her tits – what are her tits like, pal? I like redheads' milky white tits, especially when they both squint outwards.'

'Her name is Louise.'

'What did you say her name was? Louder, pal, I can't understand you.'

'Louise.'

'Listen, there's no Louise lying back there, I'd have noticed. I'd definitely have noticed a Louise, you can bet your life on that, especially if she's got such great tits.'

'No bicycle either?'

'What bicycle, yours? Yours has had it, pal.'

'The girl was riding a bicycle.'

'Louise, the redhead with the squinting tits?'

Léon shut his eyes and nodded feebly.

'On the other side of the hill? Sorry, there's nothing there. No tits, no bike.'

'Please,' Léon gasped.

'I already told you,' said the orderly.

'I beg you.'

'Fucking hell. All right, I'll take another look.'

The orderly gave the driver a sign and walked back over the brow of the hill. He returned five minutes later.

'I told you there was no one there,' he said.

'Really not?'

'Just a smashed-up bicycle.' Laughing, the man opened the passenger door. 'No tits or pussy, worse luck.'

Then the lorry, which appeared to have neither springs nor

gears, set off on its interminable journey to the Canadian military hospital at Le Tréport, of all places. The two medical orderlies stretchered their thirteen items of human freight to the emergency ward, and soon afterwards, in the tented operating theatre, Léon was anaesthetized with laughing gas by a tight-lipped, bloodstained surgeon who extracted two machine-gun bullets from his body with swift, ample strokes of the scalpel and then sewed him up with swift, ample stitches. He learned later that one of the bullets had lodged in his right lung; the other had punched two holes in his gastric wall and come to rest against his left hip bone.

Because he had lost a lot of blood and his post-operative scar was thirty centimetres long, he had to remain in the hospital for several weeks. The first thing he saw on emerging from the anaesthetic was the plump, friendly, freckled face of a nurse who was looking at her watch with her fingertips applied to his wrist, lips moving silently.

'Excuse me, mademoiselle, but has a girl been brought in recently?'

'A girl?'

'Louise? Green eyes, short dark hair?'

The nurse laughed, shook her head and called a doctor. Since he, too, shook his head, Léon spent the rest of the day questioning all the nurses, orderlies, doctors and patients who passed his bed. That evening, because they merely laughed and could give him no information, he wrote three letters to Saint-Luc-sur-Marne: one to the mayor, one to Stationmaster Barthélemy, and one to the landlord of the *Café du Commerce*. And although he knew that the army postal service was slow and he couldn't expect to receive an answer for weeks or even months, he asked if any mail had come for him the very next morning.

He stood up unaided for the first time three weeks after the operation; it was another three weeks before he took his first short-winded walk to the cliffs. He made his way along the edge of the hundred-metre drop, sat down on the grass at the western end of the beach, and looked down at the black mussel banks, the remains of the campfire, and the sandy spot among the rocks where he and Louise had spent the night.

Forty-two days had gone by since then. The sea was the same blue-grey paste as before, the wind was propelling the same rain clouds across the Channel, the gulls were frolicking in the updraughts in the same way, and the world seemed undaunted by the horrors that had occurred on land in the interval. The gulls would frolic in the updraughts tomorrow and the day after, and they would continue to do so even if not only a few hundred thousand men but all the nations on earth assembled behind these cliffs in northern France, there to slaughter each other by the billion in a last great paroxysm of bloodlust. The gulls would continue to lay their eggs and hatch them if a final stream of human blood trickled over the cliffs and into the sea; they would frolic in the updraughts to all eternity, because they were seagulls and had no reason, in their seagull existence, to concern themselves with the stupidities of human beings, hump-backed whales or harvest mice.

Three days later, because Léon, being a civilian, was not permitted to use the hospital's official phone under any circumstances, he defied the medical superintendent's explicit prohibition and struggled down the flight of steps – 400 of them – that led to the little town, where he went to the post office and put through a call to the town hall of Saint-Luc-sur-Marne. When no one answered, he called the station.

It was Madame Josianne who picked up the receiver after

much hissing and crackling and the mediation of two telephonists in succession, and Léon had to repeat his name several times before she grasped who was calling. Then she burst into a tearful sing-song of jubilation, called him her dearest angel and demanded to know where in heaven's name he'd been hiding himself all this time. She didn't give him a chance to speak, but commanded him to come home this minute. Everyone was very worried about him, although to be honest they weren't at all worried any more because – he must surely understand this – it was six weeks since he'd disappeared without trace and made no sign of life since, so they'd confidently assumed that he and little Louise, with whom he'd been seen riding out of town – that he and poor little Louise had got mixed up in the last German offensive at the end of May, the very last German offensive after four years of war – incredibly hard luck on them, because it was now clear that the Boches had been driven back across the Rhine in revenge for 1870–71 and the war was practically over already, now that the Americans, with their tanks and their negro soldiers...

'What about Louise?' asked Léon.

Everyone in the town, she said, had assumed that Léon had somehow got mixed up in the German offensive of 30 May, which was why – she hated to tell him this – his position as assistant Morse telegraphist had had to be filled by someone new – the work couldn't wait, she felt sure he'd understand – not that that must prevent him from coming home this minute – there would always be some soup and a place to sleep at Madame Josianne's. Everything else would sort itself out in due course.

'What about Louise?' Léon insisted.

'*Merde*,' sighed Madame Josianne. She spun out the vowel

sound of the uncharacteristically unladylike expletive as if to delay her inescapable answer.

'What's happened to Louise?'

'Listen, my treasure: little Louise was killed in an explosion.'

'No.'

'Yes.'

'*Merde.*'

'Quite so.'

'Where?'

'I don't know, sweetheart, no one does. They found her bag and her identity card on the road between Abbeville and Amiens. No idea what she was doing there. People say her bag was empty except for a float and four scallops, and there were spots of blood on the identity card. I don't know if that's true. You know what people are, my angel, there's always a lot of talk.'

'And her bicycle?' asked Léon, instantly embarrassed by his irrelevant question. Madame Josianne, too, fell silent in surprise, then went on in a tactful, gentle voice.

'We're all very sad, my little Léon. Everyone in Saint-Luc was very fond of Louise. She was a saint – yes indeed, that's what she was. Léon, are you still there?'

'Yes.'

'Come home now, my pet, will you? And make sure you get here in time for supper, it's ratatouille.'

❧

Léon really did get to Saint-Luc station in time for supper. He suffered Madame Josianne to kiss and feed and shower him with endearments, then dress him in clean clothes and scold him for looking as pale and gaunt as death itself. While she was doing the washing-up in the kitchen, Stationmaster Barthélemy, for his part, wanted to inspect Léon's scars and hear all about the German warplane that June morning, and the shell-holes in the road, and the length of the Canadian nurses' skirts.

However, because neither he nor Josianne could tell him anything about Louise, Léon excused himself after coffee and went for a walk along the avenue to question the gasbags in the *Café du Commerce*. When he entered the café they hailed him as if he had risen from the dead, all vociferating at once and ordering rounds of Pernod which none of them later wanted to pay for; but, when he brought the conversation round to Louise, they became monosyllabic, avoided his eye and busied themselves with their cigarettes and pipes.

The mayor, whom Léon called on next morning, was just as unable to give him any information. 'I speak on behalf of the entire town and the War Ministry when I tell you that we deeply regret the passing of little Louise,' he said in his usual, statesmanlike tone, using both hands to smooth a non-existent tablecloth in a thoroughly housewifely fashion. 'The dear girl did a great deal for our country and our war heroes' bereaved loved ones.'

'Yes indeed, *monsieur le maire*,' said Léon, who was already becoming irked by the old man's pompous manner. It struck him for the first time that the mayor of Saint-Luc had a neck like a turkey and a blue-veined nose like his opposite number in Cherbourg. 'But is it known for sure that – '

'Alas, my boy,' said the mayor, who was finding the young man's interest in his little Louise out of place, 'the facts speak for themselves. There can be no doubt.'

'Did they, er, find her body?'

The mayor subsided into his chair and emitted an audible sigh, partly in mourning for little Louise's shapely breasts and partly in annoyance at this young pup's persistence and jealousy at having to share her fond memory with him.

'You must resign yourself, my boy.'

'Did they find her body, *monsieur le maire*?'

'We ourselves continued to hope to the last – '

'Did they, *monsieur le maire*?'

'I trust you don't doubt my word,' the mayor retorted with unaccustomed asperity. And in order to silence the young man and have the last word, he impulsively informed him that they had gathered up all they could find of Louise within a wide radius of her handbag, and that her remains had, according to the Ministry of War, been interred in an anonymous mass grave.

'Thank you, *monsieur le maire*,' Léon said in a low voice. All the blood had left his face, and his body, so tense with expectation until a moment before, had gone limp. 'Can you tell me where the grave – '

'No,' said the mayor, who now felt sorry for the boy and was already ashamed of his inglorious triumph. He hadn't actually told a lie, he told himself, just pretended that an assumption bordering on certainty was a copper-bottomed fact. Being a fundamentally honest person, however, he would have given a lot to be able to retract the words that had slipped out. He now strove to salvage what could still be salvaged.

'Everything's at sixes and sevens in wartime, you know? Chin up, that's what I always say. Let's forget the past and look to the future, life must go on. Do you need a new job? Can I help?'

Léon didn't answer.

'They had to fill your position at the station, as you can understand. Do you need a new job? Can I be of assistance?'

Léon stood up and buttoned his jacket.

'Let's see, I received the War Ministry's new list of vacant positions by this morning's post. What can you do, tell me?'

It turned out that the Quai des Orfèvres headquarters of the Police Judiciaire urgently required a specialist with many years' experience of Morse telegraphy, starting at once. The mayor picked up the phone, and next day Léon caught the 8.07 to Paris.

8

Ten years had gone by since that day. At twenty-eight, Léon was still a young man. His hair might not be quite as thick, but his figure was lean and youthful and he still took the steps to the Métro two and sometimes three at a time, even when he wasn't in a hurry.

He dropped some coins in the brass bowl and took his ticket, then went through the automatic barrier and down the steps to the white-tiled tunnel. This was the hour at which his wife Yvonne, who was to become my grandmother thirty-three years later, would be preparing supper while his first-born son, who grew up to be my Uncle Michel, lay sprawled on the living room's parquet floor in the golden trapezium cast by the setting sun, playing with his tin locomotive. Léon pictured them both enjoying their strawberry tarts and hoped that this evening would pass off peacefully.

Peaceful evenings had been few and far between in recent weeks. Scarcely a night went by without some domestic drama breaking over them for little or no apparent reason and against their will, and the weekends had been one long series of bravely concealed unhappiness, spurious gaiety and sudden fits of weeping. While the train was pulling into the station, Léon recalled last night's scene. It had started after he'd put the child to bed and read him a goodnight story, as he did

---

every evening. When he returned to the living room and got out the box containing the bits of the Napoleon III wall clock he had bought at the flea market and spent months trying to restore to working order, Yvonne, seemingly out of the blue, had called him monstrously indifferent and emotionally frigid before running downstairs and out into the Rue des Écoles, where she had stood forlornly in the twilight, blinded by tears, until he caught her up and shepherded her back to the flat. He had led her over to the sofa, draped a blanket round her shoulders, shovelled some briquettes into the stove, got rid of the wall clock and made some tea, then half sincerely, half falsely begged her pardon for being inattentive and asked how he had distressed her so. Receiving no answer, he had returned to the kitchen to make some hot chocolate while she continued to sit on the sofa feeling useless, stupid and ugly.

'Be honest, Léon, do you still find me attractive?'

'You're my wife, Yvonne. You know I do.'

'My complexion's all blotchy and I wear compression stockings for my varicose veins. Like an old woman.'

'It'll pass, my dear. It isn't important.'

'You see? You don't care.'

'Nonsense.'

'But you just said it isn't important. I quite understand, in your place I wouldn't care either.'

'But I *do* care. What are you talking about?'

'In your place I'd have left me long ago. Be honest, Léon, do you have another woman?'

'No! I'd never cheat on you, you know that.'

'Yes, exactly, I do.' Yvonne nodded bitterly. 'You'd never do such a thing for the simple reason that it would be wrong. You always do the right thing, don't you? You're always so self-controlled, my conscientious Léon, you couldn't betray me however much you wanted to. It would never suit you to do anything you didn't consider right.'

'You think it's wrong for me not to want to do something wrong?'

'I sometimes wish I could throw you off-balance, don't you understand? I sometimes wish you would once, just once, lose control – hit me and the child, get drunk, spend the night with a prostitute.'

'You wish for things you don't want, Yvonne.'

'Tell me something: Why do you treat me as if I were your mother?'

'How do you mean?'

'Why do you never put your arms around me? Why have you been lying on the edge of the bed for weeks?'

'Because you flinch when I kiss you. Because you burst into tears and call me a hypocrite when I stroke your hair. Because you accused me of acting like a lecherous chimpanzee in bed and told me to leave you alone. I've done so, and now you burst into tears for that very reason. Tell me what I'm supposed to do.'

Yvonne laughed and wiped away her tears with the back of her hand. 'Poor Léon, you really don't have an easy time of it. Let's not quarrel any more, all right? But let's not lie or pretend to each other either. Let's be absolutely honest. What I want I can't expect of you, and what you want I can't give you.'

'That's nonsense, Yvonne. You're my wife, and you're a good wife to me. I'm your husband and I do my best to be a good one. That's all that counts. It'll all work out in the end.'

'No, it won't, you know that as well as I do. What won't work out, won't. One can do one's best, but one can't help what one wishes for.'

'So what *do* you wish for? Tell me.'

'Forget it, Léon. I can't expect you to give me what *I* want, and I can't give you what *you* want. We get on pretty well and we don't make each other's life a misery, but we aren't really *together*. We'll have to live with that to our dying day.'

'Why bring death into it, Yvonne? We're only twenty-eight.'

'Do you want a divorce? Tell me, do you want a divorce?'

And so it went on. It came as a positive relief to them both when Yvonne's emotional outbursts at night were succeeded by attacks of morning sickness. Subdued and filled with remorse after visiting the gynaecologist, she had begged Léon's pardon, regarded her stomach with a kind of wonder, and expressed the theory that this baby would be a girl. She said she distinctly remembered that, when pregnant with little Michel three years earlier, her mood had been one of self-satisfied, self-absorbed contentment. Léon had benefited from this to the extent that it had been spiced with frequent spasms of animal lust such as she had never displayed before.

That there could be no question of animal lust on this occasion, Léon bore with fortitude. Having matured into a man with some experience of life, he knew after five years of marriage that a woman's psyche is connected in some mysterious way with the peregrinations of the stars, the alternation of the tides and the cycles of the female body; possibly, too, with subterranean volcanic flows, the flight paths of migratory birds and the French state railway timetable – even, perhaps, with the output of the Baku oilfields, the heart-rate of Amazonian humming-birds and the songs of sperm whales beneath the Antarctic pack ice.

For all that, these constantly recurring scenes about – when you came down to it – little or nothing were gradually sapping his strength. He did, admittedly, know that Yvonne's moods were transitory, and that it was conducive to his marital happiness if he could occasionally ignore or quickly forget her temporary fits of irrationality. 'You mustn't hold it against them,' his father had once impressed on him when asked for advice by phone in an hour of need. 'They can't help it, it's like a mild form of epilepsy, you take my meaning?'

Even so, Léon was loath to equate one of his wife's main characteristics with a chronic disease. Wasn't it his duty to take her troubles seriously? Having sworn before the altar to love and honour her to the end of his days, should he belittle her agony of mind as a mere echo of whale songs?

ૐ

With his nose full of the warm, sweetish wind propelled ahead of it by the incoming train, Léon joined the tide of humanity making for the edge of the platform. A few years ago, when he was still single and living in a little attic room in the Batignolles, he had travelled to work daily by Métro and come to hate the screech of steel wheels, the heat and stench inside the carriages, the stained upholstery, the damp, slippery lathwork floors and the greasy grab handles.

In those days he had acquired the agility indispensable to the survival of the regular commuter, who can thread his way through the densest crowd of people without pushing and shoving and will always politely let the persons beside him go first without betraying that he has even noticed them. Léon knew that he could expect the same introverted consideration from his fellow passengers, and that pushing and shoving and insults occurred only when substantial numbers of tourists or elderly folk were in the vicinity.

81

He let the man on his right go first and moved into the space that opened up behind him, gave way to a woman with a pram and made it to the sliding doors in her wake. Then, in two or three quick strides, he reached the corner beside the opposite sliding doors, where there was ample standing room. He unbuttoned his overcoat and tipped his hat back, wedged himself in the corner so as not to have to hold on to a grab handle, and buried his hands in his coat pockets. While the open space in front of him was rapidly filling up, he scanned his surroundings commuter fashion, avoiding all eye contact, to satisfy himself that no potential source of annoyance lay in any direction.

Looking out of the window when the doors closed and the train pulled out, Léon watched the passengers waiting on the opposite platform, then the power cables snaking along the brownish-black tunnel wall, the red and white signal lights flashing past, and the yawning mouths of side tunnels. At the next station it became light again, then dark, and when it became light again he got out and ascended into daylight, bought his strawberry tartlets, and dived straight back below ground, where a train in the Porte de Clignancourt direction was just pulling in.

Léon allowed the tide of humanity to carry him across the platform and into a carriage as far as the same corner beside the opposite doors in which he had stood on the outward journey. When a train pulled into the opposite platform he looked at its cargo of passengers gliding by: men with newspapers, *mutilés de guerre* on crutches, women with shopping baskets. At first they were only vague, blurred figures flitting past him; then they slowed down and became more clearly defined, and when the train finally stopped he noticed, barely a metre or a metre-and-a-half from him, a young woman standing in the equivalent corner beside the sliding doors.

Wearing a black coat, a black skirt and a pale-blue blouse, she had green eyes, freckles and thick, dark hair bobbed at the back from one earlobe to the other, and she had a generous mouth and a dainty chin, and she was smoking a cigarette which she held between her thumb and forefinger like a street urchin, and she was beyond doubt, of that Léon felt instantly convinced, his Louise.

She had of course changed in the intervening ten years. The young girl's childishly soft features had developed into the firmer, more angular features of a grown woman. The eyes that looked out from beneath her fine, straight eyebrows were alert and unerringly watchful, and the corners of her mouth conveyed a look of determination that was new to him. And when she brushed a strand of hair behind her ear with her fingertips, he caught a flash of nail varnish.

Léon shook off his inertia at last. He raised his hand and waved, stepped forward into her field of view and – nonsensically – tapped on the window pane. But she, separated from him by only one metre of air and a few millimetres of window glass, pulled at her cigarette and blew the smoke downwards, flicked off the ash and stared into space. He rattled the closed doors that separated him from Louise's closed doors and tried to estimate how long it would take him to reach the other platform via the stairs. Then the open doors rumbled shut and put paid to his deliberations. He took off his hat and waved it in the air, and then, at last, she turned towards him.

Then, at last, their eyes met and his last remaining doubts vanished when the look of enquiry in her green eyes gave way successively to incredulous surprise and a smile of joyful recognition that revealed the little gap between her teeth. But then the two trains started to pull out in opposite directions, rendering the distance between them greater and the angle of view more acute, and they lost sight of each other once more.

As he plunged into the tunnel Léon desperately wondered what to do and arrived at three possible alternatives, all of which seemed to him equally sensible. He could take the next train back to Saint-Sulpice and hope that she would do the same; or he could get out one stop beyond Saint-Sulpice on the assumption that she had also got out there and was waiting for him; or he himself could wait at the next station in the hope that she would follow.

But it was hopeless in any case to try to locate someone on the crowded trains, platforms and stairs in rush hour, especially when you didn't even know whether they were waiting for you somewhere or hurriedly scouring the Métro themselves. The first thing Léon did was travel back to Saint-Sulpice, where he climbed on a bench beneath a poster depicting a bright red Citroën cabriolet 10cv B14 crossing some sand dunes and tried to get an overhead view of both platforms. Since all he could see were grey hats and strange women's hairdos, he rode the next train one station further to St.-Placide, just in case Louise had got out there and stayed put, then returned to Saint-Germain-des-Près to see if Louise was looking for him there, then went back to Saint-Sulpice and from there paid a second visit to St.-Placide.

ॐ

After sixteen such journeys Léon realized he would never find Louise that way. He was perspiring and exhausted, his suit was too tight, and pink strawberry juice and pale-yellow custard were oozing from the carton containing the *tartes aux fraises,* which had suffered appreciably from the crush on their hourslong odyssey between the same three Métro stations. He walked slowly up the Boulevard Saint-Michel beneath the autumnally golden plane trees, blinking in the glare of headlights reflected by wet cobblestones.

Feeling as if he had awakened from a chaotic dream after a restless night's sleep, he was amazed that he could have spent half the evening down in the Métro chasing after a girl whom he hadn't seen for ten years, and who was in all probability long dead. The young woman had certainly borne a remarkable resemblance to Louise, and she had undoubtedly smiled as if she recognized him. But how many green-eyed young women were there in Paris – a hundred thousand? If one in every ten had a gap between her front teeth, and if one in every fifty of those cut her own hair, wasn't it possible that one or another out of those two hundred, while travelling home in the Métro after an enjoyable day's work, would smile out of mere friendliness at a strange man waving his hat at her like a buffoon?

Léon now felt sure that he'd been chasing after a ghost, albeit a ghost that had faithfully accompanied him for ten long years. It was his secret sin that he often, while getting up in the mornings, pictured Louise leaning against a plane tree, waiting for him, and in the afternoons, when his hours in the laboratory were dragging, he amused himself by remembering that one weekend at Le Tréport. Finally, when he lay on his own, solitary side of the marriage bed, he helped himself off to sleep by thinking of his first encounter with Louise and her squeaking bicycle.

❦

He cautiously turned the key in the street door and closed it softly behind him. It was seldom that he managed to slip unnoticed past the concierge, who had taken him to her heart years ago, when her two daughters were still little, because he had made them Christmas presents of miniature lions, giraffes and hippos out of wood shavings and scraps of material. The curtain behind the glass was drawn, but issuing from the door of her lodge, which was open a crack, came the sound of frying fat and the smell of braised onions. He tiptoed past, reached the foot of the stairs, and thought he was safe when Madame Rossetos emerged in her widow's weeds, her black widow's bonnet, and her blue floral apron.

'Why, Monsieur Le Gall, you startled me! Fancy creeping into the building like a burglar at this hour!'

'Forgive me, Madame Rossetos.'

'You're late tonight, I hope there's nothing wrong?' The concierge aimed the tip of her nose at him as if taking scent.

'No, no. What should be wrong?'

'You're pale, monsieur, you look a positive fright. And what's that awful thing in your hand? Give it here. No, no arguments, give it here. I'll deal with it.'

She darted forwards and snatched the carton out of his hand. Then, never taking her eyes off him, she backed into her glassed-in den like moray eel withdrawing into a coral reef with its prey. Léon had no choice but to follow her in. He made his way into the onion fumes and watched as she deposited the carton on the kitchen table, removed the battered strawberry tartlets, put them on a floral plate, moulded them into shape with her swollen fingers, and replaced the dislodged strawberries on the custard. He smelt the aroma of onions in her troglodytic abode and the cloying smell of stale sweat that clung to the bombazine dress on her ample form, eyed the red of the lipstick that had seeped into the wrinkles around her mouth, the garish Madonna on the little family altar, the lighted candle in front of the hand-coloured portrait photograph of her late husband in his sergeant's uniform, the lace antimacassar on the armchair, the sooty grey of the wall above the stove, and he listened to the crackle of the stove and the heavy, concentrated breathing from Madame Rossetos' flared nostrils.

A heavy curtain divided the living room from the bedroom in which her two young daughters were slumbering their way to next morning under dark-red blankets and growing a quarter of a millimetre each night in the serene certainty that they would, in the not too far distant future, blossom into young ladies and, at the first opportunity, escape from their mother's clutches for ever. They would elope with some boyfriend who bought them silk lingerie or enter the service of some lady who would bear them off to Neuilly as chambermaids. But Madame Rossetos would remain behind on her own, vegetate in her lair for a while longer and wait for her daughters' ever rarer visits until one day she would fall ill, drag herself off to hospital, and soon afterwards, after a last look at the water stains on the ceiling, die a meek and submissive death.

The concierge sprinkled the tartlets with icing sugar to hide the worst of the ravages, wiped her hands on her apron, and looked up at Léon with an expression eloquent of all the guile-less vulnerability of her tormented soul.

'Here you are, Monsieur Le Gall, that's the best I can do.'

'I'm much obliged to you.'

'You must go now, your wife will have been waiting for you.'

'Yes.'

'Waiting a long time.'

'Yes indeed.'

'Two hours. You're very late tonight.'

'Yes.'

'I can't ever remember you getting home so late. Madame must be worried.'

'You're right.'

'Nothing bad happened, that's the main thing. I'll put my calves' liver in the pan now. I never eat until the girls are in bed, then I can do so in peace. Do you like calves' liver in red wine sauce, Monsieur Le Gall?'

'Very much.'

'And sautéed potatoes with rosemary?'

'It's my idea of heaven.'

'But you've got all you need at home, you lucky man. And you're really sure nothing bad happened?'

'Absolutely not. I must hurry.'

'Of course. Madame will be expecting you, and here I am, holding you up with my nonsense about calves' liver.'

'Oh, you mustn't say that, Madame Rossetos. Calves' liver in red wine sauce isn't nonsense, it's a very serious matter. Especially when sautéed potatoes with rosemary are also involved.'

'How nicely you put that, Monsieur Le Gall! You're a man of refinement, I always say. Sure you won't have a taste? Just a quick one?'

'It sounds tempting, but...'

'Madame will have your supper ready, of course, and I'm holding you up with my chatter.'

'Some other time.'

'She's bound to be worried.'

'Yes, I ought to be going.'

'Enjoy your evening and my best regards to Madame.'

9

Léon carried the strawberry tartlets up to the third floor. The stairs were freshly polished, the bright red stair carpet was free from dust, and the brass stair rods gleamed. He breathed in the scent of wax polish, which gave him a homely feeling of peace and permanency, and listened to the little sounds from the neighbouring flats, which seemed to convey a sense of belonging and security.

He paused outside his door. He could hear his wife singing a ballad in her girlishly high but slightly husky voice. '*Si j'étais à ta place, si tu prenais la mienne...*' He waited until the song had died away, then opened the door. Yvonne was standing in the hallway in a pale summer frock far too light for the time of year, arranging a bunch of asters in a vase. She turned to him with a smile.

'There you are at last! Supper's on the table. The boy's asleep already. I waited supper for you and opened a bottle of wine.'

૪ઌ

She took the plate of strawberry tartlets from him, laughing at their sorry state, sent him off to wash his hands with feigned severity and, after a quick sidelong glance at herself in the mirror, tweaked her hair into shape. Léon was surprised; this wasn't the despairing, tormented, captive creature he had left at home that morning, but the singing, laughing young girl he had once fallen in love with.

'You're looking odd,' she said when supper was over and they'd retired to the living room for coffee and the maltreated strawberry tartlets. 'Has something happened?'

'I went to Saint-Sulpice and bought the *tartes aux fraises.*'

'I know, it was very nice of you. You took your time, though, didn't you?'

'Yes.'

'Over two hours. Were you held up?'

'I saw this girl.'

'What girl?'

'I'm not sure.'

'You're not sure? You see some girl, but you aren't sure and you're two hours late?'

'Yes.'

'My dear, it sounds as if we need to talk.'

'I think it was Louise.'

'Which Louise?'

'Little Louise from Saint-Luc-sur-Marne. You know who I mean.'

'The girl who died?'

Léon nodded, then gave his wife a detailed description of his encounter in the Métro, his toings and froings along the selfsame tunnel, his doubts on the way home, and the further doubts that had arisen since then. He ended by telling her about his visit to the concierge and his subsequent ascent of the stairs, during which tears had come to his eyes – tears of pity not only for Madame Rossetos but for himself and the world in general.

When he was through, Yvonne got up and went over to the window, where she drew the curtain aside and looked down at the nocturnally silent street.

'We always knew something like this would happen one day, didn't we?' Her tone was cheerful and there was a faint smile on her lips. Her figure was silhouetted against the lamp-light and the falling rain. 'You'll go looking for this dead girl. You have to make sure.'

'She doesn't exist any more, Yvonne, either way. Besides, a lot of time has gone by.'

'You'll go looking for her all the same.'

'No, I won't.'

'You'll go looking for her sooner or later. You won't be able to live with the uncertainty.'

'The certainties I do have are enough for me,' he replied. 'I don't need any others. I don't chase after other women, you ought to know that.'

'Because you married me?'

'Because I'm your husband and you're my wife.'

'You don't want to do anything wrong, Léon, and that's to your credit. All the same, this business will prey on your mind if you don't get to the bottom of it. I don't want to see you suffer, for my own sake above all. You must look for the girl, I insist.'

§

Next morning Léon struggled with an urge to ride the Métro back and forth a couple of times, just on the off-chance. In the Place Saint-Michel he abandoned the struggle. Passing beneath the cast-iron art nouveau lamp at the head of the steps, he made his way down into the Métro station. In the hour that followed he encountered a large number of people of both sexes and every age, size and skin colour, as well as a few dogs, a cat in a wickerwork cage, and even a farmer with dull yellow canine eyes and two live sheep, who must have parked his cart at Porte de Châtillon and was taking them by Métro to market at Les Halles. But he never saw a girl with green eyes.

Nobody noticed that he was late for work. The Police Judiciaire's forensic laboratory was situated on the fourth floor of the Quai des Orfèvres building, high above the offices of the *commissariat,* the criminal police headquarters itself, which rang with shouts, lamentations and oaths at all hours of the day and night. In Léon's department, by contrast, peace reigned. There was no smell of rain-sodden police overcoats, or of the sweat of apprehensive suspects under interrogation, or of beer and *choucroute,* or of the sandwiches and cigarettes of crime reporters hanging around in the passages hoping for a scoop. Here it smelt of chlorine and Javel water, ether and acetone. The laboratory abounded in brass and glass and mahogany, and the staff worked with silent concentration to the hiss of Bunsen burners.

They padded around quietly and talked in low voices, and if some clumsy junior should happen to clatter two Erlenmeyer flasks or test tubes together, his colleagues merely raised their eyebrows in annoyance. Here superiors addressed their subordinates formally as '*vous*' and politely couched their orders in the interrogative form. Everyone made his own coffee at break time, and no one would have dreamed of even noticing a colleague's belated arrival.

It was ten years since Léon had presented himself at the Police Judiciaire's communications centre, which was situated two floors below the laboratory and one floor above the *commissariat*. In the early weeks he had found it hard to do justice to his function as a Morse expect, because all that counted there was efficiency and he couldn't disguise his incompetence by falling back on a railwayman's smart uniform and a red flag. It had clearly emerged after only one hour's work that Léon hadn't a clue about Morse telegraphy. This he had with difficulty justified to his superiors by vaguely alluding to years off work owing to war service and convalescence after being wounded in action; once he had even pulled his shirt out of his trousers to show off his cicatrized bullet wounds.

But because he proved to be extremely hard-working and pored over the official manuals of the French and international telegraph companies until long after midnight in his attic room in the Batignolles, he quickly overcame his handicap and was accounted a fully qualified telegraphist after only a few months.

However, it was soon borne in on him that Morse telegraphy, once you got the hang of it, was an extremely monotonous occupation with little prospect of variety. As luck would have it, he was rescued from the telegraph office after three years by the deputy director of the Scientific Service, with whom he occasionally had lunch and who offered him an assistant's post in the newly established forensic laboratory.

Léon's change of job did, admittedly, mean a return to a state of utter incompetence, because his total lack of interest in chemistry had consigned him to the bottom of the class at school, and he had completely forgotten the little rudimentary knowledge that had, despite himself, lodged in his brain.

By employing his tried and tested method of imposture, however, he again succeeded in remedying his ignorance in a short space of time. His colleagues forgave his initial clumsiness partly because he was friendly to them all and did not contest anyone's position in the hierarchy. By the autumn of 1928, when his second child was on the way, Léon was among the most senior members of the laboratory staff and accountable to no one. There was a good chance that he would be appointed deputy departmental director in a few years' time.

That morning he had to check a potato gratin sample for traces of arsenic, a procedure he must have carried out a hundred times before. He took the dish containing the supposedly poisoned gratin from the refrigerator, dissolved a knife point of it in hydrogen and poured the solution over a piece of filter paper to which he had previously applied a solution of auric sodium chloride. Although constant repetition had rendered every move he made second nature to him, he exercised due care when handling the samples, every second or third of which actually proved to contain enough poison to be hazardous to health. This time the result was negative. Instead of turning violet under the influence of the potato solution, the auric sodium chloride retained its brown coloration. Léon went to the sink and washed his utensils, then sat down at the black and gold Remington on his desk and typed out a report plus three copies for the investigating magistrate.

In the early years he had taken an interest in the broken vows of fidelity and cooling passions that gave rise to the poisoned potato gratins and pork chops, likewise the stories of avarice, betrayal and revenge. He had tried to imagine the desperation of the poisoners – it was nearly always women who resorted to rat poison, men having other weapons at their disposal in the fight for survival. He had also tried to empathize with the feelings of relief and disappointment entertained by those husbands who had misinterpreted their stomach-aches, giddy spells and fits of sweating as symptoms of poisoning. He used to seek out the detective inspectors on the ground floor and chat with them in order to learn something of the fate of those persons whom he, Léon Le Gall, with his pipettes and stirrers, had either set at liberty or consigned to prison or the scaffold. He had sometimes – unofficially and against his colleagues' advice – visited crime scenes or viewed the homes of female poisoners, paid his respects to their victims in the morgue, and looked into the murderesses' eyes when they were convicted and sentenced.

As time went by, however, he discovered that most of these dramas bore a terribly banal resemblance to each other, and that the same stories of rapacity, brutality and stupidity recurred again and again with only minor variations. After three years in the department at latest, therefore, he confined himself to looking for arsenic, rat poison or cyanide on behalf of the law and left any questions of guilt, motive and fate, as well as punishment, atonement and forgiveness, to others: to the judges in their august robes, or Almighty God in heaven, or the man in the street, or the beer drinkers around their favourite table. This was the attitude of professional detachment which his more experienced colleagues had advised him to adopt from the outset.

For all that, he could nearly always arrive at a clear-cut, definitive and exhaustive answer to the simple questions – Arsenic, yes or no? Cyanide, yes or no? – he had to deal with in the laboratory. This he found extremely pleasant, and after years of handling countless cases he could still subscribe without reservation to the moral principle underlying his work: that it wasn't a good thing to dispatch people from life to death by means of poison.

From that point of view, Léon still found the purpose of his job – demonstrating to potential poisoners that they might not get away with it – moral and important and right. As for the repetitive nature of his daily work, which didn't often get him down, he consoled himself with the generous salary that had enabled him to afford the move from the Batignolles to the Rue des Écoles when he married, and with the hope that if all went reasonably well he would sometime be promoted to a more interesting position.

After the potato gratin he tested a glass of white Bordeaux for cyanide, got another negative result, and took the Roquefort he was to test for rat poison from the refrigerator. A glance at the clock on the wall told him it was already eleven. He decided to save the Roquefort for the afternoon and have lunch at home for once. Being so early, he would take advantage of the spare time and make two or three Métro trips back and forth between Saint-Michel and Saint-Sulpice.

꽃

When Léon left the Boulevard Saint-Michel and turned off down the Rue des Écoles, the clouds parted. Ahead of him, the Sorbonne emitted a pale radiance such as only exists in the streets of Paris and the sky suddenly gleamed as if impregnated with gold dust. From one moment to the next the blackbirds in the trees began to sing, the hum of the traffic sounded more cheerful, the tap-tap of ladies' heels crisper, the gendarmes' whistles less peremptory.

After a few steps Léon seemed to hear, above the noises of the street, the delighted squeals of his son Michel. As he drew nearer, he saw he hadn't been mistaken: the little boy really was on the little stretch of turf beside the Collège de France which municipal gardeners had laid right below his living-room windows a few weeks ago. Cheeks flushed and eyes shining with all the *joie de vivre* of which a four-year-old is capable, Michel was riding round and round the centrepiece of the miniature park, a stone bust of the deaf poet Pierre de Ronsard, in a bright red pedal car in the form of a fire engine complete with turntable ladder, bell and spotlight.

Seated on a stone park bench, in a pose of utter relaxation, was Léon's wife. Yvonne's left arm was draped over the back of the seat, her right forearm rested horizontally against her fore-head. She had stretched out her legs and was as engrossed in the sight of her blissful child as a mother cat that has just given her litter an ample feed. She was wearing a long white linen dress that was new to Léon – her self-confidently swelling little tummy could be glimpsed beneath it – together with a pretty little straw hat and some pink-lensed sunglasses that lent her summery get-up a rather jaunty appearance.

Léon was taken aback. This wasn't the blithely singing girl he'd left at home that morning, nor the tormented domestic prisoner who had kept him company in recent months, but a woman he'd never seen before. She might have been one of those Russian aristos who strolled for hours in the Luxembourg Gardens, or an American film star on her third highball.

When Yvonne spotted him, she waved each of the fingers on her right hand in turn. He waved back, then crouched down beside his little son and got him to show off his fire engine's bell and ladder.

'Léon, how nice that you're home for lunch for once!' Yvonne said as he sat down beside her. When he kissed her, he felt her nestle against him in a way she hadn't for a long time.

'Forgive me for asking,' he said, 'but did you go mad this morning?'

She laughed. 'Because of these new acquisitions, you mean? Little Michel and I went on a shopping spree at Galeries Lafayette.'

'You bought all this stuff brand-new?'

'As you can see. Look how happy the boy is. The bell's solid brass, you know. Michel, sweetheart, ring the bell again for your Papa.'

The little boy tugged at the bell rope so hard, passers-by on the other side of the street glanced across in surprise. Léon did his best to smile at this display of childish happiness, then readdressed himself to his wife. 'Care to tell me how much that fire engine – '

'Do you like it?'

'How much did that fire engine cost?'

'No idea. It's down on the bill. Probably a bit more than you earn in a month. How much *do* you earn, actually?'

'Yvonne…'

'It's made by Renault, you know.'

'You're out of your mind!'

'A genuine little Renault, manufactured in their workshops at Boulogne-Billancourt. The salesman explained it to me. The power is transmitted from the pedals to the rear axle by a Cardan drive, just like a real Renault. You must take a look.'

'Yvonne…'

'Do you know what a Cardan drive is?'

'Yes.'

'What?'

'A drive shaft with a universal joint.'

'Correct. How do you like my dress?'

'Listen to me.'

'The sunglasses look a bit silly, I admit.'

'Kindly listen!'

'No, *you* listen to *me* now, Léon. Will you?'

'Of course.'

'What are you trying to tell me – that I've done something silly?'

'You can say that again!'

'You see? We're in agreement there. I *have* done something silly, but so have you.'

'You'll bankrupt us, you and your Cardan drive.'

'And you did a fair bit of travelling on the Métro today, didn't you?'

Léon didn't answer.

'I know you too well – I knew you would before you knew it yourself. I watched you from behind when you left the building this morning. I could tell you'd go on the Métro today from the guilty way your neat little boyish buttocks waggled to and fro.'

'And that's why you took our son to Galeries Lafayette?'

'Exactly.'

'Forgive me if I fail to see the connection.'

'Léon, your Métro rides are a disgrace and an insult – an insult to you and me and us both. I don't want you committing such pathetic little stupidities. You're making a fool of yourself, and you're making me look a laughing stock to myself. It's got to stop. Either you go looking for that dead girl, or you don't.'

'You're right.'

'But if you go looking for her, you must do it properly. Otherwise, I'll show you how to commit some really big stupidities, not pathetic little ones. If you continue to go on your pathetic little Métro rides, I'll commit some stupidities that'll make your hair stand on end.' She took his right hand and clamped it between her knees, then rested her head on his shoulder.

'Am I going to lose you, Léon?' Her voice had gone suddenly reedy and her expression was as pained as if she were plucking her eyebrows or ripping a depilatory off her leg. 'Are you going to leave me? Am I losing you?'

'How can you even ask such a thing? I certainly won't leave you, it's out of the question.'

'Nice of you to say so, but we know better, don't we? You probably won't leave me, that's true, but either I've already lost you or I never had you. That's the way it is. From now on, things can get either worse or a little bit better. It's entirely up to us.'

'I'm sitting here beside you, Yvonne, surely you can see that? I'm here because I want to be. I won't leave you, I promise.'

'And you always keep your promises, I know.' She sighed and patted his flank like a dog. 'For all that, Léon, you mustn't waste any time. Go looking while the trail is fresh.'

'There's no point.'

'I order you to. Think of some way of finding the woman. After all, you're with the police.'

They sat there in silence for a while, watching little Michel circling the gravel path in his fire engine. When the pressure of her knees relaxed he took her right hand and pressed it firmly to his lips. Having released her, he nodded as if in confirmation of some decision he'd come to. Then, without another word, he rose and walked swiftly, resolutely off. It felt as if the Rue des Écoles were leaving him behind, not the other way round.

10

The express to Boulogne was heading out into Picardy. Seated on his own in an overheated second-class compartment, Léon was trying to read the afternoon edition of *Aurore* but looking out at the autumnally brown countryside every few moments. After leaving his wife in the park and returning to the Boulevard Saint-Michel, he had only briefly contemplated calling in at headquarters and enlisting police assistance in his search for Louise. Then he realized that nothing good could come of it. For one thing, he would make himself look a fool in front of his colleagues; for another, if the police actually launched a search contrary to all expectations, it would very probably yield no result. Thirdly, if Louise were actually run to earth, she wouldn't find it very romantic if the first sign of life made by the long-lost friend of her youth was to send a posse of uniformed gendarmes chasing after her.

So Léon had decided to look for Louise by himself. Although the detective methods employed by the Police Judiciaire were known only in broad outline to him, who spent his days in the seclusion of the laboratory, he was familiar with one basic rule of criminology: that a perpetrator often returned to the scene of the crime. And since he and Louise were both, in a sense, perpetrators and accomplices as well as victims and investigators, he took the Métro to the Gare du Nord and bought a ticket to Le Tréport. The direct route via Épinay was closed for construction work in September 1928, so he had to make a detour by way of Amiens and Abbeville.

Like most townsmen, Léon seldom left the city. Like all Parisians, he always swore that he would, if only it were possible, gladly exchange the noise, dirt and bustle of the City of Light for a quiet, peaceful life somewhere in the provinces, and that he would happily exchange the Opéra, the Bibliothèque Nationale and all the theatres in Paris for a glass of burgundy in the southern sun, a game of *pétanque* with friends, and a long walk through the woods and vineyards with the dog he would then acquire – possibly a black and white cocker spaniel by the name of Casimir or Patapouf.

But because there were no jobs for Léon in the vineyards of the South and he secretly realized, like all Parisians, that he would very soon get bored to death in the provinces, he stuck it out in the unloved city. Once or twice, at the best time of year, he would take a *bateau mouche* trip down the Seine with his wife and child or picnic in the woods at Saint-Germain-en-Laye, and at Christmas and the New Year he took the train to Cherbourg to visit his father and mother. The other three hundred and fifty days he spent within the city limits, and on three hundred of them he saw little more of the city itself than the handful of streets between the Rue des Écoles and the Quai des Orfèvres.

Not for the first time, Léon was surprised at how abruptly the sea of buildings petered out and the green and brown undulations of field, meadow and ploughland began. At Porte de la Chapelle the railway line was still flanked by factories and warehouses and the banks of the Seine by sheds and barns; but immediately beyond the gasometer at Saint-Denis, where dense smoke billowed from tall chimneys, a farmer's boy could be seen herding some cows across a meadow, a dead straight avenue of poplars stretched away to the horizon, and golden yellow willows were bending before the keen north-east wind.

Léon experienced an almost irresistible urge to get out at the next station, buy a bicycle – or, better still, steal one – and ride to the sea beneath the open sky, in the fresh air and rain and against the wind. His buttocks would hurt as they had then, his muscles would ache as they had then, and he would collect some strange odds and ends on the way and keep an eye on the horizon in the insane hope that a girl with a red and white polka-dot blouse and a squeaking bicycle would appear. He would buy some bread and ham and drink water from a fountain, relieve himself behind a hedge like a farmer's boy, and seek shelter from storms in empty barns like a tramp. And it would all be pointless and nonsensical – a pathetic little stupidity unworthy of his Yvonne, unworthy of his Louise, and unworthy of himself.

The journey took two hours thirty-five minutes. Between Amiens and Abbeville the track followed the asphalted highroad he had cycled along with Louise. He thought he could remember this or that farmhouse or corn mill, maybe also some lone lime tree or particularly pretty villa, and he kept a sharp eye open for the range of hills on which Louise and he, only a stone's-throw apart, had lain in their respective shell-holes. The most noticeable traces of devastation had disappeared in the ten years since the war's end. Roads had been repaired and houses rebuilt, and nature had filled in the trenches and clothed the shell-holes in merciful greenery.

At Abbeville he changed to the little tourist tram, which lurched along to Le Tréport. He was the only passenger apart from some schoolchildren and a girl in clogs with a basketful of cabbages on her lap. It was clear from the state of the train that Parisian holidaymakers had stayed away because of the war, inflation and the Depression. The lilac-upholstered seats were worn and torn, the window panes cloudy, the leather straps cracked and the chrome-plated grab handles tarnished. The track was warped and weeds were growing up between the rails. Nobody got in or out on the way. It wasn't until they got to the terminus on the Quai François Ier that the schoolchildren made a noisy exit and the girl in clogs shuffled after them.

On the quayside Léon looked round as if there were the smallest chance that a girl with green eyes might appear from a side street, at a window, or on board a fishing boat. They had left their bicycles beside that lamp post and she had slipped her arm through his somewhere near that bollard. Here they had tossed the strips of white fat from their ham sandwiches into the harbour basin, there she had thrust her last morsel into his mouth with her fingertips, and there she had criticized the holidaymakers for putting on airs. That was the fountain she'd drunk from and those were the cobblestones, which now had grass and moss growing between them, on which she'd walked in her shabby black lace-up shoes.

The tourist boats that had sailed in and out, belching steam and smoke, were now tied up against the harbour wall with weed-encrusted hulls and boarded-up hatches. There were no white lace parasols to be seen on the quayside, no pink bootees or gleaming spats, just scrawny seagulls, shaggy dogs and a horde of barefoot urchins playing football with an old tin can. The fishermen were still there, repairing their nets, puffing at their pipes and stroking their wrinkled necks with gnarled hands.

Léon walked out to the lighthouse, sat down on the sea wall and shuffled around until he had a distinct feeling that he was sitting just where Louise had. Then he rested his hands on the wall and caressed it. It suddenly struck him that he was hungry. He hadn't eaten a thing since breakfast.

The *Café du Commerce,* where Louise had explained the difference between rich bores and poor, was shut. The doors and windows were barred and wind-blown autumn leaves and faded sheets of newsprint were lying in front of the entrance. A yellow dog trotted past, cocked a hind leg and urinated against the wall, hobbling along on three legs as it did so.

Léon overtook the dog and walked past a closed lacemaker's shop, then a closed newsagent's, a ramshackle private house and a brightly painted shop called *Aux Quatre Vents,* which used to sell beach toys. Beyond it was an ironmonger's. The lights were on inside, so Léon pushed the door open and went in. He acquired a blue enamelled saucepan, then set off up the Rue de Paris, where he had once bought bread, wine and vegetables.

An hour later he was sitting between the two boulders that lay at the southern end of the beach, massive, immovable and immutable. The tide was out, the waves were feebly, sullenly lapping the grey shingle, and seagulls were frolicking in the updraughts. Léon realized only now how much he had missed their harsh screams. He poked the embers of his campfire, put on more driftwood, and stirred his saucepan, which was filled to the brim with mussels, carrots, onions and sea water.

The church clock struck five. Then came the distant bell of the tram. Having studied the timetable, Léon knew that it was the last incoming tram of the day, and that the last train back to Paris would be leaving in less than an hour.

He scanned the shingle beach with its row of bathing huts, once white but now peeling and covered with algae. The smart seaside villas behind them had been freshly whitewashed and were bravely standing their ground, but their closed windows and rigidly motionless curtains made them look as if the course of world events had taken their breath away. If she wanted to eat some mussels today, Louise would have to appear at the other end of the esplanade in the next few minutes, in the gap between the Hôtel des Anglais and the casino.

When the church clock struck five-fifteen, Léon took the saucepan from the fire and started eating, at first hesitantly and with many a sidelong glance at the esplanade, but then quickly and resolutely. He tossed the empty shells on to the beach. Then he went down to the water's edge, rinsed out the saucepan and deposited it beside the ashes of his fire upside down.

He didn't return by way of the beach but took the direct route across the esplanade to the Rue de Paris, then up the hill to the Église Saint-Jacques. The Virgin Mary was still standing in her niche on the right of the entrance. Her cheeks were just as red and her boot button eyes just as black, but her blue and gold robe had faded a little and her figure was no longer studded with folded and rolled-up slips of paper. What was new was the money box at her feet, into which people could put donations for the widows of drowned seamen.

Léon considered kneeling down in front of the Virgin and trying to murmur a prayer, but being unsure whether he could even recite the whole of the Lord's Prayer from beginning to end, he decided against it and dropped a coin into the money box instead. Then he took out his notebook, scribbled a few lines and tore out the page, rolled it up and stuck it in the Virgin's right armpit, exactly as before.

But because his slip of paper was the only one, it resembled a thermometer inserted in her armpit and made her look as if she had a temperature, so he pulled it out and stuck it behind her ear instead. There it looked like a carpenter's pencil, in the folds of her blue robe like a dagger, between her lips like a cigarette, and at her feet like a bone left there by some dog. So he replaced it in her right armpit, left the church and made his way down to the harbour. He would have to hurry if he wanted to catch the last tram.

ଛ

Three days later, Léon was sitting on the terrace of the *Café de Flore* far too early. It was Saturday afternoon, and the Boulevard Saint-Germain was thronged with strollers and tourists. He had already drunk three cups of coffee and skimmed five newspapers twice over, and he still had twenty minutes to kill before five o'clock finally came. He buttoned and unbuttoned his jacket, stretched his legs and withdrew them under his chair again, asked the man at the next table for the exact time and set his pocket watch three minutes slow. Then he folded the newspapers into a neat pile, never taking his eyes off the stream of passers-by.

ଛ

If the truth be told, he was sitting there against his will. It was Yvonne who had compelled him to keep this assignation, not that he was even sure it was one. When he had returned to the Rue des Écoles late at night two days ago, he had managed, contrary to his expectations, to sneak unnoticed past the concierge's door. However, Yvonne had been waiting for him on the landing, ready to leave in her hat and coat with a suitcase at her feet. Clutched in her hand was a crumpled handkerchief, which she was pressing to her lips.

Léon was taken aback yet again. This wasn't the tipsy *demimondaine* in pink sunglasses whom he had left behind in the park that lunchtime, nor the blithely singing young girl, nor the tormented housewife. This time Yvonne was the self-sacrificing heroine of a Greek tragedy.

'Well?' she said.

'Nothing,' he replied, taking the suitcase from her. 'I'm an idiot. Forgive me.'

'What?'

'I went to the church at Le Tréport. Like that time, you know. It was just a hunch. Please let's go in.'

After he had told her everything she wiped her eyes on her handkerchief and said, 'Five o'clock at the *Café de Flore* the day after tomorrow?'

'Yes, but…'

'No buts. You're going, Léon, you hear me? Just to make sure. You must, I insist.'

❦

It was ten minutes past five when he sensed Louise's presence. He couldn't see or hear her, just sensed her like a current of air wafting down the street or a ray of sunlight falling on a building when the clouds overhead disperse. He looked around enquiringly at the café's other customers and scanned the windows on the other side of the street, simultaneously keeping an eye on the passers-by.

Then he noticed a pretty but rather battered sports car standing on the other side of the boulevard in the Place du Québec with its engine running. It was a lime-green Peugeot Torpedo 172, easily identifiable by the sharply tapering back to which it owed its name. Léon had fallen in love with the smart, speedy little two-seater when it was all the rage in the streets of Paris a few years earlier, and for a while he had secretly calculated for how many months he would have to set aside a quarter, a third or a fifth of his salary in order to afford the down payment.

Being a sensible soul, however, he had never lost sight of the fact that a family man like himself had no legitimate reason for spending a quarter, a third or even a fifth of his salary on a two-seater. When Yvonne poked fun at the yearning looks he cast at passing Torpedoes, as she sometimes did, he always claimed that he was looking, not at the car, but at some pretty woman on the other side of the street.

He hadn't seen the Torpedo arrive, so it must have been standing there for a while. The hood was up, the exhaust smoking, and a vague figure could be glimpsed behind the windscreen. It was as if the little round headlights above the battered wings were winking at him, the dark, round hole in the dented radiator grille calling to him, and the whole of the little car trembling with impatience for him to get up at last, cross the street, and get in.

He rose hesitantly, put some coins on the table with one hand and raised the other in a tentative wave. At that, the battered passenger door sprang open and a woman's arm on the driver's side beckoned him over.

Léon had one foot inside the car and the other still on the running board when the Torpedo took off and threaded its way neatly into the stream of traffic in the Boulevard

Saint-Germain. Meantime, he flopped down on the seat and opened his mouth to greet Louise but couldn't get a word out because he felt that a commonplace '*Bonjour*' or '*Salut*' would seem too banal in such an exceptional situation.

So it was Louise who got in first. 'We won't kiss,' she said. 'We won't fling our arms around each other's neck, all right? We won't burst into tears and dry them for each other, and we won't carve hearts in age-old lime trees and swear eternal love.'

'If you say so,' said Léon.

Louise was wearing a leather helmet and goggles with green lenses. She vigorously double-declutched, changed up from second to third, and turned sharp right into the Rue Bonaparte.

While the Torpedo was slithering over cobblestones wet with rain, Léon wedged himself between the dashboard and the passenger door with his arms and legs. Lying at his feet, slightly soot-stained, was a blue enamel saucepan. Louise drove the car with swift, unerring movements. Her face was flushed.

'Don't gawp. Keep your eyes on the road.'

'I'm not gawping, just looking. A snappy little roadster, you've got.'

'Four-cylinder, does sixty k.p.h. with ease.'

'I know,' he said. 'A Torpedo won the Coupe des Alpes a few years back.'

'Two years running. It was a present to myself to celebrate the anniversary of my employment by the Banque de France. I got it cheap – it already had a few dents.'

'The name doesn't really suit it, though.'

'Why not?'

'A torpedo's pointed at the front, not the back.'

'I'll drive around in reverse if you like.'

'You work for the Banque de France?'

'Have done for five years.'

'Congratulations.'

'Congratulations aren't appropriate. They treat me like a serf.'

'Why?'

'Because that's what I am. I spend the whole day typing out tabular computations, and I have to produce five copies of each.'

'Hence the Torpedo?'

'Exactly.'

'You don't ride a bike any more?'

'If I have to go somewhere I take the car. And if I don't have to go somewhere I also take the car.'

'And if you go to the seaside?'

'Then I certainly take the car.'

'So why did I see you in the Métro?'

'The car was in for repair.'

'You work at head office?'

'Yes, Place de la Victoire.'

'I've been working at the Quai des Orfèvres for the last ten years. That's only a few hundred metres away.'

'Well, well,' said Louise, 'so we've been polishing the seats of our chairs in pretty close proximity for quite a while. Some people would call that bad luck.'

'Yes.'

'Don't let's talk now. We'll drive out of town for bit, if that's all right with you. We'll talk later.'

Louise changed up from third to fourth and drove past the Luxembourg Gardens with her foot hard down, then further south past the Observatory and into the Avenue d'Orléans. She let her left arm dangle over the door and steered the car with her right hand. She overtook horse-drawn vehicles and buses on the left or right, wherever a gap presented itself, and when the street came to an intersection she shimmied between pedestrians, bicycles and cars at breakneck speed. Whenever a bus or a lorry refused to give way she thumbed her horn and cursed and swore until the startled driver pulled over, and when she shot through the gap she thrust her arm out of the window and made a gesture that would normally, if directed by one man at another, have resulted in a punch-up.

Léon stared with delighted horror at the lethal obstacles flashing past the Torpedo on either side. He also stole sidelong glances at Louise, who, now that the traffic had thinned and the road was flanked by fields, was leaning back and looking ahead with her eyes half shut.

She had removed her leather helmet and goggles. The corners of her mouth conveyed a suspicion of a smile, her chin was tilted expectantly, and her neck made a softer impression than it used to. A little furrow ran from the dip below her ear to her throat, and this, combined with the silver strands above her temple, lent her still girlish appearance a hint of womanly dignity. Léon would dearly have liked to know if the ironical twinkle in her eyes related to the other drivers on the road or her sudden togetherness with him in the cramped confines of the little sports car. Both her hands were now resting on the steering wheel, and he noted she wasn't wearing a ring.

'Now stop staring,' she said, putting a cigarette between her lips. 'We'll stop in half an hour, then we can talk.'

11

The nearby forest of Fontainebleau was a dark ribbon below the night sky. Cowering on the plain were little hamlets in which only a scattering of lights still burned late that evening. In the *Relais du Midi*, which stood beside the road between two nameless villages, long-distance lorry drivers and travelling salesmen were drinking beer in the stifling heat given out by the stove in the middle of the taproom.

Léon and Louise were sitting close together beside the window in the corner. He had his right arm round her waist. She was leaning against his shoulder with his right hand in her left. A cold draught coming through the cracks in the window was blowing the smoke of her cigarette horizontally towards the stove.

'We still haven't talked,' he said.

'Do you want to talk?'

'No,' he said. 'Do you?'

'We have talked a bit.'

'But not about that.'

'No.'

'Only about cars.'

'And *Metropolis*.'

'And Kellogg and Fitzmaurice.'

'And Chanel dresses and stupid cloche hats. And about your concierge and your mangled *tartes aux fraises*.'

'And about inflation and the Banque de France.'

'And elephants. How did that joke about elephants go again?'

'Do you still read Colette's novels?'

'Oh, that silly cow. I've never been so disappointed by anyone. I'm out of cigarettes.'

'Are there some left upstairs?'

'In the car.'

'I'll get them for you.'

'Stay here,' she said, squeezing his hand. 'Don't leave me. Not yet.'

He drew her closer and kissed her.

'I'm hungry,' she said. 'Let's order before the kitchen shuts.'

'I'll have steak and *frites*,' he said.

'Me too.'

Léon beckoned the landlord over and ordered, then told Louise a story to make her laugh.

It was the story of the tramp who sat outside the Musée Cluny day in day out, year after year. Léon used to drop a coin in his hat every morning on the way to work. The man smelt of red wine but was usually clean-shaven, and one could tell that he tried to keep his shabby clothes clean. They always said a friendly good morning and sometimes exchanged a few words, wishing each other a nice day before Léon walked on.

Every few months, the museum gateway would be deserted when Léon went to work. When that happened he would anxiously wonder whether something had happened to the tramp overnight and wave to him in relief when he saw him sitting in his usual place at lunchtime. Having grown attached to the man over the years, he worried about him as he would have worried about a distant uncle – one with whom he wasn't on very intimate terms but who was somehow 'family'.

Léon didn't know the man's name nor did he want to, nor did he want to know where he spent the night and whether he had some relations somewhere. Over the years, however, he had gleaned a few scraps of information about him. He knew, for instance, that the tramp had a predilection for *foie gras* and suffered from an arthritic hip in the winter, and that he had once had a wife named Virginie and a job as verger at a church somewhere in the suburbs, plus a flat to go with it, before his own or other people's debts had deprived him first of his wife or his job or his flat, and that he had subsequently lost the rest of this petty bourgeois trinity because you had to have them all or not at all.

Conversely, the tramp had built up a picture of Léon. When a flu epidemic was going round he enquired after the health of Léon's offspring and his lady wife, and when a poisoning was making headlines in the press he wished him success at the laboratory.

The tramp had become one of the most important people in Léon's life as years went by, because there weren't very many other individuals with whom he daily exchanged a few words in the confident assumption that they were well disposed towards him for no ulterior reason. He had become Léon's personal tramp in the course of time – so much so that Léon felt almost jealous when he chanced to see another passer-by put some money in his hat.

In October of the previous year the tramp had not been sitting in his usual place for three days in succession. On the fourth day he was back, however, and Léon was so relieved that he'd invited him to the nearest bistro for a coffee. There the man told him that four nights earlier, when a vicious north wind was driving sleet through the streets of the Latin Quarter and he was dead drunk and looking for a place to sleep, he had found an unlocked, empty cattle wagon in the vicinity of the Gare de Lyon. Sliding the door open, he climbed into the agreeably windless interior, shut the door again, wrapped himself in his blanket in the straw, and fell asleep within seconds.

So soundly had he slept that he didn't wake up when the cattle wagon jolted into motion, and he slept on at dawn, when the train complete with locomotive and twenty empty cattle wagons pulled out of the Gare de Lyon and headed southwards out of the city. Anaesthetized as he was by several litres of cheap red wine, the incessant rocking and lurching kept him profoundly asleep throughout the day like an infant in a cradle. Meantime, the train continued on its way through the French provinces. The tramp slept on while traversing Burgundy from north to south, and he slept on in the vineyards of the Côte du Rhône, and he slept on at dusk, when the train was steaming past the wild horses of Provence, and he slept on in Languedoc and Roussillon and at the foot of the Pyrenees. It wasn't until the next morning, when his wagon had been stationary for quite a while and was becoming ovenlike in the southern sun, that he awoke with a furry tongue and a head like a block of wood.

The tramp crawled out of the straw and wiped his sweaty face on his sleeve. Sliding the door open, he saw – when his eyes had grown accustomed to the dazzling sunlight – a deserted cattle-loading station and beyond it, stretching away to the horizon, a shimmering plain completely bare except for a few isolated cacti. It was a while before he grasped that he wasn't in Paris any longer, nor even in the north of France, but somewhere very far to the south. He had no money, no papers, and presumably no knowledge of the local language.

Impelled by agonizing thirst and a raging headache, he climbed down on to the permanent way and trudged north-east along the track for an hour-and-a-half until he came to the nearest railway station, where a level-crossing keeper in an operetta uniform disclosed in broken French that he was on the banks of a river named Arga, not far from Pamplona.

୫ଛ

Louise laughed. Then the food came.

They didn't talk about their weekend together at Le Tréport ten years earlier, nor about their night on the beach and the shellfire next morning, nor about the years they'd been apart.

Earlier that evening, when they were still lying in bed, mutually exploring the scars left on their bodies by shrapnel, machine-gun bullets and surgeons' scalpels, Louise had told him that a wine merchant from Metz, who had also got mixed up in the bombardment, had picked her up and driven her in his van to the women's hospital at Amiens. There, after undergoing an emergency operation, she had lain among the hopeless cases for a whole month, contracted pneumonia and Spanish flu, and not been discharged until six months after the war ended, only semi-recovered even then.

She went straight back to Saint-Luc-sur-Marne and called on the mayor, who gave her a rapturous welcome and told her straight out that Léon had also paid him a visit a few months earlier, looking gratifyingly restored to health. Seated on the very chair on which Louise was sitting now, he said, Léon had described his own misfortunes, then suddenly jumped up and walked out. No one had seen him since.

When Louise asked the mayor if he knew Léon's address, he

gave a regretful shrug, and when she overcame her embarrassment and asked if Léon had enquired about her, he patted her hand, shook his head sadly, and made some profound remark about the capriciousness of young people in general and the fickleness of young men in particular.

§a

When Léon ordered two coffees after the meal, the landlord ostentatiously squinted at the clock on the wall. After bringing the cups he toured the taproom with his purse and put the unoccupied chairs upside down on the tables. Léon and Louise talked in low voices, eyeing one another as intently as if they were engaged in difficult negotiations about decisions of the greatest moment, when they were really only talking of trivia and carefully avoiding anything weighty and important.

Léon began by describing the gigantic airship that had recently floated past his laboratory window, almost close enough to touch. Then Louise told how her Torpedo had conked out on the way back from Le Tréport and refused to start until she had rid the air filter of dust with a drop or two of petrol from her spare can. After that they discussed the advantages and disadvantages of asphalted and paved roads, and Louise went on to mention that her route to work took her past the Place de Clichy, which had been freshly paved, and that nearly all the prostitutes there had worn mourning since the war. She wanted to know if Léon thought they were really all war widows. Probably, was his rather bemused response, whereupon Louise said she hoped so, because if the only other possible explanation were true – namely, that the whores affected widows' bonnets as a business-boosting form of costume because homecoming soldiers relished the idea of screwing their fallen comrades' wives – if that were true, she wanted nothing more to do with men for the rest of her days. He couldn't judge, said Léon, because he had no statistically relevant information about the Place de Clichy's whores or the emotional state of homecoming *poilus*. All he knew for sure was that the idea wouldn't appeal to him personally.

'I know it wouldn't,' said Louise, and she quickly described how she had once skidded in freezing rain in the Place de l'Étoile, almost glissading under the Arc de Triomphe and over the Tomb of the Unknown Soldier.

য়ঽ

The Torpedo was back on the road shortly after midnight. Louise was now driving slowly while Léon stroked the nape of her neck and gazed at the headlights' twin yellow beams on the road ahead. They didn't speak for a long time. Then Louise cleared her throat.

'Listen, Léon,' she said, harshly all of a sudden, 'we'll be back in Paris an hour from now. You must promise me something.'

'What's that?'

'I don't want you stalking me.'

'Stalking you?'

'You know what I mean. We won't see each other again, it would be pointless – it would get us nowhere. You don't know where I live and I'm not going to tell you, but you know where I work.'

'So?'

'Don't act dumb, it doesn't suit you. I don't want you hanging around outside the Banque de France in the hope of seeing me. You're not to loiter in the Rue de Rivoli or the Place de la Victoire either, or set some detective on me, or bump into me by chance when I'm buying a pound of potatoes in the vegetable market, or happen to sit down beside me in the cinema. Will you promise never to do that?'

'Coincidences happen,' said Léon. 'Paris isn't as big as people think, you know. It's always possible our paths will cross. In the Métro, in the street, at the butcher's...'

'Don't talk nonsense,' she said sharply. 'We don't have the time. You must promise not to do anything silly. Never, not once. If our paths ever do happen to cross, we can say hello in passing if you like, but we won't stop. For my part, I promise I'll never set foot in the Rue des Écoles or the Quai des Orfèvres. I can't leave the Boulevard Saint-Michel to you entirely – I have to go that way from time to time.'

'So do I. Twice a day at least.'

'Be a man, Léon. Promise me.' She took her right hand from the steering wheel and held it out. 'Do you promise?'

He turned to her and smiled as if to say, 'Give me a break!' Then he took her hand, looked out of the side window, and said, 'No.'

For a few seconds Louise drove through the darkness in silence. Then she braked and put the car into neutral. As soon as it was stationary she applied the handbrake, got out, and walked round the bonnet to the passenger door.

'Move over. You're going to drive now.'

'Louise, I've never – '

'Go on, move!'

'I can't drive.'

'Then you're going to learn. You're driving from now on, otherwise we'll beat about the bush for ever and – who knows?

– maybe burst into tears. This is the accelerator and this is the brake. I'll handle the gear changes to start with. Now depress the accelerator a little – only a little, that's right. Now take your foot off the pedal and depress the clutch. That's first gear, see? I'll release the handbrake and you slowly release the clutch and, at the same time, gently depress the accelerator, gently, gently…'

⁂

Once they were in third, Léon maintained a speed of fifty k.p.h. Keeping to the middle of the road, he drove northwards through the darkness and headed for the city. He tried turning the headlights off and on, blew the horn, and let his left arm dangle in the airflow outside the window. Louise helped him to steer only on very tight bends, and when the road ran uphill she took the gear lever and changed down. As they breasted one of the last hills before the outskirts of the city, the strings of lights on the Eiffel Tower came into view in the north-west. The moon was visible above a dark strip of forest to the north-east.

'Look,' said Léon, 'the moon is exactly half-full. Know what that means?'

'No, what?'

'It means the moon is precisely in the same place in the solar system as we were four hours ago.'

'What?'

'Four hours ago, the earth was where the moon is now.'

'We were up there four hours ago?'

'That…' – he glanced at his watch – '…is precisely where I tore the last button off your blouse four hours ago.'

They drove on in silence for a while, looking at the moon through the windscreen.

'It's moved on a bit now,' he said. 'Now it's reached the place where your knickers – '

'Leave my knickers out of it,' she broke in.

Léon explained that when the moon was half-full, the earth, the moon and the sun formed a perfect right angle, which meant that the moon, on its orbit around the sun, followed in the earth's wake, so to speak, at a mean distance of three hundred and eighty thousand kilometres and a speed of a hundred thousand kilometres per hour. 'That means that we were there just short of four hours ago, and that the moon will be here in four hours' time.'

'Four hours?' said Louise. 'Hang on, let me check.' She put her head back and looked up at the sky while the Torpedo puttered peacefully through the darkness. After a while she said, 'You're right. Three hours, fifty-two minutes and a few seconds. But is the moon waxing or waning?'

Léon laughed in surprise, then hung his head. 'No idea,' he said ruefully. Perhaps it depends whether you're looking at it from north or south of the equator.'

'Nonsense. All men are the same – astronomically speaking, at least.'

'Anyway, there are two possibilities: the moon is either four hours behind us or four hours ahead.'

'If it's ahead of us, it's now where we'll be in four hours' time.'

'I don't want to know that,' said Léon. 'Let's assume it's trailing after us.'

'The odds are fifty-fifty,' said Louise. 'So where would the moon be now?'

'At the place where I carried you from the table to the bed.'

'And we stopped beside the wardrobe on the way.'

'Beside the coat hooks, you mean.'

'Which weren't properly screwed to the wall.'

For a while they silently regarded the moon, which was lifting above the skyline at a surprising rate.

'Actually,' said Louise, 'you wouldn't need a rocket to get to the moon. You'd simply have to stay put for four hours.'

'Just jump into the air, hover there, and let the earth sail on.'

'And wait for the moon.'

'And then climb on.'

'Tell me, Léon, where has the moon got to now?'

'Where the bedside light fell over and smashed. And you started moaning my name.'

'You're a conceited ass.'

'I can still hear you,' he said. 'I've got you in my nose, too. I can smell the two of us. Here, smell.'

She sniffed his neck, his shoulder and her own forearm. 'We smell exactly the same.'

'Our smells have mingled.'

'I wish they could stay that way.'

'For evermore.'

Louise laughed. 'That's ambitious of you.' She undid the bottom button of his shirt and slid her hand beneath it. 'You're feeling very smug – you think you're a hell of a fellow, don't you?'

He nodded.

'But do you also know, master of the universe, where a car's footbrake is?'

'I can accelerate, turn the lights on and off and sound the horn. I don't want to be able to brake.'

'But I do. Apply the brake, you lord of creation. Now, right away, go on. Take your foot off the accelerator, then depress the clutch and put the car into neutral. No, that's the hand-brake, not the gear lever. Now the footbrake, just next to the accelerator. Pull over to the right, go on, quick.'

While Léon was still busy with the steering wheel, clutch and brake, she kissed him and tugged at his clothing until the car bucked and lurched to a halt. The engine hissed softly under the bonnet. An owl hooted in the distance. The valley between them and the outskirts of Paris was wreathed in mist. They fetched two blankets from the boot and, closely entwined, made their way to the edge of the woods, where they lay down on the soft turf between two bushes and made love until dawn by moonlight.

12

Léon and Louise never saw or heard from each other again in the ensuing eleven years, eight months, twenty-three days, fourteen hours and eighteen minutes. Léon kept the promise he'd refused to give and never, not once, went near the Banque de France, nor did he undertake any pointless Métro rides or loiter in the Boulevard Saint-Michel for no good reason.

It was inevitable, however, that he went to work in the morning and came home in the evening. He couldn't keep his eyes shut en route but had to keep them open, so there were bound to be occasions when his heart beat faster at the sight of a pair of green eyes in the Boulevard Saint-Michel or the back of a neck surmounted by dark hair bobbed from one earlobe to the other. Even after years had gone by, he would still give a start when a Renault Torpedo rounded a bend, or when, in the corner of a Métro carriage, he sighted a woman in a raincoat smoking.

He once left the laboratory during working hours, climbed to the top of the Palais de Justice, and located a north-west-facing window among the roof beams. Opening this window, which was black with the dust of centuries and white with cobwebs, he found to his relief that, although he could look across the Seine towards the Banque de France, the bank itself was obscured by several rows of buildings.

Another time, while he was on his way home on a Thursday

evening, a vague figure disappeared behind the circular bookstall in the Place Saint-Michel. Instantly convinced that it must be Louise, he dashed over to the bookstall and circled it twice, scanned the people hurrying past, then circled the bookstall once more in the opposite direction. But the figure had vanished as mysteriously as if it had soared into the sky or been swallowed up by a trapdoor.

Before going to sleep at night Léon continually relived his ride in the Torpedo, being with Louise at the *Relais du Midi,* and those last few hours before dawn on the edge of that wood within sight of the Eiffel Tower. He was surprised to discover that his memories didn't fade as the weeks, months and years went by; on the contrary, they became stronger and more vivid. The touch of her lips on his neck seemed ever warmer from year to year, the thrill that ran through him at the thought of her whispered 'Touch me there – yes, there!' ever more powerful, the scent of her ever sweeter. He could actually feel his hands on her supple and wiry but unyielding and demanding body, which was so different from that of his soft, warm, yielding wife. In his heart he preserved the feeling he had only ever known with Louise – the sense of being completely at one with himself and the world and the little time allotted him.

By day he dutifully went off to work, and at night he joked with his wife and was an affectionate father to his children; fundamentally, however, he always felt most alive when devoting himself to his memories like an old man. His outward appearance had changed little in the twelve years since his excursion with Louise. He had neither gained nor lost weight, and although his hair was receding, his body at forty was much the same as it had been ten or even twenty years earlier.

But he wasn't, he had felt of late, a young man any more.

He still had no aches and pains and still wasn't given to melancholy, his memory wasn't failing and he still found the sight of a woman's shapely pair of legs disturbing. For all that, he felt that the sun had passed its zenith. He had no wish to look young any more and no longer felt the need to make himself look interesting in gleaming spats and a jaunty bowler hat. Having recently bought a classic tweed suit, he was surprised and rather amused, when trying it on, to find that he looked the spitting image of the father of his childhood years.

His wife didn't complain. When he had kissed Louise for the last time that Sunday morning in the Place Saint-Michel and got out of the Torpedo prior to dragging himself back to the Rue des Écoles like a condemned man on his way to the scaffold, Yvonne had behaved as if he hadn't been out all night but had just got back from the baker's or popped downstairs with some shirts for Madame Rossetos to iron. The door of the flat was open, the scent of coffee was drifting out of the kitchen, and when he took her hand and started to try to explain, she released herself and said, 'Skip it, Léon, we both know the score. Let's not waste any words on the subject.'

To his boundless amazement, they then spent an agreeably unemotional Sunday like the happiest of families, went walking in the Jardin des Plantes in the milky light of the November afternoon, showed Michel the stuffed mammoths and sabre-toothed tigers in the Natural History Museum, ate lemon ices at the *Brasserie au Vieux Soldat,* and treated their little son to a motorbike ride on the carousel at the entrance to the Luxembourg Gardens. And all the while Yvonne had clung to his arm, her soft, pregnant hips following his every movement like a cuddlesome cat, as if they had always had the same goals, desires and intentions in life.

Léon was puzzled at first by the absence of the seemingly inevitable scene. He felt surprised by Yvonne's magnanimity on the one hand, and, on the other, by how quickly he could become unfaithful to his own infidelity. But then he grasped that Yvonne had vanquished him by taking possession of his escapade and turning it into an episode in her marriage. So far from coming between them, his reunion with Louise would in future be a mutual bond, a shared memory. At the same time, he also realized that her magnanimity stemmed ultimately from cruel implacability: from the certainty that she was dependent on him for better or worse, and that a moral person like him would find it impossible, in times of crisis and inflation and in a Roman Catholic country like France, to desert his first-born son and his God-entrusted, five-months-pregnant wife purely in order to seek happiness at another woman's side.

It did, in fact, seem so natural to Léon to stay with Yvonne that it wasn't even a duty; he had no need to give it a second thought. They would stay together and never get divorced – not, in the first place, because they were insufficiently passionate by nature to lend themselves to such a final catastrophe, but because they lacked the requisite measure of unscrupulousness and egocentricity peculiar to all marital dramas despite their emotional exaltation. Secondly, because for all its alienation and detachment their marriage was sustained by a sibling-like feeling of affection, goodwill and respect which neither of them had ever betrayed. And this, thirdly, was how it came about that they had never really discerned the strongest and most important bond that keeps most couples together: the fear of hunger and hardship in an unheated attic.

It was dark by the time they came home from their Sunday outing. After a supper of bread, ham and eggs in the kitchen, they put little Michael to bed and went to bed too. Under the bedclothes they were closer, in their mingled grief and happiness, than they had been for a long time, and Léon, heavy-hearted though he was, felt bound to his wife by fate. But, when he moved still closer to her and pulled up the hem of her nightdress, she said, 'No, Léon, not that. Not any more.'

※

Next morning he went to work just as he had on a thousand other mornings. The grass in the park across the way was fluffy with snow, the streets were wet and the plane trees black, and the Métro rumbled beneath their roots as usual. At Christmas 1928 he went to the Rue de Rennes and spent all their savings on a pearl bracelet at which Yvonne had more than once cast hopelessly covetous glances in passing, not that she had meant him to notice. A springlike New Year's Eve was followed by the harsh winter of 1929. In April, when Yvonne gave birth to a healthy boy, the Rue des Écoles was still covered in hard-frozen snow stained with coal dust.

One Friday morning three months later, Léon's mother died while buying some perch for supper in Cherbourg's fish market. She had just been handed the fish wrapped in newspaper when an extremely important artery in her competent brain, which had functioned perfectly for fifty-eight years, was occluded by a blood clot. She said 'Ow, what's that!', clasped her forehead with her left hand, and sat down abruptly on the icy wet pavement, which smelt of fish, knocking over a basketful of oysters as she did so. When the fishmonger's wife, shocked by her customer's deathly pallor, called loudly for a doctor, she made a dismissive gesture and said in a matter-of-fact tone, 'Don't bother, that won't be necessary. Better call the police, they'll notify the medical officer and...' Then she shut her eyes and mouth as if she had now seen and said all she wanted, lay down on her side, and died.

The funeral took place on a stormy spring morning when cherry blossom was whirling through the air like snowflakes. As he stood beside the open grave, Léon marvelled at how smoothly the ritual ran its course – at the positively insulting simplicity with which persons who had, after all, been loved, hated or at least needed during their lifetime, could be simply buried, consigned to the past and removed from everyday life without more ado.

He left the next day, although it was only Saturday and he could have stayed longer. He was surprised at himself for being in such a hurry to return to Paris and annoyed that he blurted out an excuse to his father like a sixteen-year-old boy caught playing truant. It didn't dawn on him until later that his mother's death had finally set the seal on his youth, and that no link remained between Cherbourg and the man he now was.

Yvonne stayed on in Cherbourg with the boys for a few weeks to help her widower father-in-law to pack up the house and move to a small flat near the harbour.

She returned to Paris having developed a new habit which Léon initially found disturbing. Its outward manifestation was a notebook with a black oilcloth cover and red-lined pages in which she recorded her dreams every morning before getting up. Léon suspected that the oilcloth-covered notebook presaged renewed marital turbulence. When this failed to materialize he construed it as a belated effect of childbirth or an aftershock of his extramarital escapade.

For her part, Yvonne neither concealed nor made a fuss about the notebook, which she always left open on her bedside table. For a while Léon suspected that this was because it contained messages addressed to himself, so one day, when Yvonne was out, he picked it up and leafed through it. 'Train journey by night through snowy winter countryside,' he read, or: 'Something to do with a horse, then Papa on the sofa.' And, under another date: 'Léon practised shooting in the garden, but what garden, where did he get the pistol and what was he firing at?' Or: 'I and the little boys in the Métro. Hole in stocking. Yves screamed like a stuck pig. Indignant glances. Terribly embarrassing. The train went on and on along the dark tunnel – it just wouldn't stop. Back into the womb of Mother Earth?'

Such or similar were the fragments Yvonne's memory had salvaged in her waking state. All she had written one morning was: 'Nothing, absolutely nothing. Was it really just dark all night long?' Léon did his level best to develop an interest in his wife's nocturnal peregrinations. At first he also strove to interpret their inherent symbols and imagery, whose meaning tended to be dismayingly obvious, and make inferences about Yvonne's mental well-being, the state of her marriage, and her idea of himself. Because he never learned anything really new, however, he eventually came to the conclusion that dreams were merely waste products of the mental metabolic process. A young girl might find it entertaining to examine them for a while, but he found it profoundly surprising that a grown woman like Yvonne could take such an obsessive interest in her nocturnal phantasmagoria.

In July 1931, by which time he was well past his second birthday and had aroused the family doctor's incipient concern by failing to utter a single word – really not a word, not even 'Mama' or 'Papa' – little Yves at last enunciated, loud and clear, the resonant word 'Roquefort', complete with long-drawn-out vowel sounds and a guttural, unmistakably Parisian R.

That was also the summer when the Great Depression began, somewhat belatedly, to ravage France as well. In accordance with ministerial orders to economize, the Police Judiciaire had to shed twenty per cent of its staff. Léon escaped redundancy because he had two children to feed, and his wife, who, motivated by natural good nature, pleasure in forgiveness and self-interest, had not maintained her sexual embargo for long, was three months pregnant.

In April 1932 Yvonne gave birth to a third son, who was christened Robert. In the second week of July, when the summer holidays began, Léon's father retired from the teaching profession after spending exactly forty years sitting on the same chair behind the same desk in the same Cherbourg classroom. Ten days later he put a thoroughly proactive end to his lonely widower's life by discreetly purchasing a coffin of the appropriate size and setting it up in his living room. Having donned a white nightshirt and imbibed a hefty dose of castor oil, he emptied his bowels in the lavatory before taking a sufficient dose of barbiturates and lying down in the coffin, where he pulled the lid over himself, shut his eyes and folded his hands. The housekeeper found him next morning. On top of the coffin lay a note addressed to her, a five franc coin intended to compensate her for the shock, and a notarized will that settled all matters relating to his estate and gave full details of his funeral, which had already been arranged and paid for.

Yvonne and the children again spent the summer in Cherbourg, where she took possession of her father-in-law's flat for use as a holiday home, and also of Léon's inheritance, which proved to be quite substantial. After all expenses had been deducted, they acquired a nice financial cushion in the Société Générale amounting to several months' salary. Because they managed this nest egg cleverly, it maintained its value for decades with only minor fluctuations and guaranteed them a modest but financially carefree way of life.

While walking on the beach shortly before she returned to Paris, Yvonne made the acquaintance of a handsome, dark-eyed youth named Raoul, who had no regular job, cadged some money off her after only a few minutes, and had the audacity, when the children were asleep that evening, to visit her at her late father-in-law's almost empty flat. She slept with him the same night and the two nights thereafter, doing things she had never done in the connubial bed she shared with Léon.

She bitterly reproached herself on the train journey home to Paris, uncertain whether she had committed adultery in retaliation for Léon's affair with Louise or from feminine vanity and fear of growing old. It wouldn't have been worth it for sexual pleasure alone – that had been borne in on her after the first time at latest. She was still convinced, even when the train pulled into the Gare Saint-Lazaire, that she would have to make a clean breast of it to Léon, but when she saw her blue-eyed, unsuspecting husband standing on the platform in a suit creased and crumpled by two months of enforced bachelor-hood, she couldn't bring herself to do so. Instead, she rushed at him and took refuge in an embrace whose duration and intensity should have aroused his suspicions. It would be almost thirty years, and with death staring her in the face, before she owned up to her one and only fall from grace.

In May 1936 the Popular Front won the election and Léon got paid holidays for the first time. He went to Cherbourg for two weeks with the boys and Yvonne, who had given birth to a girl named Muriel a short time before. Although he failed to meet up with his boyhood friends, he did hire a sailing dinghy and take the family on trips to the Channel Islands. Yvonne, who spent the whole fortnight secretly dreading the possibility that her handsome beau might surface at some stage, did not relax until they were sitting in the train on their way back to Paris.

One evening in April 1937, great agitation reigned in the Rue des Écoles. Just before suppertime, Madame Rossetos ran screaming through the building in search of her two daughters, now aged sixteen and fourteen, who had disappeared into the blue together with their clothes, bedclothes and their mother's savings, which she'd kept for many years in a sugar basin in the kitchen cupboard.

In January 1938, Léon Le Gall was appointed deputy laboratory director of the Police Judiciaire's Scientific Service, and on 1 September 1939, the day the Germans invaded Poland, he had to undergo an operation for haemorrhoids at the Salpêtrière Hospital.

The day on which Louise first sent him another sign of life was one of the most bizarre in French history. It was Friday, 14 June 1940. That first springtime of the war, which had so far passed almost unnoticed in Paris, was unprecedented in its beauty and *joie de vivre*. Throughout the month of April, while thousands of young men were once more dying in the East, women in short floral dresses had gone around beneath the dark-azure skies with their hair cascading down their backs. The pavement cafés were crowded until late at night because the boulevards still glowed with the heat of the sunlight stored up during the day. It was as if some gigantic, warm-blooded creature were hidden beneath the flagstones, breathing gently and imperceptibly.

Radios broadcast Lucienne Delyle's wistful *Sérénade sans Espoir,* customers in Galeries Lafayette and the Samaritaine competed for white linen suits and beach pyjamas, the air was laden with the beguiling scent of expensive perfumes in minuscule bottles, and at dusk lovers' shadows blended with those of the plane and chestnut trees blossoming in the parks. To be sure, the Parisians' thoughts occasionally turned to the *drôle de guerre,* the so-called phoney war, between two kisses or two glasses of wine, but should they have drunk one glass, bestowed one kiss or danced one dance fewer? Whom would it have benefited?

That sweet dream of a springtime came to an abrupt end when it turned out that the Maginot Line was incapable of holding the Hun at bay. After 10 May, tens of thousands of Belgians and Luxembourgers fled from the Luftwaffe's huge steel dragonflies and the saurians of the Panzer brigades, which descended on the countryside like a biblical plague, at horrific speed and with an ear-splitting din, and sprayed their leaden poison over the streams of refugees. When German armoured columns broke through at Sedan as well, Paris succumbed to a universal spirit of *sauve qui peut.* It was led by the government and its generals and ministers and industrialists, who made off with their workers' wages, followed by parliamentarians, civil servants, lickspittles, toadies, diplomats, businessmen, and the ruins of the army. With them also went the *beau monde* of the journalists, artists and academics who felt obliged, for the sake of humanity and in the interests of the future, to save their own skins by all available means and as a matter of the highest priority.

They were joined by hundreds of thousands of women, children and old men who fled southwards in overcrowded trains and along traffic-choked roads, on foot and on bicycles, in taxis and cars drawn by teams of oxen for want of petrol and travelling bumper to bumper, their roofs laden with mattresses, bicycles and leather armchairs; on horse-drawn wagons, lorries and handcarts piled high with the entire contents of craftsmen's workshops, grocery stores and private households.

After three weeks the stream of refugees dried up. Paris had lost two-thirds of its population. Those who remained included the wealthiest of the wealthy and the poorest of the poor, as well as anyone forbidden by law to desert his or her post for professional reasons: hospital staff, financial and fiscal administrators, post office, telegraph office and Métro employees, the staff of power stations and gasworks, firemen, and the French capital's 20,000 policemen.

And so, while newspapers were carrying reports of the retreat to Dunkirk, the collapse of rail traffic and the capitulation of the Belgian government, Léon continued to go to the laboratory every day as if nothing had happened. He was assigned the same sort of work as he had performed in peacetime: almond tarts impregnated with cyanide, champagne laced with rat poison, mushroom risotto made with deadly fly agaric. To his surprise, although Paris was two-thirds depopulated, cases where poison was suspected had considerably increased in number rather than diminished. It seemed that, in times of chaos and mass panic, many female poisoners had ventured to do what they would have lacked the courage to perpetrate in more stable circumstances.

On Monday, 10 June 1940, however, my grandfather's professional routine was rudely interrupted. When he turned up for work at eight-fifteen as usual, the Quai des Orfèvres was thronged with members of the Police Judiciaire: uniformed gendarmes, plainclothesmen, forensic chemists, pathologists and office staff were sullenly standing around on the pavement in the morning sunlight, smoking, muttering together in small groups, or reading newspapers in the shade of doorways or projecting roofs. The doors of the main building were shut, but the lights were on inside.

'What's up? Why isn't anyone going in?' Léon asked a young colleague whom he vaguely knew from having shared a coffee break with him.

'No idea. Room 205 is being cleared, apparently.'

'The Ministry of Shame, you mean?'

'Seems so.'

'Are they shutting it down?'

'No, the records are being evacuated, that's all.'

'The whole of the aliens' card index?'

'It'll be quite a job. We're supposed to lend a hand.'

'You lend a hand, then. I've got a mass of stuff to do in the lab.'

'You won't be working there today, I reckon. Emergency decree. All departments are suspended from their normal duties and have to pitch in.'

'Fair enough. At least we won't be turning over those records to the Nazis. It's a humanitarian act.'

'Humanitarian my eye!' the young man said, flicking his cigarette end into the Seine. 'They want to save their card index, that's all.'

'From the Nazis?'

'Yes, because they're afraid they'll mess up their nice, tidy Room 205, seeing they can't even speak French.'

'You don't say.'

'Yes.'

'That's typical.'
'Room 205 is even keener on being tidy than the Germans.'

❧

The Service des Étrangers in Room 205, the department responsible for supervising foreigners and refugees, had become notorious in France and far beyond its borders as the 'Ministry of Shame'. It comprised a team of junior civil servants whose sole job it was to spy on, supervise and bully all the refugees who were seeking asylum in the home of human rights and make it as hard as possible for them to obtain permanent residency. Originally established from the worthiest of motives to assist the human jetsam of the First World War, the Service des Étrangers had mutated over the years, seemingly of itself and without outside help, into a Moloch that fed on the blood of those it should really have protected, its supreme aim being to know all about anything and anyone that wasn't one hundred per cent French.

The grandest hotels in Paris and the shabbiest suburban boarding houses had to submit their guests' registration forms to Room 205 every day. Every labour exchange had to report its foreign applicants, every judicial authority had to submit relevant information, and every anonymous informer received a ready hearing from conscientious officials who carefully entered every denunciation on an index card and filed it away for all time.

There were millions of red index cards recording foreign residents' addresses, millions of grey index cards that classified them by nationality, and millions of yellow index cards containing political information. Jews, communists and freemasons were listed in separate indexes. So numerous were the index cards that they had to be collated into central registers, which in turn were collated into one big, comprehensive register, and all these card indexes and registers were methodically stored in wooden boxes and suspension files kept on the ceiling-high shelves that lined every wall in the spacious office.

Outside the door of Room 205 were some long benches polished to a high gloss by the trouser seats of hundreds of thousands of Polish Jews, German communists and Italian anti-fascists who had spent many hours, days and weeks tremulously hoping that their name would at last be called and they would be admitted to Room 205, where a junior civil servant, having eyed them suspiciously over the top of his glasses and consulted some red and grey cards, would pick up his rubber stamp and – please God – renew their resident's permit for another week or month.

The bells of Notre Dame had just struck half-past eight when a black Citroën Traction Avant pulled up on the Quai d'Orsay. The passenger door opened and out got Roger Langeron, the French capital's prefect of police. Putting a megaphone to his mouth, he addressed the army of waiting men over the top of the car.

'MESSIEURS, YOUR ATTENTION PLEASE. ALL POLICE JUDICIAIRE PERSONNEL ARE HEREBY ASSIGNED TO SPECIAL DUTIES UNDER THE PROVISIONS OF MARTIAL LAW. YOU ARE ALL TO PROCEED TO THE FIRST FLOOR BY WAY OF STAIRCASE F AND HOLD YOURSELVES IN READINESS IN THE PASSAGE OUTSIDE ROOM 205. KINDLY HURRY, THE GERMANS HAVE ALREADY REACHED COMPIÈGNE!

At his young colleague's side, Léon climbed Staircase F to the first floor and sat down on a bench in the passage. The door of Room 205 was open. Usually renowned for its cathedral hush and positively robotic working methods, the big office was as filled with noise and bustle as a flea market. Standing on tall ladders, men in oversleeves were removing card indexes from the shelves and handing them down to other men in oversleeves, who carried them over to a big central desk at which the prefect of police himself was seated. Having examined each card index in turn, he slid it to the left- or right-hand side of the desk. Those that went left were destined for immediate destruction, whereas those on the right were to be taken to a place of safety.

Lined up on either side of the desk were two human chains for the removal of the card indexes. Running parallel to each other, they led out into the passage and down Staircase F to the ground floor, then out through the main entrance and across the Quai des Orfèvres to the banks of the Seine. The card indexes destined for disposal were taken a little way downstream and thrown into the river, where individual cards drifted away on the current like outsize autumn leaves; the material to be preserved was loaded into two specially requisitioned barges moored further upstream.

Léon joined the chain responsible for jettisoning card indexes. For eight hours he stood on the steps passing thousands of folders and box files from hand to hand. Documentary evidence relating to millions of human lives floated away on the turbid waters of the Seine, there to disintegrate, dissolve and sink to the bottom of the river, where mud-eating invertebrates would ingest it, digest it, and reintroduce it to the life cycle.

Urged to hurry by their superiors, the members of the human chains did little talking. Room 205 had been cleared by the evening of the second day, and the last of the records were removed from the basement overnight. At half-past eight the next morning, exactly forty-eight hours after the operation began, the barges cast off and disappeared under the Pont Saint-Michel, heading upstream for the unoccupied South of France by way of rivers and canals.

♣

Three days later, on Friday, 14 June – in other words, the day on which Louise sent him a first sign of life – Léon awoke long before dawn as usual. He lay there listening to the ticking of the alarm clock and his wife's regular breathing until the morning light showing through the sun-bleached linen curtains changed from pale blue to orange and pink. Then he slipped out of bed, bundled up his clothes, and tiptoed out into the passage, inadvertently making a noise because some small change fell out of his trouser pocket. In the kitchen he lit the gas and put some water on, then washed and shaved at the sink. When he went to fetch the *Aurore* from the landing, he was surprised to find that it wasn't lying on the doormat as usual. This had never happened before.

For want of anything else to read, Léon took the last three days' papers from the hall table and went back into the kitchen, where he opened the first of them and read an article he'd previously missed on sheep farming in the Outer Hebrides. Shortly before seven o'clock he buttered ten slices of bread for the whole family, his customary chore. The first to make a bleary-eyed appearance was his eldest son Michel, now sixteen and at secondary school. While Léon was pouring two cups of coffee, Yves, the next in age, tottered off to the lavatory.

Léon put a saucepan of milk on the stove. A little later, when Yvonne came into the kitchen holding four-year-old Muriel in her arms and leading eight-year-old Robert by the hand, he found himself hemmed in between the stove and the sink. Having kissed his wife on the corner of the mouth and the two youngest children on the top of their heads, he took his second cup of coffee and retired to the armchair beside the living-room window, which had a nice view of the Rue des Écoles and the École Polytechnique.

He had only just sat down when he caught sight of a soldier who had made himself comfortable on a bench in the little park outside. Blinking in the morning sunlight, he was eating an apple and a big slice of bread with his legs stretched out in front of him. His helmet was lying beside him on the bench, the butt of his rifle planted on the gravel path. A box camera was hanging from his neck by a strap, an absurdly large holster attached to his belt.

'Yvonne!' called Léon, retreating behind the curtain so as not to be seen from outside. 'Please come and take a look.'

'What is it?'

'That soldier over there.'

'Yes, how odd.'

'Don't stand in front of the window.'

'Where would he have got that apple?'

'What about the apple?'

'At this time of year there isn't an apple to be had anywhere in Paris. The new crop doesn't come on the market till late July.'

'I'm talking about his helmet and his uniform.'

'Look, now he's getting out another apple. And feeding bread to the pigeons – real white bread made with wheat flour.'

'The uniform, Yvonne.'

'The stuff we eat is like sawdusty cardboard – you can hardly call it bread – and that fellow's feeding good bread to the pigeons. He'll be eating meat, next. If we want meat we have to hunt squirrels in the Luxembourg Gardens.'

'The squirrels have been exterminated, I heard.'

'All the better.'

'But forget about apples and squirrels, Yvonne. Look at his uniform.'

'What about it?'

'It's grey. Ours are khaki.'

'But… that's impossible!'

'I'll go to the baker's and scout around.'

The nearest two bread shops were shut, but a tour of the Latin Quarter left Léon in no doubt: the Wehrmacht had tiptoed into Paris in the course of that early summer's night. Not a shot had been fired, not an order shouted or a bomb dropped. At dawn the Germans had simply materialized like some recurrent seasonal event – like the arrival of swallows from Africa at the end of May, or the Beaujolais nouveau with which landlords swindled tourists in the autumn, or the latest novel by Georges Simenon.

As if it were the most natural thing in the world, they had introduced themselves into the urban scenery and were now standing around with their steel helmets and Mauser pistols, queueing up like tourists at the foot of the Eiffel Tower, sitting in the Métro, studying their Baedeker guides with Agfa cameras suspended from their necks in brown leather cases, and photographing each other's grinning faces as they stood on their own or in groups outside Notre Dame and Sacré-Cœur.

Battle-hardened Panzer grenadiers gallantly helped elderly ladies to board buses, tipsy infantrymen loosened their belts as they ate steak and *frites* in the pavement cafés, complimented the chefs and tipped the waiters generously. Dapper Luftwaffe officers, who might just as well have been fobbed off with tomato juice, exhausted the stocks of Châteauneuf-du-Pape, and many of the newcomers, being Austrians, spoke remarkably good French. All that rendered the occupying power unpleasantly conspicuous was its insistence on holding a big parade in the Champs-Élysées, of all places, at precisely half-past twelve every day.

§ა

'They're all over the place,' Léon whispered to Yvonne when he returned with two baguettes. He kept his back to the children so as not to alarm them. 'I saw two sitting in a car in the Place Champollion and one drinking coffee on the terrace in the Rue Valette. There are huge swastika flags hanging from the Panthéon and the Sorbonne. On the way back I actually bumped into one coming round a corner, and you know what? He apologized. In French, what's more.'

'What do we do now?' asked Yvonne.

Léon shrugged his shoulders. 'I must go to the lab. The children must go to school.'

'You're going to work?'

'Duty calls, Yvonne. We already discussed this.'

'We could escape.'

'Where to, Cherbourg? For one thing, the Germans will

soon be everywhere, if they aren't already. For another, the police would promptly arrest me – the French police, too, not even the Germans. Thirdly, if I went to jail you and the children would be out on the street within a month, starving.'

'We could hide here in the flat.'

'Where? Under the sofa?'

'Léon...'

'What?'

'Let's think it over.'

'What's to think about? There's nothing to think about. You can only think things over if you've got some information, and we don't know a thing. We can't see or hear anything, we've no idea what's going on. We don't know what happened yesterday, and we know even less about what's going to happen tomorrow.'

'At least we can see a bit,' said Yvonne, pointing out of the window.

'The soldier, you mean? A Wehrmacht soldier eating two apples, one after the other, and enjoying the sun? All right, what does that tell us?'

'That the Germans are here.'

'Yes, and we can also hazard a guess that the fellow will get diarrhoea if he eats a third apple. But apart from that it tells us nothing. We don't know how numerous the Germans are and what they intend to do, settle in or move on, or whether the British will come to our aid or the Germans have already landed in England, or if Paris will be spared or razed to the ground. We don't know a thing. Events have overtaken us, that's all. There's no point in thinking or arguing about them.'

'But things could get dangerous here. For us and the children.'

'They could, but blindly rushing off somewhere is almost certainly the most dangerous thing we could do. That's why the children must clean their teeth and wash their faces. I'm off. There's a lot of work waiting for me at the lab.'

At that moment a loudspeaker van came down the street. On behalf of the German authorities, it informed the city's inhabitants that they were to remain in their homes for the next forty-eight hours, and that France would observe German time from now on, so all clocks should be put forward one hour.

13

Léon didn't find it unpleasant that his internal clock woke him one hour later than usual. The *Aurore* wasn't lying on the doormat the next morning either, so his time at the kitchen table would have dragged in any case. It felt good for once, not roaming around in the dark like a zombie but lying in bed for as long as his wife and children in the unaccustomed silence that had descended on the city. Besides, the two days' house arrest decreed by the occupying power was long enough in any case. The Le Gall family devoted them to reading, eating and playing cards. Michel, the eldest boy whose present resemblance to the boy Léon had been in the days of his boat trips on the English Channel was positively absurd, spent hours twiddling the radio's tuning knob in search of news when all the stations were playing nothing but music. Léon and Yvonne sought to disguise their concern by being exaggeratedly cheerful and aroused the children's suspicions by trying to kiss them at the most inappropriate moments.

Whenever Léon went to the window, Michel abandoned the radio and came and stood beside him with his hands clasped behind his back, chewing his lower lip in silence and looking down at the street. Now and then a German army lorry would drive past, or sometimes an ambulance, hearse or police car, and once even a sewage tanker going about its indispensable business.

It was so quiet outside that, when a patrol marched down the street, the tramp of boots could be heard through closed windows. And because, after two months of almost uninterrupted sunshine, the sky that day was veiled in cloud, the birds had fallen silent as if in obedience to German orders.

Every two or three hours, Léon would leave the confines of the flat and sneak downstairs. He ventured out on to the pavement and peered right and left, listened to the silence and sniffed the air. But he never saw, heard or smelt anything that conveyed even the least idea of what was happening in the outside world.

On the third morning, house arrest was over and Paris came to life again. At dawn Léon wondered which would be wiser, to go to work as prescribed or spend another day in the haven of the flat. He could hear a faint hum of motor traffic and the occasional clip-clop of horses' hoofs. So as not to wake Yvonne, he tiptoed to the window and drew the curtain aside. A taxi drove past, followed by a Léclanché van and a woman on a bicycle. A hairy youth in a sleeveless vest trundled a mobile vegetable stall over the cobblestones.

But there was still no evidence of the war. No dark clouds of smoke stained the sky, no armoured vehicles were standing in the Rue des Écoles, the magnolias were flowering in the park across the way, and there were no trenches, soldiers or signs of combat and devastation to be seen.

'The Germans are making themselves invisible,' thought Léon. 'Either that or they've moved on. It doesn't look dangerous out there, anyway.'

He decided to go to work, calculating that it would probably be more dangerous for him to stay at home and risk a court martial for dereliction of duty. That morning he shaved a trifle more carefully than usual and put on clean underwear and his new tweed suit; if anything happened to him he wanted to cut a good figure in hospital, prison or the morgue. He wrote a note for Yvonne while drinking his coffee in the kitchen, then took his hat and coat from the hooks in the hall and closed the front door quietly behind him.

On the ground floor he noticed that Madame Rossetos' glass door was ajar. He paused to listen but heard nothing, so he sidled nearer and called the concierge's name. Her gloomy abode was deserted. In one corner stood a broom, and beside it a pail with a floorcloth draped over it to dry. Where once Sergeant Rossetos' photograph had hung, the floral wallpaper displayed a conspicuous pale rectangle. The air smelt of braised onions and pungent cleaning fluids, and Madame Rossetos' eternal apron was hanging on a hook behind the door. On the stove, which was unlit, lay a big bunch of keys and beside it a handwritten note:

Please destroy all incoming mail unopened, I rely on your discretion. You can all go to hell as far as I'm concerned, you idle, self-important nit-pickers. Mesdames and Messieurs, please accept my most respectful salutations.

Josianne Rossetos,
concierge of No. 14
Rue des Écoles from
23 October 1917 to
6 a.m. on 16 June 1940.

No swastika flags were hanging up outside the Quai des Orfèvres and no SS men lounging around in the passages. The laboratory, where everyone had turned up for work, was its usual hive of silent industry.

To Léon's surprise, the refrigerator was overflowing with tissue samples – something that had never happened before in his fourteen years' service. When he commented on this to a colleague, the latter shrugged and pointed out that a clothes locker had been converted into a makeshift refrigerator, and that this was also chock-full.

The reason was that, in the two days since the Germans marched in, the medical officers of Paris had discovered 384 cases where death by self-administered poison was suspected, all the deceased being assumed to have left life's dinner table to avoid a bitter last course of humiliation, mortification and anguish. The doctors had cut a hen's-egg-sized lump out of each liver and sent it off to the Police Judiciaire's Scientific Service in a preserving jar. Léon Le Gall and his colleagues would spend three weeks testing this backlog of human tissue. They detected 312 instances of cyanide, 23 of strychnine, 38 of rat poison, and 3 of curare. Only in the case of one sample did the despairing man's method of suicide remain a mystery, and none yielded a negative result.

After a busy but uneventful day in the laboratory, Léon set off for home. There were fewer cars than usual in the streets, almost as if it were a Sunday, not a working day, the streams of home-goers on the pavements were sparser than usual, and the buses were half empty. The second-hand booksellers had locked up their stalls and the pavement cafés had cleared away their chairs and tables. Strollers, proprietors, waiters, customers – all had disappeared, but there were no roadblocks, tanks or machine guns to be seen. Paris appeared to be resuming its traditional, thoroughly Gallic way of life – with one minor difference: the park benches and *bateaux mouches* were occupied by German soldiers.

The wooden, iron-bound door of the Musée Cluny was also shut. Seated in front of it as usual was Léon's personal tramp, into whose hat he had dropped the customary coin that morning. Léon raised his hand in greeting and was about to walk on when the tramp called, 'Monsieur Le Gall! If you please, Monsieur Le Gall!'

Léon was surprised. It was anomalous and contrary to the rules of the game for the man to know his name. That he had addressed and called after him was positively improper. Reluctantly, he turned back and went up to him. The tramp scrambled to his feet and removed his cap.

'Please forgive me for troubling you, Monsieur Le Gall. It'll only take a moment.'

'What is it?'

'It's cheek of me to ask, but needs must...'

'I gave you something this morning, remember?'

'That's just it, monsieur. That's why I'm begging your indulgence and taking the liberty of politely enquiring – '

'What do you want? Speak up, let's not waste time.'

'You're right, monsieur, time is of the essence. To put it in a nutshell, I wanted to ask you this: Will you be giving me another fifty centimes tomorrow morning?'

'What a question!'

'And the day after that?'

'You've got a nerve! Are you drunk?'

'And next week, monsieur? Will I be getting fifty centimes from you every day next week and in a month's time?'

'That's enough! Who do you think you are?' Feeling that the man had taken advantage of his good nature, Léon turned to go.

'Just another moment, please, Monsieur Le Gall. I realize how impertinent this must seem, but I can't help it.'

'What is it, man? Tell me.'

'Well, the Nazis are here.'

'So I've seen.'

'Then I'm sure you must have heard what they've been doing to my kind in Germany.'

Léon nodded.

'You see, Monsieur Le Gall? That's why I've got to get out. I can't stay.'

'Where do you propose to go?'

'To Jaurès bus station. Buses leave from there for Marseille and Bordeaux.'

'Well?'

'If you'd advance me the money you were going to give me in the immediate future…'

'Well, really! How long will you be gone?'

'Who knows? I'm afraid the war will be a long one. Three years, maybe four.'

'And you want your daily fifty centimes for all of that time?'

The tramp smiled and gave an apologetic shrug.

'Two hundred working days a year for four years would make eight hundred times fifty centimes.'

'Quite right, Monsieur Le Gall. Of course, a considerably smaller sum would also get me off the hook.'

Léon rubbed his neck, pursed his lips and stared at his toecaps for quite a while. Then he spoke as if to himself. 'Now I come to think of it, I can't see any good reason not to give you the money.'

'Monsieur…'

While waiting, the tramp had been staring at the ground and humbly kneading his cap in both hands. Léon also removed his hat and looked in both directions as if waiting for someone to advise him on the matter. At length he put his hat on again and said, 'Make sure you're here just before noon tomorrow. I'll bring you the money.'

'Thank you, Monsieur Le Gall. What about you? What are you going to do?'

'We'll see. Anyway, mind you take that bus. My name is Léon, incidentally. That's what my friends call me – or did when I still had some. And yours?'

'My name is Martin.'

'Pleased to meet you, Martin.'

The two men shook hands.

'See you tomorrow, then. Take care.'

'You too, Léon. See you tomorrow.'

And then – neither of them could have said how it happened after the event – they stepped forwards and exchanged a hug.

৪৯

On getting home, Léon was amazed how noticeable Madame Rossetos' absence already was. The pavement outside the front door was strewn with cigarette ends, pigeon feathers and dog turds, a stinking dustbin was standing in the hallway, and the route to the stairs was obstructed by five gas cylinders. Because no one had sorted and left it outside the various flats, most of the tenants having fled to the south, the day's mail was lying on the big radiator beside the door leading to the inner courtyard.

৪৯

My dearest Léon,

It's me, your Louise, writing to you. Are you surprised? I am.
I was very surprised how badly I wanted to write to you as soon
as I knew for certain I was leaving Paris and would be very far
away for a long time. For the last week I've spent every spare
moment jotting down a whole mishmash of stuff for you. This is
the fair copy – reasonably coherent, I hope – which I plan to post
tomorrow.

I can't pretend I've thought of you constantly these past twelve
years. You can't remain in that state for longer than a few
months; sooner or later you come up against the limits of your
capacity for single-mindedness. Then, quite unexpectedly, for
instance during the digestive process in your lunch break, you
draw a deep breath and give the subject a rest, and from then on
you just go on living and enjoy your little pleasures. You go to the
cinema on Saturdays and drive out into the country on Sundays
and treat yourself to lunch in some country inn or other.

What sort of life have I been living in the interim? For a while
I had a tomcat named Stalin, but he slipped off the icy window
sill and impaled himself on some railings four floors below. At
the Musée de l'Homme there's a very young man with a face like
a dyspeptic monkey who suffers from verbal diarrhoea, thinks
I'm a lady, and courts me with hot tea on cold winter days. He
occasionally writes me love letters, very polite and never too long,
and if I'm assailed by sneaking doubts about the meaning of life,
my feminine charms or humanity in general, he takes me for
walks and feeds me chocolates.

I have a pretty good life. I don't miss you, you know. You're just one of the many gaps in my existence. After all, I've never become a racing driver or a ballerina, I can't draw or sing as well as I'd have liked to, and I'll never read Chekov in the original. It's been a long time since I thought it was too bad of one's dreams not to come true in real life; that could soon become a bit too much.

You get used to your gaps and learn to live with them. They're a part of you, and you wouldn't want to be without them. If I had to describe myself to someone, the first thing that would occur to me is, I can't speak Russian and I can't perform a pirouette. So your gaps gradually become characteristic traits and fill themselves with themselves, so to speak. I'm still completely full of you and my longing for you – or just my knowledge of you.

Why? No idea. It's something you get used to, that's all.

I was all the more surprised, while sitting in the taxi on my way to Montparnasse Station, to feel such an urgent desire to write to you, like a teenager before her first date. I was even more surprised when I said your name aloud on the back seat of that cab while preparing to leave you far behind. I scolded myself for being a silly fool, but I got out some notepaper and my fountain pen, and later on, during the endless train journey to Lorient in an overcrowded, underheated compartment, I tried to put down what I thought of to tell you.

I'm now sitting on the edge of the bunk in my sweltering cabin, notepad on lap, having carefully locked the door, and I still don't know what to say. Yes, I do: everything and nothing, neither more nor less. The one thing I know for sure is, I won't send this off until the last moment, when the postman is going ashore and the engines have steam up and the ropes are being cast off and I can be certain there's no possibility of my being ordered ashore and sent back to Paris.

As you read these words you're probably standing on the mat outside your front door and scratching the nice, flat back of your head. I picture the concierge handing you the letter with a conspiratorial frown, and you staring incredulously at the sender's name on the back of the envelope as you climb the stairs and slit it open with your forefinger. In a moment Yvonne will appear in the doorway and ask if you're coming in. She's bound to be worried, seeing you standing there with an envelope in your hand. Perhaps she's afraid it's a death notice, or your marching orders, or a termination of tenancy, or a notice of dismissal. So you hand the letter to her without a word, I imagine, then follow her in and shut the door behind you.

(Hello, Yvonne, it's me, little Louise. No need to worry, I'm writing this far away and addressing it to the Rue des Écoles on purpose, to rule out any secrecy.)

You know, Léon, I admire your wife for her diplomatic skill, but also for the courageous way she puts up with your good behaviour. I'd have sent you packing ages ago, doubtless very much to my own detriment, because I couldn't have put up with your impeccable conduct any longer.

Because you really have behaved well these past twelve years, that I grant you. You've never stalked me or tried to waylay me, never phoned the Banque de France or sent me billets doux addressed to the office. Yet you've suffered just as I have, I'm sure.

It would of course have been childish of us to act out all the lovers' little rituals in secret. Apart from being pointless, it would have been distressing for all three of us, and I'd have taken it amiss if you'd failed to keep yourself to yourself. On the other hand, there were many times when I wondered if I oughtn't to be rather annoyed with you for complying so fully and completely with the communication ban I imposed on you. I haven't been as well-behaved as you, by the way. One can get a good view of your living room from the rising ground in the little park near the École Polytechnique, did you know? Fourteen times in the past twelve years I've taken the liberty of standing there and peering through your lighted window as if I were looking into the interior of a doll's house. The first time was the night after our excursion together, the second the Sunday after that, and then at irregular intervals roughly once a year. It was always in winter, because I needed to do it under cover of darkness – I know the dates by heart. The last eight times I took a pair of binoculars with me.

I felt rather silly, playing the detective hidden behind a tree trunk, but thanks to the binoculars I was able to see everything: your three boys playing soldiers in the living room, your little daughter's gap-toothed smile – once, even, your wife's nice breasts; the new bookcase, too, and the fact that you now wear glasses when you tinker with your funny bits and pieces. You and your funny bits and pieces, Léon! I think it was partly them that made me fall in love with you in the old days. A rusty pitchfork, a worm-eaten window frame and a half-empty can of paraffin… You're one of a kind!

I never skulked behind my tree for longer than fifteen or twenty minutes, by the way – I couldn't have even if I'd wanted to. Somehow, the news that a woman was all on her own in the dark spread like wildfire – every lonely lecher in the Latin Quarter got wind of it. Once I had to explain to a gendarme what I and my binoculars were up to in the park so late at night. I talked my way out of it by claiming to be an ornithologist – spun him a yarn about sparrows roosting close together for warmth on winter nights and taking it in turns to stand guard.

Anyway, I enjoyed seeing you in the bosom of your family.

Every time I did, it was like a trip to another dimension, an insight into a parallel universe or into the life I myself might have led, but for that shell-hole in the road or the mayor of Saint-Luc's infatuation with my incomparably graceful, swanlike neck. To me your family is a subjunctive made flesh, a three-dimensional subjunctive, a living, life-size doll's house, the only disadvantage being that I can't play with it.

Don't get me wrong, I'm content with my life and I'm not looking for another. Besides, I wouldn't know what to say or which I'd choose if I had the choice between indicative and subjunctive. The question doesn't arise in any case, because no one has that choice.

You've got a good-looking family and you're a good-looking man, Léon. Middle age suits you. Earlier on, when you were younger, one might have found your serious cast of mind a trifle dull, but now it suits you admirably. Have you started drinking a bit? It seems to me you're usually holding a glass of Ricard. Or is it Pernod? I'll refrain from commenting on the fact that you've taken up pipe-smoking since last winter. It does age you rather. If you were my husband I'd forbid you to smoke a pipe, indoors at least. I still smoke Turmacs, incidentally. I'll have to see if one can buy them where I'm going. If not, you'll have to send me some.

Strange to say, it's only now, when we'll be separated by so much — an ocean, a war, maybe a continent or two, not forgetting all the years that have already gone by and are still to come — that I can be really close to you again. It's only now, when a few thousand kilometres will insulate us against deceit, lies and underhandedness and we very probably won't see each other for a long time, that I feel really close to you once more. Only far away from you am I really at home with myself, only far away from you can I dare to open my heart without losing myself. Can you understand that? Of course you can. You're a clever boy, even though such feminine dilemmas and paradoxes are alien to your masculine heart.

You take a more straightforward view of all these things, I know. You do what you must and refrain from doing what you shouldn't. And if, for once, you do do something you shouldn't, you remain on good terms with yourself simply because a man sometimes has to do what he shouldn't. You stand by what you've done and take responsibility for it and make sure life goes on.

Incidentally, it isn't true you've never seen me all these years. I feel sure you spotted me that time you chased me round the bookstall in the Place Saint-Michel. I simply ran faster than you – I always was the quicker of us, wasn't I? – so I ended up chasing you, not the other way round. When you came to a stop and scanned the square, I was standing right behind you; I could have put my hands over your eyes and called peekaboo! And when you turned on the spot I turned too, keeping behind your back. It was like a Chaplin film – people laughed. But you didn't notice a thing.

So now I'm going overseas, I don't have the least idea where to. I don't know if it'll be dangerous or if I'll ever come back, and they still haven't explained what they expect me to do. I suppose I'll have to play the office girl somewhere, what else?

Last Saturday I drove to work as usual in my Torpedo, which is showing its age a bit (the bearings and gearbox have had it and the rear axle is bent out of true). I was intercepted at the main entrance by Monsieur Touvier, our general manager. The god of the demigods who inhabit the executive floor of the Banque de France, he normally takes no notice of lower forms of life like office girls from the ground floor. This time, however, he not only took me by the arm but inclined his majestic head and murmured in my ear in his soft but imperious voice:

'You're Mademoiselle Janvier, aren't you? You're to go home at once and pack. Leave your car here and take a taxi.'

'Yes, monsieur. Right away?'

'This minute. You've an hour. Light luggage for a long journey.'

'How long?'

'A very long journey. Your tenancy has already been terminated. We'll take care of your furniture.'

'What about my car?'

'Don't worry about that, we shall compensate you. Be quick, you're expected at the Gare Montparnasse an hour from now.'

That was a statement, not an order, so I went home, packed a few clothes and some books and said goodbye to my worldly goods. I haven't left much behind, just a decent walnut bed with a horsehair mattress and a swansdown duvet, a chest of drawers, a leather armchair and a few kitchen utensils. But no broken heart, in case you're interested, and no faithfully waiting swain.

I've had a few romances and affairs over the years – nobody likes getting bored – but alas, they all became dull and insipid very quickly. Besides, I came to realize that I get less bored on my own than I do in the company of some man who doesn't altogether appeal to me.

So I'm still unattached, as they say – partly, no doubt, because by some miracle I've never become pregnant. Besides, it's amazing how easily you can live among a city's four million inhabitants for ten or twenty years without getting to know anyone apart from the greengrocer on the corner and the cobbler who nails new heels on your shoes twice a year.

And somehow – I don't know why, my dear Léon – you're the only man I've ever really fancied. Can you understand that? I can't. Do you think we would have made a go of it if we'd had *more time together? My head says no, my heart says yes. You feel the same, don't you? I know you do.*

On the way to the station all the streets were choked with refugees. So many panic-stricken people! I don't know where they thought they were going. There can't be enough ships to hold them all or places far enough away for the war not to catch up with them. The station and the trains were overcrowded, and our train for Lorient made a certain amount of progress only because, being a Banque de France special, it took priority throughout the rail network.

While I'm sitting writing in my cabin, soldiers are unloading our goods train. You won't believe it, but my luggage includes the bulk of the gold reserves of the French national bank, plus thirty and two hundred tonnes of gold respectively from the Polish and Belgian national banks, which we've been holding for them for the past few months. Two to three thousand tonnes of gold in all, I estimate. We're to take it to a place of safety.

Our ship, the 'Victor Schoelcher', is a banana boat requisitioned by the Navy and converted into an auxiliary cruiser. It still looks a touch Caribbean for a naval vessel, with its green, yellow and red colour scheme. The only thing that's navy grey is a silly little popgun in the bow. I'm the only woman on board, so my cabin is forward near the bridge, immediately aft of the captain's.

It's as hot and stuffy in here as if we were already in the Congo or Guadeloupe. The condensation trickling down the lime-green steel walls collects into quivering lilac puddles on the red steel floor. Every ten seconds a plump, non-European cockroach crawls out of the plughole of my washbasin (I try to kill the creatures with my shoe). I'll spare you a description of the lavatory I share with the captain. I'm told there's a second lavatory below deck for the eighty-five members of the crew. God grant I never have to go anywhere near it!

We're supposed to be sailing tonight, or tomorrow morning at the latest. Everyone's in a tearing rush. German tanks are said to be in Rennes already, and a few hours ago a Heinkel flew over us and dropped some mines in the harbour mouth to prevent us from leaving. The captain intends to wait for high tide at 4.30 a.m. and reach the open sea at dawn by keeping to the extreme edge of the fairway, between the mines and the mud banks.

This is all top secret, of course – I shouldn't be telling you any of it. But be honest, who on God's good earth cares what a typist writes to a humble Paris police officer? Anything I tell you is very probably outdated already and consequently unimportant, and by tomorrow it's bound to be over and forgotten and utterly irrelevant. What's more, nothing I see can remain secret in any case. Or do you think it's possible to conceal the existence of twelve million refugees? Can two thousand tonnes of gold escape notice? Can Heinkels zooming overhead remain a secret? What's the point of all this mystery-mongering, when everyone can see everything and understands none of it? The bell is sounding for dinner, I must fly!

It's dark now. I had a bite to eat in the wardroom with the captain, the ship's officers and my three superiors from the bank. We had perch and fried potatoes. Conversation revolved around the strength of the Wehrmacht, which is apparently bearing down on us in a great hurry and can be expected here tomorrow afternoon, if not before. I also learned that the man the 'Victor Schoelcher' was named after was responsible for abolishing slavery in France and her colonies in 1848. Nice, no? Over coffee the gentlemen flirted with me a little in a friendly way, though rather too perfunctorily and with insufficient enthusiasm for my taste.

After that I went into town to buy some emergency supplies for the long voyage. We don't know what we're in for, after all. I had to walk the darkened streets for quite a while, the street lights being masked with blue paint and the buildings blacked out, before I found a grocer's shop. Without much hope, I asked the grocer for some condensed milk. He pointed to a well-stocked shelf and asked how many tins I wanted. A dozen, I said on impulse, and you know what? The man sold them to me without turning a hair. I also bought some chocolate and bread and a sausage, and he didn't even ask me for any coupons. That just shows you – everything's in a state of flux and nobody knows what tomorrow will bring. So why all the secrecy?

I'm now sitting outside on the gangway, where a cool evening breeze is blowing, looking down at the quayside. Like a vast swarm of bees, soldiers are busy stacking heavy wooden boxes on top of each other. Working in teams of four to a box, they heave them out of the goods wagons, whose sliding doors are open, and carry them over to the loading area. I'm wondering how many boxes there will be. They'll be calling me any minute. Then I'll have to go down to the freight gangway and begin my office girl's night shift counting boxes of bullion. I shall spend all night seated at a little table with a well-sharpened pencil, and for every box that disappears into the 'Victor Schoelcher's hold I'll make a tick on a form I've personally designed and produced for the purpose.

Perched on the wall behind the goods station are some boys in caps and short trousers, watching. Their faces are expressionless and they're sitting quite still. It's hard to tell if they guess what a fortune is lying under their noses.

Officially the boxes contain explosives, but nobody here believes

that. Standing behind me at this moment, smoking, are two
young seamen. They've been bragging to each other that this is
the biggest gold shipment ever to sail out into the Atlantic. They
may even be right. I can't imagine that the Spanish conquistadors
ever collected two thousand tonnes of gold into one big heap. Or,
if they did, their wooden ships would have had to sail back and
forth a couple of dozen times to transport it all across the ocean.

The wardroom radio is churning out music – no news
broadcasts any more. Only the radio operator can listen to
the BBC. His name is Galiani, and just to hear him roll his
Italianate Rs makes you feel hungry for a bowl of bouillabaisse.
He's so hirsute, curly black hair escapes from every chink in his
uniform. In his spare time he enjoys strutting around the deck
in his role as the best-informed man on board. He'll stroll past
behind my back and say, 'Have you hearrrd, mademoiselle?
Norrrway has surrrendered.' Then he screws up his face into an
expression of disgust, sticks a Gauloise in one corner of his mouth
and spits out of the other. That's how he has kept me up to date
with the course of world history in the last few days. 'Have you
hearrrd? Hitlerrr has bombed London.' Gob. 'Have you hearrrd?
The Wehrrrmacht has marrrched into Parrris.' Gob. 'Have you
hearrrrd? Rrroosevelt intends to rrremain neutrrral.' Gob. And
he pulls his disgusted face every time and expects me to express
my admiration, which I do – or rather, overdo. And because,
although he's a show-off, he's also a sensitive southerner, he sees
through me every time and walks on looking offended.

They're calling me, so I must stop. This may be my last spare
minute before we sail. Tomorrow morning I shall give this letter
to the postman, and then we'll be off. Strangely enough, and
contrary to all reason, I'm feeling quite footloose and fancy-free.
Just because I've no idea where this ship will be taking me, I

have the deceptive sensation that the world is my oyster. That's a misapprehension, of course; in reality, the whole world is closed to me — with the exception of some desk on whichever continent the Banque de France has decided to send me to. Whatever happens, it can't be worse than dying. I love you and I'm very worried about you, my Léon — I haven't said that before. I dearly hope the Nazis don't do anything nasty to you. Take care of yourself and your family and steer clear of anything dangerous. Be as careful and as happy as possible, don't play the hero and keep fit and don't forget me!

Yours ever, Louise

P.S. Six hours later. It's 4.20 a.m. All the boxes are on board after a long night's pencil-ticking. 2208 of them, nett, gross and tare weight unascertained because of the sheer quantity and the rush, so not known, The ship has had steam up for the past two hours, the postman is leaning against the gangway and drumming his fingers on the rail. It's already getting light in the east, or is it my imagination? I must finish off this letter at once, right away, or it'll never get to you. Into the envelope, lick the flap and stick it down. Au revoir, my dearest, au revoir!

14

A few days after the German occupation the surge in suicides abated and peace returned to Paris. But the invaders didn't render themselves invisible, as Léon had supposed they would. On the contrary, they spread themselves all over the place: in the parks and streets, in the Métro and cafés and museums, and above all in department stores, jewellers', art galleries and junk shops, where they spent their army pay, which had multiplied in value thanks to the new exchange rate, on buying up anything that could be had for money and wasn't nailed down.

It seemed in those days as if the Germans' arrival in Paris had introduced an almost normal daily routine. The Wehrmacht presented public concerts in the Bois de Boulogne and distributed bread to the poor behind the Bastille, ensured that the streets were cleaned and, because all the municipal gardeners had fled, sent working parties to tend the flower beds in the Tuileries. The nightly curfew scarcely differed from the blackout imposed by the French government when in office, given that its start was put forward from nine to eleven p.m., and if some night owl failed to make it home in time he had little more to fear than a few hours' polishing boots or sewing on buttons until dawn in a military police post.

At the end of June the cinemas of Paris reopened their doors, newspapers remarkably similar in title and layout to prewar

Parisian dailies appeared, and chorus girls high-kicked once more at the Moulin Rouge. Landlords, tailors and cabbies did good business, and more prostitutes than ever lay in wait for customers, most of them now in field-grey, between the Place Blanche and the Place Pigalle.

In the absence of an apocalypse, refugees returned to the unscathed city, at first hesitantly and in dribs and drabs, embarrassed by the seeming futility of their precipitate flight, but then in whole hordes; by mid-July the population of Paris had doubled within a month. The first to reappear were shop-keepers unable to afford to let their businesses stagnate any longer, then workers and junior office staff summoned back by their bosses, Jews who hoped that things wouldn't be so bad after all, and journalists, artists and actors who scented oppor-tunities in the advent of a new era. The end of summer saw the return of pensioners hankering after their wing chairs, their family doctor and their favourite bench in the park around the corner, and finally of the children for whom the beginning of September marked the end of the longest summer holiday of their lives.

❧

Léon kept his head down and went on living as best he could. He didn't read the new newspapers like *Le Petit Parisien*, *L'Œuvre* or *Je suis partout* because, although written in French, they were German in thought. He didn't go to the cinema either, but spent his evenings listening to the radio. He heard Marshal Pétain's speech on the French radio and General de Gaulle's riposte on BBC France, and he heard the Swiss Press Agency's reports of the fighting in Finland, North Africa and

Norway; he pinned a map of Europe to the kitchen wall and marked the fronts with coloured pins, drew out nine-tenths of his savings, bought some gold bars on the black market, and concealed them beneath the living room's parquet floor, and he hoped every day for another sign of life from Louise in whatever corner of the world her colourful Caribbean banana boat might have conveyed her to.

But he didn't receive another letter from her all summer, and newsreaders made no mention of the *Victor Schoelcher* or a Banque de France gold shipment. It was ironical, he felt, that the same girl should disappear without trace in both the world wars he had so far experienced. The longer his uncertainty lasted, however, the more he forced himself to interpret the lack of news as a good sign.

In August it struck him that the plane trees were losing their leaves earlier than usual. It had been a hot summer; now autumn was coming early.

§ə

It is a documented fact that the *Victor Schoelcher* succeeded in getting away at the very last minute on the morning of 17 June 1940. According to eye-witness reports, the Wehrmacht's advance guard could still see the ship's plume of smoke beyond the harbour mouth when it entered Lorient. Once out at sea, the *Schoelcher* linked up with three Marseilles-Algiers Cruise Line passenger steamers that had also been converted into bullion transporters and set a course for Casablanca. From there she was to sail on to Canada, where the French, Belgian and Polish gold was to be stored in the strongrooms of Ottawa until the end of the war.

But the four vessels had only just crossed the Bay of Biscay when the news that France had surrendered came over the radio. That posed the question of who was now legally entitled to dispose of the gold: the Vichy government, which ultimately meant Nazi Germany; the French government-in-exile in London under General de Gaulle; or still the Banque de France, which came under the Ministry of Finance but was a limited company, not the property of the French state.

This was how it came about, on the day of the surrender itself, that the German admiralty radioed the four ships threatening to torpedo them unless they headed at once for the nearest port in occupied France. Only hours later, General de Gaulle threatened to torpedo them unless they headed at once for London. No transatlantic voyage could be contemplated under those circumstances, so the convoy maintained its southerly course and, after an intermediate stop at Casablanca, reached Dakar on 4 July 1940.

There it was safe from German destroyers for the time being, but a British fleet was lying off the coast of Senegal with the avowed intention of helping General de Gaulle to take possession of the French West African colonies on behalf of Free France. Consequently, the Banque de France authorities decided to load the 2–3000 tonnes of bullion entrusted to them – no one has ever discovered the exact amount – into goods wagons and transport them as far as possible into the African interior via the Dakar-Bamako line.

The entire cargo was unloaded by four p.m., and three days later the last shipment left Dakar station. A preliminary check at Thiès revealed that one box had lost thirteen kilograms on the voyage. Another, from the bank's branch at Laval, was filled with pebbles and scrap iron, and two or three had vanished altogether.

※

On Sundays Léon went for walks with his wife and children as if nothing had happened. If a Panzer brigade paraded down the Boulevard Saint-Michel, however, he instructed his children not to stare, but to turn round and look at the shop window displays.

'All right, so they beat us and they've behaved pretty well up to date,' he told his eldest son, Michel, who couldn't stand being cooped up in the flat any longer and was impatient to explore the occupied city on his own. 'But if one of them speaks to you, you say *bonjour* and *au revoir*, and if he asks the way to the Eiffel Tower, you tell him. But you can't speak German – you've forgotten what you learned at school – and even if he can speak French, that doesn't obligate you to chat about the weather with him. If he spells his name for you, you're entitled to have poor hearing and a bad memory, and if he asks you for a light, don't hand him your lighter, offer him the end of your cigarette. And you never – never, you hear? – take off your cap to a German. You merely tap the peak with your forefinger.'

※

Léon himself went to the Quai d'Orfèvres day after day, keeping his head down, and performed his work in the same old way. He didn't exactly have a great deal to do because cases of poisoning with fatal consequences were now few and far between. It seemed that all the city's murderers and suicides had put their plans into effect during the days of chaos and mass panic, so there was no one left to dispatch with the aid of poison.

Léon used his spare time to embark on a long-cherished project and write a scientific article the length of a licentiate's essay or shortish doctoral thesis. He had for some time regarded it as one of his life's greatest failures never to have acquired an academic qualification, or even to have finished school.

Although it would naturally have been impossible and absurd to try to make up for what he'd missed out on as a young man, he wanted to prove he was a serious person and prepared to use his brains. As the subject of his dissertation he had envisaged a statistical evaluation of murders by poisoning in Paris, 1930–1940. If there was any expert in this field, it was Léon. Equally, this was the only subject he really knew something about.

His first step was to stack the laboratory diaries for the last ten years on his desk and embark on their statistical evaluation. He classified the perpetrators and their victims according to sex, age and social status and recorded their degree of relationship or form of acquaintanceship, the type of poison used and the way it was administered, the geographical dispersion of the cases across the twenty-one *arrondissements* of the city of Paris, and their seasonal distribution over the year. He planned to produce tables and diagrams, and he would sketch profiles of perpetrators and their victims and send his essay to the *Journal des Sciences Naturelles de l'École Normale Supérieure,* and perhaps, when the war was over, he would spend a few weeks making guest appearances at the police academies of France as a lecturer and expert on murder by poisoning.

To Léon's surprise, the early summer of 1940 followed a monotonous and uneventful course. The one date he would remember to the end of his days was 23 June, a Sunday morning when fleecy little pink clouds were glowing in the sky. Léon was on his way back from the baker's to the Rue des Écoles with three baguettes under his arm when he heard the full-throated hum of a powerful car bearing down on him from behind. He turned to see an approaching Mercedes convertible with the hood down, and seated in it five men in German uniform and Adolf Hitler. The man beside the driver was quite definitely Adolf Hitler – there was no mistaking him. Followed by three smaller vehicles, the Mercedes drove past swiftly but without undue urgency, and it goes without saying that neither Hitler nor his companions took any notice of my disconcerted grandfather standing on the pavement with three baguettes under his arm as the wind of world history ruffled his hair.

Historians would later record that the Führer had only three hours earlier landed at Le Bourget airport on his first and last visit to Paris, accompanied by his architects, Albert Speer and Hermann Giesler, and the sculptor Arno Breker. He had paid lightning visits to the Opéra, the Madeleine and the Place de la Concorde, had driven up the Champs-Élysées to the Arc de Triomphe, along the Avenue Foch to the Trocadéro, and on to the École Militaire and the Panthéon. When he drove past Léon he must already have been on the way back to his plane and would only make a brief stop at Sacré-Cœur, where he cast a last glance at the conquered city that lay, waking up ignorant of his presence, at his feet.

If Léon had had a pistol on him, he often thought later, and if the pistol had been loaded and the safety catch off and he himself capable of firing it with relative accuracy, and if he had summoned up the requisite presence of mind and wasted no time on debating whether Christian and Western codes of conduct rendered it morally justifiable, he might possibly have performed a deed of historic importance. As it was, he merely stood there with his mouth open and the three baguettes under his arm, and their two- or three-second encounter had absolutely no effect on his or the Führer's future existence. Even decades later, Léon used to shake his head in disbelief that this insignificant incident was still one of the most memorable in his life, and that the colours and light of that summer morning had etched themselves into the depths of his psyche, whereas the really important events in his life – his wedding, the births of his children, his parents' funerals – lived on within him as vague memories, nothing more.

But the laboratory remained devoid of exciting incidents. It was only every few days that he had to interrupt his statistical labours to examine a suspect specimen for rat poison or arsenic. He performed these tasks with his habitual care in the certain knowledge that, even under German occupation, he was serving the cause of justice, for whoever currently ruled the roost at the Hôtel Matignon or the Élysée Palace, the same basic principle held good: that no person should administer poison to another.

Being a kind of police officer, Léon realized that he was, like it or not, a subordinate of Marshal Pétain and ultimately under German command, but as long as his duties were restricted to the technical investigation of suspected poisonings he could hope to preserve a relatively clear conscience.

But then came the morning when he turned up for work at his usual time of eight-fifteen and once more found the Quai des Orfèvres black with policemen. They were standing sullenly on the cobblestones in the morning sunlight, smoking, and moored to the quayside was a barge which Léon recognized as one of the two that had fled downstream on 12 June, laden with several million index cards.

Standing near Léon by chance was the same young colleague whom he had asked for information a month earlier.

'What's going on?'

The young man shrugged. 'What do you think?' he growled. 'The Germans captured the barge.'

'Only the one?'

'The other got away to Roanne.'

'And this one?'

'Got stuck.'

'Where?'

'At Bagneux-sur-Loing, near Fontainebleau.'

'So near?'

'An ammunition ship blew up ahead of it and blocked the canal. Our people concealed it under trees and bushes as best they could, but the Germans found it. What do you expect? A barge like that is big and easy to spot. It was stuck in the canal. It couldn't take off across country or fly away.'

'All the same, it's surprising the Germans are so well-informed about our canal system.'

'And about what our barges are carrying.'

'What are you implying?'

'Nothing. What are *you* implying?'

'Nothing.'

The bells of Notre Dame had just struck half-past eight when the black Traction Avant belonging to the prefect of police pulled up on the Quai des Orfèvres. Roger Langeron himself got out of the left-hand rear door; the right-hand rear door disgorged a tall young man wearing a mustard-yellow hat and mustard-yellow trenchcoat, rimless glasses and a red swastika armband. His plump, clean-shaven face lent him the appearance of an amiable, short-sighted schoolboy. Going over to the men standing nearest him, he genially proffered a packet of cigarettes, then replaced it in his coat pocket when none of them helped himself. Meanwhile, the prefect of police had mounted the car's running board with a megaphone in his hand.

'MESSIEURS, YOUR ATTENTION PLEASE. ALL POLICE JUDICIAIRE PERSONNEL ARE HEREBY ASSIGNED TO SPECIAL DUTIES UNDER THE PRO-VISIONS OF MARTIAL LAW. THE DOCUMENTS ILLEGALLY REMOVED FROM ROOM 205 ARE TO BE RETURNED TO THEIR RIGHTFUL LOCATION. ALL AVAILABLE PERSONNEL, FORM A DOUBLE LINE FROM THE QUAY TO ROOM 205 BY WAY OF STAIR-CASE F, AND BE QUICK ABOUT IT!'

❧

A murmur ran through the crowd, and the men were slow to discard their cigarettes. They could see no reason for excessive speed now that the Germans were no longer advancing but had been on the spot for quite some time. The greyish-black sea of hats and coats formed two human chains as requested, but sluggishly and without enthusiasm. Patently resentful at having to replicate the chore they had already performed in June, but in the opposite direction, the men now took three or four times as long to carry out every part of the operation, with the result that, although there were only half as many docu-ments as before, it took nearly twice as long to return them as it had to evacuate them.

In Room 205, Prefect Langeron and the man in the yellow trenchcoat sat at the big desk, opened sundry cartons and found that the documents had suffered considerable damage. Canal rats, beetles and worms had nested in them during the barge's one-month absence and water had leaked through the hull. The humidity resulting from summer storms had made ink run, paper swell, and cartons and wooden boxes disintegrate. Even before the lunch break, Langeron and the young German had decided that the whole archive, all three million index cards and other documents, must be copied and neatly stored in new card indexes and suspension files to be delivered within a week by the Ministry of Information.

But preliminary mental arithmetic indicated that it would be quite impossible for Room 205's hundred-strong staff to complete this job in a reasonable length of time because each of them – in addition to recording the new entries that came in every day – would have to produce around 30,000 copies apiece. Consequently, their colleagues in the other departments of the Police Judiciaire would have to shelve all but their most urgent work and help to copy the documents as a matter of priority.

For Léon Le Gall this meant that he had to lay aside his scientific article for the time being. He locked up his notes and the laboratory diaries in a cupboard and resigned himself to the fact that his professional existence would, for the foreseeable future, revolve around smudged pink index cards curling up at the edges.

The time passed quickly. Before he knew it, he had already spent three weeks deciphering Slav names, transcribing them on to snow-white cards, and depositing these in brand-new card indexes. The names, addresses and categories were legion: Vichnevski, Wychnesky, Wysznevscki, Wichnefsky, Wijschnewscki, Vitchnevsky, Wishnefski, Vishnefskij; Aaron, Abraham,

Achmed, Alexander, Aleksander, Alexei, Alois, Anatol, Andrej, Andreji; Rue de Rennes, Rue des Capucins, Rue Saint-Denis, Rue Barbès; Jew, Jew, Jew, Jew, Jew, Communist, Communist, Communist, Communist, Freemason, Freemason, Freemason, Freemason, Gypsy, Anarchist, Homosexual, Amoral, Work-shy, Alcoholic, Aggressive, Schizophrenic, Nymphomaniac, Racially Impure.

Léon devoted himself to this job with an abhorrence which he had last felt at the age of sixteen, when made to copy out pages of Virgil in detention on half holidays, while the sea was washing up objects of great interest on Cherbourg beach. The difference this time was that the punishment additionally felt as if the teacher had gone mad and was holding a loaded gun to his head.

At the same time, he had to admit that the Germans were exquisitely courteous in their personal dealings. Every afternoon, shortly before the end of working hours, the man in the mustard-yellow trenchcoat toured the various departments of the Police Judiciaire and collected the copied cards like a bee-keeper collecting honey. His name was Knochen, Helmut Knochen. He padded around softly, always said an amiable hello, and was as touchingly considerate towards his worker bees as any good apiarist should be. In his correct but rather guttural French he almost daily enquired how Léon was, shook his hand, enquired if he had enough coffee, and wondered whether he didn't need a brighter desk lamp. And all the while he looked him artlessly in the eye with his own pale-blue eyes, which the glasses strongly magnified.

Léon murmured his thanks and said he was content with his coffee and desk lamp. He had remembered enough of his German lessons at school to appreciate the poetry inherent in

Knochen's surname, which meant 'Bone' or 'Bones'. On the other hand, he found it hard to take the young man seriously as a potential threat, even though he was a Hauptsturmführer, or SS captain, and head of the Security Police. Given his age, which couldn't have been much more than twenty-five, and his Boy Scout's crew-cut, Léon found it impossible to imagine that this puppy could actually bite him with its sharp little milk teeth.

One day in September, however, Knochen turned up early in the morning. Having jocularly tapped the opening bar of Beethoven's 5th on Léon's door, he opened it a crack and put half his face round it.

'Good morning! May I intrude at such an unusually early hour? Am I disturbing you? Should I look in later?'

'Come in,' said Léon.

'No false courtesy, please!' Knochen exclaimed, baring the other half of his face as well. 'This is your personal domain – the last thing I want is to keep you from your work. If this is an inconvenient time, I can always – '

'Please come in.'

'Thanks, very kind of you.'

'But I'm afraid I must disappoint you. At this hour of the morning I've only got two copies ready for collection.'

'The cards? Oh, let's forget about them for the moment. Look, I've brought us something. May I?' Knochen sat down on a chair and clicked his fingers, whereupon a soldier outside in the passage took a tray from a trolley and deposited it on Léon's laboratory table. 'Look – or rather, smell! Genuine Arabian mocha from an Italian mocha jug. Quite unlike the wartime stuff you filter through roasted acorns and brew on your Bunsen burner.'

'Thank you, but our coffee is just the thing for me. My circulation – '

'Nonsense, a little mocha never killed anyone. May I pour you a cup? Cream, sugar?'

'Neither, thanks.'

'Just black?'

'Please.'

'Oho, you're a hard case! Is that your Norman blood? Or your profession? Have all those poisonings immunized you against the bitterness of life?'

'Not in the least, I'm afraid.'

'It's more the other way round, isn't it? I thought as much. One becomes thin-skinned in time – I'm just the same, or will be when I've had as much, er… experience as you. How do you find the coffee?'

'Excellent.'

'It is, isn't it? I must make a note to send your department a packet every week. I'll leave the mocha jug here, it sits on your Bunsen burner perfectly. Is there anything else I can offer you? A croissant, perhaps?'

Léon shook his head.

'You're sure? My orderly has some. Absolutely fresh, made with real butter.'

'Really not, thank you. Please don't go to any trouble.'

'As you wish, Monsieur Le Gall. But tell me, your place of work…' – Knochen made a sweeping gesture with his slender, well-manicured hands – '…is it all right, as far as it goes?'

'Oh yes, I've had many years to get used to the facilities here.'

'I'm glad to hear that, because it really matters to me that you should be able to work in the best possible conditions.'

'Thank you.'

'A man can only do a good job of work in decent conditions, I always say. Isn't that so?'

'Yes indeed.'

'You must be sure to let me know if I can do anything for you.'

'Thanks very much.'

Knochen rose and went over to the window. 'You have a splendid view from up here. Paris is a wonderful city – the loveliest in the world, in my opinion. Compared to Paris, Berlin is just what it always has been: a provincial Prussian dump. Am I right?'

'If you say so, monsieur.'

'Ever been to Berlin?'

'No.'

'Well, you haven't missed much, so far at least. I myself come from Magdeburg, which has even less to recommend it. But tell me something: Do you, as a Parisian, appreciate the beauty of the City of Light? Do you still notice the view at all?'

'One gets used to it. After twenty years – '

'Magnificent – the view is simply magnificent. In here, though, the lighting is – how shall I put it? – a trifle dim, a little on the faint side. Are you sure you have enough light to work by?'

'I manage.'

'Really? I'm glad to hear that, because the thing is, a minor problem has arisen.' Knochen clicked his fingers again and his orderly came in with two card indexes. 'I hate to waste your time on trivia, but I'd like you to take a quick look at something. Know what I have here? These...' – he indicated one of the card indexes – '...are the last hundred copies you produced. And these…' – he pointed to the other – '…are the originals. Know what struck me when I compared the two?'

'No, what?'

'This is the unpleasant part. You mustn't take offence.'

'Please go on.'

'I noticed that you make rather a lot of mistakes when you're copying. That's why it occurred to me that the lighting conditions in here might not be of the best. Please forgive me for asking, but how is your eyesight?'

'Pretty good.'

'Really? You don't need reading glasses yet?'

'Fortunately not.'

'That's good, because you aren't as young as you were, are you? How old are you actually, if I may ask? Forty?'

'I regret the mistakes, monsieur.'

Knochen brushed this aside. 'They're only minor matters – venial sins, of course – so don't take this too hard. At the same time, I'm sure you'll agree with me that even tiny errors can have disastrous administrative repercussions.'

'True.'

'I knew I wouldn't have to explain that to you, being a scientist. Look: here, for instance, you've written "Yaruzelsky" instead of "Jaruzelsky". If this card were filed alphabetically under Y, we'd never be able to locate the man. Or here: "Rue de l'Avoine" instead of "Rue des Moines" – a street of that name doesn't exist at all. Or this date of birth: "23 July 1961" – the man wouldn't have been born yet. You see what I mean, Monsieur Le Gall?'

'Yes, monsieur.'

'I took the liberty of comparing all these hundred cards with the originals and totting up the defective ones, and do you know how many there were?'

'I regret – '

'Guess! Go on, have a guess! How many do you think: eight? Fifteen? Twenty-three?'

Léon shrugged his shoulders.

'Seventy-three! Seventy-three out of a hundred, Monsieur Le Gall! In percentage terms that makes, let's see, just a minute – oh, of course, I'm an idiot: seventy-three per cent! That's a lot, isn't it?'

'It is.'

'Nearly all the errors are minimal, but as Lichtenberg said, the most dangerous untruths are truths that have been slightly distorted. Do you agree?'

'Certainly.'

Knochen made another dismissive gesture. 'Don't take it too hard, we all make the occasional mistake, though I'm bound to say your own mistakes are remarkably numerous. Do you know what your colleagues' average percentage is?'

'No.'

'Eleven-point-nine.'

'I see.'

'I'm glad you see. What matters now is to eliminate the source of your errors and thereby improve your performance, isn't it? Isn't it, Monsieur Le Gall?'

'Yes.'

'Have you an explanation for your high percentage?'

'Many of the cards are hard to decipher.'

'Certainly,' said Knochen, 'but your colleagues have to contend with equally damaged material, don't they? Or do you think it conceivable that you're allotted a statistically significant preponderance of badly damaged cards? If so, is that preponderance fortuitous, or should we look for some underlying reason?'

Léon shrugged.

'That's why I was concerned about desk lamps and reading glasses, you see. There must be some reason why you make so many mistakes. Needless to say, my SS colleagues are quick to suspect sabotage and high treason if they see a percentage like yours. Are you acquainted with any other members of the SS?'

'No.'

'Just between ourselves, some of them are thoroughly reprehensible hotheads – not the kind I'd care to meet in a dark alley some night. Do you know what they do to saboteurs? To start with, all kinds of unmentionable things. Then they take them to Drancy internment camp and put them up against a wall. Or throw them into the Seine in handcuffs. Or dump them in the nearest ditch with a bullet in the back of the neck. It's martial law. They're entitled to.'

'I see.'

'They're hot-headed youngsters, as I say. Ill-bred, some of them, but what can one do? Don't worry, though, Monsieur Le Gall. For the time being, I still decide what happens in this establishment, and I say my staff must be provided with good working conditions if they're to do a good job.'

Knochen clicked his fingers yet again, and the orderly brought in a big desk lamp with a reflecting shade.

'Say what you like, but one needs a good light to do good work by. Just because you've got used to your old thing, that doesn't mean it gives a good light. Mind if we disconnect it and plug this one in instead?'

'If you insist.'

'This is a Siemens, the Mercedes of desk lamps, so to speak – no comparison with that old thing of yours. If you'd just sign for it as a matter of routine. Administrative routine is important, is it not?'

'Yes, monsieur. What about the coffee?'

'What about it?'

'Don't you need a receipt for that too?'

'Now you're poking fun at me, Le Gall. That's unjust. I'm not a pettifogging pedant, so don't get me wrong. Personally, I need no receipts for anything at all. My own view is that life demands an unsolicited receipt from us all, sooner or later. But the bureaucrats can't wait for our demise, they need receipts before that. And to be fair, administrative routine is never an end in itself; ultimately, it exists for our own benefit. Isn't that so?'

'Of course.'

'So administrative errors can have grave consequences, I always say. But here I am, standing here chatting when you've a great deal of work to do. Au revoir, Le Gall. See you this evening.'

'Au revoir, monsieur.'

Knochen hurried out into the passage, coat tails fluttering, and pulled the door to behind him. A moment later he opened it again.

'I almost forgot. At lunchtime you must look in at the kindergarten in Rue Lejeune – the headmistress called. It's about your little daughter – the four-year-old, what was her name again? Marianne?'

'Muriel.'

'Apparently, little Muriel threw a cobblestone at a third-floor lavatory window and smashed it.'

'Muriel did?'

Knochen made another of his dismissive gestures. 'It's all

nonsense, of course. I mean, how could a girl of four throw a cobblestone at a third-floor window? A mix-up, no doubt – just a typical administrative error. Still, perhaps you'd better look in there at lunchtime. I was told that the little girl has been locked up in the coal cellar – in durance vile, so to speak – and she's crying her eyes out.'

Léon pushed his chair back with a jerk and made to get up, but Knochen gripped him by the shoulder and forced him down again.

'No rush, Monsieur Le Gall, no fuss. The best thing we can do is let matters take their course in the routine way, don't you agree? One's work takes priority over one's private life. Put in another two hours' conscientious copying, then it'll be lunchtime and you can go to the Rue Lejeune. The headmistress is a hidebound martinet, I'm told. If she won't let your little daughter out of the coal cellar, tell her Hauptsturmführer Knochen sends his regards, that should help. Au revoir, monsieur, and happy copying. Have a nice day.'

15

Then came the winter of 1940–41, and Paris turned cold. In summer the switch to German time had granted the city's inhabitants long, light evenings on which the sun didn't set until after ten o'clock and residual streaks of daylight still glimmered on the horizon at midnight. They paid for this now because the working day began in the middle of the night. Léon rose when it was pitch-dark and shaved by dim electric light. At breakfast he could see his reflection in the black window pane, and on his way to work the stars twinkled in the sky as if it were already dusk, not early in the morning.

That winter, where his work at the Quai des Orfèvres was concerned, Léon realized that right had become wrong and wrong was now the law; the scum had risen to the surface and the laws were made by rogues. In the passages at headquarters, policemen exchanged whispered reports of the latest doings of the most notorious hoodlums in Paris – 'Pierrot la Valise', 'François le Mauvais' or 'Feu-Feu le Riton' – who had exchanged their ten-, fifteen- or twenty-year prison terms for freedom, cars and petrol, not to mention firearms and German police permits. Things had yet to reach the stage where they turned up at the Quai des Orfèvres in broad daylight and arrested the policemen who had arrested them, but everyone knew that day would soon come.

Although it was to Léon's advantage that he did his work anonymously and out of contact with the outside world, he could literally smell danger whenever he passed the various departments on the stairs every morning, and he realized that any colleague, secretary or gendarme could be in cahoots with the villains and murderers. He could see no way out of this situation, so he took refuge in his laboratory, performed his duties, and carefully avoided all non-essential contacts.

As early as November, a big depression flooded the city with cold air from Siberia. Petrol and diesel became so scarce, the streets were dominated by bicycles, pedicab rickshaws and horse-drawn vehicles. If an occasional car did drive past, you could be sure that the person behind the wheel was a German or a collaborator. Most noticeable of all was the silence in the streets and the cold, unspeaking silence of those who trod the pavements. The old street noises were no more. Now, all that could be heard was the crunch of hurried footsteps on hard-frozen snow, an occasional cough, a perfunctory greeting, or the listless cries of a newspaper seller who had long abandoned hope of selling his German-dictated papers.

Silent queues stood outside shops and policemen on street corners behaved as if they weren't there. In cafés, people crowded into the warmth of the coffee machines, silently staring at the bottles of colourful liqueurs, most of which were dummies, the faded Martini calendars and the statutory notices proscribing public drunkenness. Many of them had red noses and cheeks flushed with fever, most wore hats, scarves and gloves, and all were clearly refugees from homes in which it was little warmer than outside in the street.

The Le Galls went to bed in long stockings, gloves and woollen sweaters. In the mornings they scraped their frozen breath off the window panes. When Léon came home with a bundle of firewood bought on the black market, as he sometimes did, they spent the evening seated around the open fire in the living room. Lulled by the unaccustomed warmth they would fall asleep, one after the other, on the sofa, in the armchair, or on the Persian rug. Long after midnight, when the fire had gone out and the cold had crept back into the flat through cracks and crannies, Léon and Yvonne would carry the younger children to bed one by one.

It was on one of those nights that they begot Philippe, their little afterthought, who in his turn, almost exactly twenty years later, in September 1960, would meet a young girl from Switzerland who was passing through on her way to Oxford University but prolonged her stay. One mild autumn night she accompanied Philippe back to his attic room in the Rue des Écoles, with the result that nine months later she gave birth to a little boy who was baptized in my own name at the church of Saint-Nicolas du Chardonnet.

❧

They all remained healthy, however, nor did they have to go hungry. Because Léon and Yvonne retained vivid memories of the First World War, they had, from the day war broke out onwards, amassed as much as they could in the way of emergency supplies of food. Prices had risen only moderately by the autumn of 1940, so they filled their cupboards with sacks of rice, flour and oats. They also, behind an inconspicuous curtain in the light shaft over the lavatory, where no looter would have suspected the presence of food, stashed scores of tins of beans, peas, condensed milk and apple purée.

Even eggs, butter, meat and sausage appeared on the table regularly once Michel, their eldest son, began visiting Rouen on the first weekend of every month to see Aunt Sophie, who maintained a cordial relationship with various Normandy dairy farmers. The sixteen-year-old youth much enjoyed setting off for the Gare Saint-Lazare on Saturday morning with his pockets full of money and boarding the Rouen train with all the aplomb of a seasoned traveller. Somewhat less enjoyable was his return journey on Sunday with a bulging suitcase. Forever on the qui vive for gendarmes and German soldiers, he had to lug this three long kilometres from the station to the Rue des Écoles.

The winter of 1940 was hardest of all for Yvonne. Ever since the school authorities had thought it necessary to confine little Muriel in the coal cellar and turn her into a persistent bed-wetter, Yvonne's keen intelligence had been devoted day and night to keeping her family fit and intact. The entries in her dream diary ceased, and gone were the days of pink sunglasses, filmy summer dresses and light-hearted singing. From now on her thoughts revolved around nothing save how to keep her husband and children safe until the war's end, to feed and warm and shield them from sorrow and affliction.

She pursued her aim with the guile of a secret agent, the courage of a goddess of war and the ruthlessness of a Panzer grenadier. In the mornings she accompanied her children to school one by one – even big Michel, who vainly jibbed at being escorted by his mother – and in the afternoons she collected them all again. Before she let Léon leave the building in the morning she went to the living-room window and peered in both directions, on the lookout for potential dangers; and when he was a few minutes late back from work she went to meet him and reproached him bitterly. If one of her children developed a cough she procured honey, lime-blossom tea and Sirolin cough syrup with the aid of lies, counterfeit money, and her décolletage. When the water in the kitchen froze, she felled a small acacia outside the Romanian Orthodox church, in broad daylight and under the eyes of several curious onlookers, then hauled the whole tree home and chopped it up into firewood in the inner courtyard.

The day after she heard strange noises on the stairs one night, she bought a black market Mauser 7.65 automatic plus ammunition and informed her disapproving husband that, if anyone set foot in their flat without her consent, she would shoot him without warning. When Léon pointed out that a pistol hanging on the wall in the first act of a play had to be fired in the second act, she shrugged and retorted that real life and the Russian theatre followed different rules. And when he asked why she had opted for a German pistol, she explained that if the German authorities found a German bullet in a German corpse, they would very probably go looking for a German perpetrator.

Whether these hard times welded Yvonne and Léon even closer together because they had to supply renewed proof of their mutual loyalty and dependability every day, or whether they forfeited their last hope of romantic love because they had quite pragmatically to function as comrades-in-arms – in other words, whether they grew closer under these circumstances – is hard to tell, but it's conceivable that they never asked themselves that question. What mattered was not the label on their partnership, but sheer daily survival. All metaphysics apart, time had simply created certain facts that weighed more heavily than any words.

It was, for instance, a fact that they were both over forty and had, with a fair degree of probability, passed the midpoint of their lives. It was also an arithmetical fact that they had spent half their lives together and would soon have spent more nights sleeping together in the same marriage bed than alone. It was furthermore foreseeable that their children would grow up in a surprisingly short time and go out into the world as living proof that Léon and Yvonne had been passable parents. Before long their remaining days on earth would speed by ever faster, and the sum of their shared memories would soon be so great that it offered greater comfort than any prospect of a life without each other, whatever form that might take.

Of course, something or other might one day cause Yvonne to run out on Léon or him on her. But it wouldn't be a new beginning or a new life, just a continuation of their previous lives under new circumstances. There was no such a thing as a second life; you only had the one. Although this seemed shattering at first sight, closer inspection revealed it to be comforting in the extreme, for it meant that their lives to date, far from being unimportant, were the essential prerequisite of all that was to come.

Léon was the man in Yvonne's life and she was the woman in his. She had no further grounds for jealousy. Nothing would change this even if they did lose one another in consequence of some disaster or senile folly. There simply wasn't enough time left for them to spend as many nights sharing another marriage bed with someone else as they had already spent together.

For Léon, who had long grown used to having two wives, one at his side and one in his head, nothing much changed, but Yvonne's soul found peace at last. For her too, the question of whether or not they were destined for one another had now been settled, and it no longer mattered whether they were really passionately or only half-heartedly in love, or whether they only pretended or wrongly believed that they loved one another. All that mattered was the actual status quo. It was as simple as that.

Without putting her feelings into high-flown words, Yvonne had to admit that she was still attracted – perhaps even more so than before – by Léon's stolid masculinity. She liked to hear his light-footed tread when he came up the stairs and his firm footsteps when he crossed the landing, and she liked the unaffected good nature in his voice and the strong but never acrid body odour given off by his overcoat when he hung it on the hook at the end of a day's work.

She liked it that the children, although they were really too old for it, still climbed on his lap and sat quietly there, and she liked the fact that he didn't cross his hands on his stomach as men of a certain age tend to do, and that he didn't yet groan when getting to his feet and still showed no signs of becoming a know-it-all who delivered long-winded lectures.

She liked it that malice and cruelty were foreign to his nature, and she still liked it when he wrapped his long arms around her in his sleep. And even if it happened that he sometimes embraced another woman in his dreams, the weight of the facts was on her side. In truth and actuality, *she* was the woman in his arms, no one else.

Medina
on the banks of
the Senegal River
24 December 1940

My dearest Léon,
Are you still alive? I am. I've just thrown the remains of a
preternaturally tough chicken over the terrace wall and into
the Senegal River. Now dwarf crocodiles are tussling for them
while hippos look on with bored expressions and open their jaws
for those funny little birds with sharp beaks to pick strands of
chewed-up waterlily from between their teeth.

Soon the sun will set and the muezzin will utter his call to
evening prayer. Then comes mosquito hour. I spend it in our
fortress in the officers' mess smoking room, which has thick stone
walls and thick mosquito netting over the windows. The mess
is the only still semi-habitable building in this dilapidated
old colonial town. All the other European buildings are ruins
in which young trees are growing and the Africans erect their
huts. My companions in the smoking room include the fortress
commander, his two sergeants, and my two colleagues from the
Banque de France. Another member of the party is Giuliano
Galiani, the expectorating radio operator from the 'Victor
Schoelcher'. You remember, he was assigned to us as a liaison
officer (although there's nothing and nobody here to liaise with).

Until dinner we sit in cane chairs and smoke. Meanwhile,
outside in the other ranks' quarters up against the fortress wall,
the ninety Senegalese riflemen who guard our precious cargo (of
which I'm not allowed to speak) sing melancholy songs of love,
death and homesickness. When the bell sounds for dinner we
repair to the dining room, where a loudly shrieking fan with
rust-eroded blades rotates above the table. One day in the not too

far distant future it's bound to fall from the ceiling and neatly behead us all within the same hundredth of a second.

Until that happens we sit there submissively and sweat, curse the heat, and vie with each other in fantasizing about wagonloads of chilled beer and champagne. When nothing else occurs to us, one of the men will present an account of his day's doings, its inevitable theme being the Africans' chronic unreliability and aversion to work.

Our overseers do, in fact, have great difficulty in keeping their native labourers hard at it. As soon as the sjambok is out of sight, any African promptly retires to the shade of the nearest baobab tree. I can sympathize with this, personally, because the work they have to do for us – breaking stones, carrying water, felling trees – is really no fun in a temperature of fifty degrees. This climate is enough to make the likes of us collapse under our own body weight.

It's also true that the Malinké, Wolof and Toucouleurs have never been keen competitors for the privilege of working for us, nor, to the best of my knowledge did they invite us here in the first place, bid us welcome, or beg us to stay once we were here. Even so, it surprises us every day that our overseers have to extort the requisite hospitality again and again with the aid of the sjambok.

The everlasting floggings and beatings, the screams and the blood and humiliation are a trial to everyone here – mainly to the victims, of course, but also to the floggers themselves, with whom I sit in the smoking room night after night. For the first few weeks I often wondered how these whip-wielders could bring themselves to have so little compassion and be so brutal and lacking in humanity. Since then I've realized that, if no one restrains them, floggers succumb to a sort of mania that impels them to go on flogging more and more brutally because only constantly repeated violence confirms their superiority over their victims and provides a justification for the obvious injustice of brutality.

But there's something else involved. Because I'm with my whip-wielding colleagues every hour of the day, I've got to know them pretty well. I hear them cry out at night when they're tossing and turning in their own sweat, racked by nightmares. I hear them whimper and cry out for their mothers, I hear them bellow commands and throw grenades, and I hear them running along the trenches of the Chemin des Dames to which they've returned night after night for the past quarter of a century, fleeing from German bayonets and poison gas and searching for their lost humanity.

It's particularly sad that the floggers were not on their own at the Chemin des Dames; many of their black victims were there too, side by side with their present tormentors. Even sadder is the prospect that the victims will one day rise and reach for the sjambok in their turn, and that, if no one intervenes, the flogging will be perpetuated from generation to generation.

Generally speaking, I'd say we're in much the same position here as the Germans occupying Paris. From what I hear, they're also rather sad that the French don't wholeheartedly welcome them as guests even though they've left their tanks outside the city and are behaving quite well in other respects. It's a curious fact that floggers, when they lay the whip aside for ten minutes, always expect their victims to love them at once.

One night in the officers' mess, between the starter and the main course, I expressed the idea that we in Senegal are suffering the same fate as the Germans we fled from; in other words, that we're the Germans of West Africa, so to speak. That didn't go down at all well. Since then I've learnt that it's better to keep your thoughts to yourself – or, better still, not to reveal that you think of anything whatever.

I shouldn't really be writing to you at all, everything out here still being extremely hush-hush. I suppose I was rather cheeky in my last letter, when I recounted the whole saga of our cargo in the belief that none of it mattered. Since then the commandant has given me several lectures. He impressed on me that it matters a great deal what some humble office girl gives vent to over her milk and biscuits on a quiet night when she's feeling bored, and that even a little careless talk in times like these can easily put one up in front of a firing squad. Since then I've pulled myself together and kept a bridle on my tongue because la patrie is, after all, la patrie. On the other hand, you and I still exist, and I still feel closer to you the further away from you I am.

I'd dearly like to know why this has never changed over the years. After all, let's be honest: you aren't such a uniquely magnificent individual. Anyway, I'm glad of the little pang the thought of you always gives me. For one thing, pain is comforting because only the living can feel it, and, for another, I know for sure you feel it just as I do.

Not an hour or a day goes by that I don't want to tell you this or that, and that I don't wish you were here and could see what I can see, and that I could hear what you had to say about it all. So if I'm writing you another few lines in defiance of regulations, it's because it may be a long time before such a favourable opportunity recurs: my colleague Monsieur Delaport, who has contracted yellow fever and been issued with a travel permit for Dakar, will take this letter with him and make sure it reaches the Rue des Écoles unopened.

It's six months since I wrote to you from Lorient harbour.

———

Time goes fast, especially when lots of things are happening, and even faster when nothing is… Just as I wrote that, a bird that's driving me mad started up again. 'Ruuku-dii', 'ruuku-dii', 'ruuku-dii', it goes for hours and days and nights on end. Just 'ruuku-dii', 'ruuku-dii', 'ruuku-dii', with a persistence that really ought to exceed its strength, always just 'ruuku-dii', 'ruuku-dii', 'ruuku-dii' until I go to sleep late at night with my nerves shredded and my fingers in my ears. That's why I can't be sure whether or not the creature takes an hour's rest occasionally. Don't get me wrong, I'm sure it's a perfectly harmless bird and just as naturally entitled to its niche in Creation as the rest of us. Its cry probably isn't especially loud or piercing, objectively speaking, but it drives me to such a pitch of fury that I've more than once rushed outside with my pistol (yes, I've got one here) and would have shot it dead if only I'd been able to spot it in the branches of the acacia where I suspect it roosts.

The bird has done me no harm. It's probably vegetarian and goes 'ruuku-dii', 'ruuku-dii' for laudable reasons. It may be defending its territory, hoping to pass on its genes, or simply having fun. In search of explanations for its incredible stamina, I hit on the possibility that it might be down to the avian respiratory system, which differs in some way from that of us mammals. At college I had to make pretty drawings of it in red and blue crayon, but I can't recall the details. Air flows through birds' lungs in one direction only, right? Fine, but how the hell does it find its way out again? Needless to say, there's no one here with even a smidgen of ornithological knowledge and no Larousse I could consult. Both exist in Dakar, no doubt, but that's a thousand kilometres west of here and inaccessible without a travel permit, and I'm unlikely to get one of those before the war ends.

If I were at home in Paris and the bird was perched on my window sill, I'd probably pay it little attention. But here in the sameness of these red, ferruginous hills with their unvarying acacias and baobabs, where I'm irked by the uneventfulness of my hours and days of idleness and the silence of the nights when nothing can be heard but the distant cackle of hyenas, the footfall of shadowy human figures shuffling past nearby, the nightmare whimpers of my companions, and the 'ruuku-dii', 'ruuku-dii', 'ruuku-dii' of this same bird, I sometimes become so bored that I long for some catastrophe – a tornado, an earthquake, a German invasion – to sweep it all away.

Incidentally, I can't give you any descriptions of the scenery. There are hills and plains and the river and all manner of flora and fauna here, for sure, and at night the sky is pitch-black and sprinkled with stars. I could no doubt produce some quite edifying thoughts on the subject if I were an English lady passing through in a train. However, circumstances have decreed that I'm not an English lady and not passing through; I've got out here and stayed, which is why I relieve myself behind bushes and take my weekly bath in the river, watching out for crocodiles and hippos… What I mean to say is this: When you're in the middle of a landscape it ceases to be a suitable subject for aesthetic contemplation and becomes a damned serious matter.

There are moonstruck NCOs here who try to drag me into the bushes. I have to avoid direct sunlight and get into the dry before the next cloudburst. I'm annoyed with my typewriter because the A, V, P and Z have been sticking for some time. I ought to clean my teeth using sterilized water, and it would be to my advantage if I could exchange a friendly greeting with the Malenké king's wives in the vegetable market, all five of whom are insufferably haughty… In short, if I want to survive here I have to keep my wits about me however bored I am, so I can't afford to poeticize about trees, mountains and baobabs.

By contrast, Galiani, our radio operator with nothing to radio, seems to be enjoying himself hugely. He sports an old French pith helmet which he wears cocked at an angle when he goes shooting early in the morning, so it doesn't hamper his aim. At lunchtime this overgrown Napoleon with the sunny disposition – he's more likely to die of high blood pressure than cancer of the liver – returns from the bush with an antelope over his shoulder, and in the afternoon he struts around the market and winks at the Fula girls with their long legs and firm little breasts, who smile, blushing faintly, as if they've already made his acquaintance elsewhere and at quite other times of the day. In the evenings he sits cross-legged beside the villagers' fires and converses volubly in a wide variety of native languages, having acquired a smattering of each, and sometimes the darkness swallows him up and he doesn't reappear until next day or the day after that. I ought to take a leaf out of his book.

I'm sure you worry about me. You mustn't, I manage all right. My greatest worry is my digestion. After that come boredom and the fact that I'm the only white woman within a radius of fifteen kilometres. Where the white men in the vicinity are concerned, that earns me a popularity I could happily do without.

And you? Are you still alive, my little Léon? Are you going hungry while I'm complaining about my stringy chicken? Are your children condemned to shiver while the sweat runs down my forehead and into my eyes? Are you living in daily fear and trembling while I suffer from boredom? Are shots being fired in the streets of Paris and bombs falling from the sky?

I'd so much like to know all these things, but I know you can't reply. You needn't even try to – it's months since we received any

*mail and the telephone and telegraph have been out of action for
ages. I worry about you terribly – all the more terribly because I
have no news of you and there's nothing I could do for you if you
needed my help.*

*We're separated by 4500 kilometres, an ocean, and the biggest
desert in the world, by Nazis and fascists and the Allies and –
as if that were not enough – by Marshal Philippe Pétain and
General Charles de Gaulle and Francisco Franco and Adolf
Hitler. And nearly all of them have it in for us – for me, at least,
or so I tell myself.*

*'Ruuku-dii', 'ruuku-dii', 'ruuku-dii', goes the bird while the
red hills glow in the setting sun. I never hear any other bird
from my room, always just this one going 'ruuku-dii', 'ruuku-
dii', 'ruuku-dii', and I wonder whether it really is just one lone
individual, or if several members of the same species have joined
forces and are taking it in turns to drive me crazy.*

*In favour of the first alternative is the fact that 'ruuku-dii'
always rings out singly, never in a chorus. What argues against
it is sheer probability: why should there be only one example of
the species for kilometres around? Because it's the last of a dying
breed? Because it has lost its way and really belongs somewhere
quite else, Finland or the Balkans, perhaps? Was its courtship
display so exuberant that it drove all others of its kind away,
male and female alike, and is it now, with a perseverance
born of loneliness and despair, trying to call them back? Is the
bird perched in the acacia not an exotic creature at all, but a
perfectly ordinary wood pigeon that calls 'ruuku-dii' instead of
'groogroo' only because it was born with a misshapen larynx?
Does the pigeon persist so desperately because other pigeons can't
understand its distorted mating call?*

One goes soft in the head out here. We're cut off from home

*and from those we love, we get no mail or newspapers, we haven't
been paid for ages and have no idea when or if we'll ever be
relieved. It isn't the heat or the omnipresent dust during the dry
season and the mud during the rest of the year that gets me down,
it isn't the hyenas and snakes or the strangeness of the natives, to
whom we'll never be close however used to them we get because
the sjambok keeps us apart and is bound to do so until that
inevitable day when the black man sends the white man home;
nor is it the sameness of the surrounding plain with its everlasting
acacias and baobabs, which extends for hundreds of kilometres
and is only rarely enlivened by little hills scarcely worthy of the
name. No, what gets me down is the absence of concrete and
electric light, of bookshops and bakeries and newspaper sellers, of
park benches and rainy Sunday afternoons at the cinema. I miss
chocolate éclairs and casual conversations in the office and quick
steak-and-chips lunches and good dinners at Chez Graff near the
Moulin Rouge. I miss the screech of the trams and the rumble
of the Métro, and how much I'd like, on a mild evening in late
summer, to go for a long walk in the Tuileries on the arm of my
youthful admirer from the Musée de l'Homme, who isn't so young
any more but still, I hope, regards me as a lady.*

*Because I miss all these things, I study the phenomena on offer
here. For instance, it surprises me anew every day that mashed
potato takes far longer to cool down, here in the African heat
than in Europe, to a temperature your mouth can stand. On the
other hand, you need never hurry over breakfast because your
coffee stays hot for hours. I also find it amusing that Africans are
almost invisible in the dark, whereas whites like us can be seen
from far away in the faintest starlight.*

*Then there's the highly individualistic ana tree (Acacia
albida), which sheds its feathery leaves in the middle of the*

---

rainy season, when everything around it is green and luxuriant, and stands there with its pale trunk looking dead. During the dry season, by contrast, when everything around it withers and shrivels up, it comes back to life. It blossoms and puts out the lushest of tender green leaves, triumphantly demonstrating to everyone in sight that life goes on even under the most adverse circumstances, after long periods of drought and seemingly endless spells of death and destruction. I hope that isn't too much for you in the way of metaphor and allegory. It is for me.

Before I embark on a description of the long, sluggishly flowing Senegal River, or of the gardens that thrive on its banks, in which orchids bloom and birds of paradise breed, passing on the spark of life, I'll give it a miss and bring this letter to an end. Just one more poetic aperçu for you: When the Africans develop a fever – I've been assured of this more than once – they treat it by stuffing a pepper pod up their anus. I kiss you tenderly, my dearest Léon, and firmly believe that we'll meet again some day.

Yours, Louise

PS. On my bosses' instructions, I had the enclosed photo-booth picture taken a few minutes before our train left the Gare Montparnasse. We each had to take twenty passport photos with us for visas and passport extensions and so on. Please note the strands of white on my left temple – I think they look very stylish. I'd very much like a photo of you. Please send me one addressed to Medina, French West Africa, perhaps it'll miraculously get here in spite of everything. Oh yes, and – if you can – enclose a few packets of Turmac cigarettes.

16

One day in the spring of 1941, Madame Rossetos suddenly reappeared. Léon noticed a preliminary indication of this on coming home from work, when he was still outside on the pavement and spotted it from a long way off: the brass handle on the front door, which had become dull and tarnished in the past year, was as lustrously golden as it had been in peacetime. Not only did the marble floor of the entrance hall sparkle with cleanliness, but hanging once more over the glass door of the concierge's lodge, which had been a dark, blank rectangle for a year, was a floral curtain with light showing through it, and – unless it was his imagination – Léon could again smell braised onions.

He paused and listened, then decided to walk on and took a few steps towards the stairs. When his shadow fell on the glass door, however, the clatter of saucepans ceased, to be replaced by the sort of an unnatural silence of which a person is capable only when asleep or dead or listening intently. Léon couldn't help smiling at the thought that two grown-up people were listening to each other with bated breath, and that one could see the shadow of the other on the pane. To put an end to this ludicrous situation, he went up to the door and knocked. Silence. He knocked again and called Madame Rossetos' name. When still no sound issued from the interior, he felt sure it really must be her who had slunk back into her lair. What had happened to her in the meantime? How much unhappiness and dismay, how much horror and hardship must she have experienced before she brought herself to humbly return to the Rue des Écoles and throw herself on the mercy of the tenants she had scathingly abandoned barely a year earlier?

Léon debated whether to bid her welcome through the unopened door. Then, realizing that she would only think he was being sarcastic, he made for the stairs with deliberately heavy tread. He would respect Madame Rossetos' invisibility for as long as she needed, and on the day she crept out of her lair he would say a casual hello, acting as if nothing had happened and she'd never been away.

♨

On 8 June 1941, little Philippe was born. When Yvonne's labour pains began at 3 a.m. Léon summoned a pedicab, accompanied her to the Maternité in the Boulevard du Port-Royal, and took the same taxi home, there to watch over the sleeping children and get them off to school on time. He spent the rest of the night in his armchair beside the living-room window. Having at first tried to read, he turned out the light and divided his time between looking up at the star-spangled sky and down into the deserted street.

Once he heard a faint whimper from the nursery, probably from little Muriel, who was prone to nightmares since her incarceration in the coal cellar. By the time Léon opened the door she was already snoring her high-pitched, rapid, childish snores. He waited until his eyes had grown used to the darkness, then surveyed his children's sleeping forms beneath their light summer duvets.

Eight-year-old Robert and eleven-year-old Yves were lying as far apart as possible in the bed they shared beside the window, arms and legs dangling down on either side. Little Muriel lay sprawled on her back in the middle of her little bed with her limbs flung out in that vulnerable but regal pose characteristic of drunks and infants. Sixteen-year-old Michel no longer slept in the nursery. On one of the first warm spring days, he had moved into the unoccupied attic room upstairs and underlined his independence by spending some of his pocket money on a second-hand alarm clock at the flea market. The first night her first-born spent on his own had been a wrench for Yvonne, who wept, but Léon welcomed the fact that Michel had bought the clock at the flea market instead of investing in a new one.

Like Léon himself, the children had developed the habit of bringing home bits of old junk salvaged from rubbish dumps and backyards – rusty horseshoes, jute sacks with exotic inscriptions, and curious pieces of wood or metal that might once have been the components of something. Léon admired these treasures and joined the children in speculating about their original purpose, previous history and former owners. Meanwhile Yvonne, who was less susceptible to the charm of useless objects, stood ready with disinfectant and awaited her opportunity to rid these gems, if they had to remain in the flat at all, of microbes and other sources of infection.

It pleased Léon that his children were genuine Le Galls. True, they had each been endowed from birth with characteristics unmistakably their own. Robert was fair-haired, Yves auburn, and Muriel on the dark side; the first had inherited his father's inoffensive stolidity, the second his mother's acumen and tendency to hysteria, and the third possessed a talent for diplomacy hitherto unknown in the family. But the backs of all their heads were flat, they were amiably rebellious, and even the youngest ones displayed a propensity for cheerful melancholy.

While surveying his sleeping children, Léon silently recapitulated his highly personal argument in favour of the immortality of the human soul, which he had cobbled together with the aid of basic theoretical physics and probability calculus. The foundation of his theory was the obvious fact that human beings aren't soulless automata – his children certainly weren't, he would have staked his life on that – but are quite clearly endowed with a soul from the moment of their birth.

From that, in conformity with the law of conservation of mass, Léon inferred that the soul could not have created itself out of nothing. And this, in turn, meant either that it must have existed as an entity before birth – and thus probably before conception as well – or that it took shape from previously inanimate particles or sources of energy in the course of incarnation.

Léon determined by process of elimination that only the first of those alternatives was feasible. This was because the second possibility – that the soul of each of the millions of human beings born every day was spontaneously formed every time out of previously inanimate particles or sources of energy – was just as unacceptable according to the laws of probability as if the miracle of the genesis of life out of lifeless mud had not occurred just once at the beginning of all time many millions of years ago, but was forever recurring a million times over in every puddle and rivulet throughout the world.

Still in his armchair when dawn broke, Léon sat up with a start. He went to the baker's and bought some bread, then put some water on for coffee. Shortly before seven he woke the children and laid out clean clothes for them. Then he climbed the stairs to the attic to wake Michel, who never heard his alarm clock ring. Back in the kitchen again, he poured the coffee water through the filter, put some milk on and buttered some slices of bread.

Then the morning hush outside was broken by the squeak of bicycle brakes. Muffled voices could be heard, followed by the sound of a woman's heels on the pavement. Léon opened the living-room window and looked down. Outside the front door was a bicycle taxi, and standing beside it Yvonne. Less than four hours had elapsed since Léon had left her at the Maternité in the care of a nurse. He ran downstairs and hurried to meet her in the entrance hall, relieved her of her bag and thrust aside a fold of blanket so as to be able to see the little face of the baby she was carrying bundled up in her arms.

'All in order?'

'Absolutely. Two kilos eight hundred. Flat occiput.'

'What is it?'

'A little Philippe.'

'Philippe like the Marshal?'

'No, no, just Philippe.'

'What about you? All well?'

'Oh yes, it was an easy birth.'

'Still, you should have had three or four days bedrest at the Maternité.'

'What for?'

'We could have managed.'

'Don't worry, I'm not going to die on you.'

'What would I do without you?'
'Or I without you?'
'Yvonne?'
'Yes?'
'I love you.'
'I know. I love you too, Léon.'
'Let's go up, the milk will be boiling over.'

ge

This exchange took them both by surprise, it was so many years since they'd uttered the words. Perhaps that was why they still sounded so fresh and pristine that morning, and why there was nothing false or contrived or affected about them. With Léon's arm around her waist, Yvonne climbed the stairs carrying the peacefully sleeping trial of patience who would be their guest for the next few years.

ge

The next day Léon went back to the laboratory, where he would soon have been engaged in copying index cards for a year and was taking good care not to let the job drive him insane. Lying on his desk at half-past eight every morning would be a pile of a hundred smudged, curly, dog-eared index cards whose inscriptions he had to decipher and transcribe on to new, snow-white cards. At some stage after office hours, when most of the offices and laboratories in the Quai des Orfèvres were deserted, Hauptsturmführer Knochen's orderly went the rounds and collected up both copies and originals.

Léon sometimes managed only seventy or eighty copies in

a day because he'd had to test an almond tart for arsenic or a bottle of Campari for rat poison. When that happened he left the twenty or thirty unprocessed cards on his desk and the orderly would add another seventy or eighty overnight, so that he again found a hundred waiting for him next morning.

Out of consideration for his family, Léon now refrained from making too many mistakes. For a while he had tried staging an unofficial go-slow by poring over each card for as long as possible, drafting the text in pencil, and inscribing the final, ink version in schoolboy calligraphy. Although he succeeded in reducing his output to twenty cards a day, the calligraphy gave him writer's cramp and the go-slow became boring in the long run. After a few days' strenuous inactivity he gave his temperament free rein and reverted to working at his normal speed.

But he never drank the mocha which Hauptsturmführer Knochen, with malicious regularity, made sure was delivered to him week after week. He put the unopened red, white and black packets, each of which contained a quarter of a kilogram, in the cupboard where he had also kept the Italian mocha jug. Furthermore, he banished the new desk lamp to the window sill beside his desk, and, when the captain hadn't shown his face for several months, exchanged it for an old lamp he'd found in the attic.

֍

But one sunny morning in late summer, after a shower of rain during the night, everything changed again. On his way to work Léon had kicked chestnuts across the glistening wet cobblestones and looked up at maidservants wielding their feather dusters in the open windows; on the Pont Saint-Michel he picked up the last of the chestnuts and flung it zestfully into the Seine, and when he turned into the Quai des Orfèvres he ran a few steps from sheer exhilaration.

When he entered the laboratory, however, his old lamp had disappeared and the Siemens lamp was back on his desk. He searched high and low, went out into the passage and peered in both directions, scratched his head and frowned. Then he returned to his desk, picked up the index card on top of the pile, and began his day's work.

It wasn't until late afternoon that his fears materialized. On returning from a visit to the lavatory he found Knochen sitting in his chair. The German had propped his elbows on the desk and was massaging his face with both hands. He was looking thoroughly world-weary.

'What are you standing around for? Come in, Le Gall, and shut the door behind you.'

'Good afternoon, Hauptsturmführer. Long time no see.'

'Let's not fool around, I'm sick of playing games. We're both grown men.'

'Whatever you say, Hauptsturmführer.'

'Sturmbannführer. I've been promoted.'

'Congratulations.'

'I'm here to caution you, Le Gall. You've been indulging in sabotage again, and I can't let it pass. Take care, I warn you.'

'But Sturmbannführer, I'm doing my best.'

'Don't talk nonsense. You're too much of a coward for genuine sabotage, of course, you merely play the *résistant* so no one gets hurt. You want to assuage your conscience, so you deliberately make schoolboy howlers. In your place I'd be ashamed.'

'May I be quite frank, Sturmbannführer?'

'By all means.'

'In your place I would also be ashamed.'

'Really? Why?'

'You come here and throw your weight about, knowing you've got all those tanks and guns behind you.'

'At least I *do* have them behind me.'

'If you were in my place and I in yours – '

'Who knows, Le Gall? The fact is that last autumn, when you still had the wind up about your little daughter, your errors averaged eight per cent. Now that a few months have gone by and she's probably peeing the bed only every other night, you get cocky again and allow yourself fourteen per cent.'

'I didn't realize – '

'Shut up, don't talk nonsense. You aren't back to seventy-three per cent of errors, not yet, but they're on the increase. While we're on the subject, what was the matter with this desk lamp? What harm did it do you?'

'It's just a lamp.'

'Does it bother you that it's a Siemens?'

'I've got sensitive eyes, it's so bright it dazzles me. The old lamp – '

'Shut up, the lamp stays where it is. Take this as a final warning.' Knochen sighed and planted his boots on the desk.

'May I ask you a question, Sturmbannführer?'

'What is it?'

'Why me?'

'What do you mean, why me?'

'I'm the only person in the building you've treated to coffee and a new desk lamp.'

'You've asked around?'

'Why me, Sturmbannführer?'

'Because you're the only one that makes difficulties.'

'The only one in the Quai des Orfèvres?'

'You're the only one out of a staff of five hundred who plays the hero. And now make me some coffee, I'm tired. Nice and strong, please.'

'Coffee?'

'Yes, right away.'

'Filter or mocha?'

'Mocha. None of that wartime pigswill of yours. And use the mocha jug, not that funny filter thing.'

'It's just that – '

'What?'

'The mocha you send me isn't ground.'

'Well?'

'I don't have a coffee mill.'

'Then use a mortar, man! This is a laboratory, after all, you must have something of the kind. And stop playing these girlish games.'

Knochen watched Léon open the cupboard. Neatly arrayed on the top shelf were two or three dozen quarter-kilo packets of coffee printed red, white and black. The German sighed and shook his head, then clasped his hands behind his head and stared out of the window over his boots.

Léon ground up a handful of coffee beans in the mortar, filled the reservoir and emptied the coffee into the funnel, screwed the top on, put the jug on the burner, and turned on the gas, which ignited with a faint plop. While the water was heating up he laid out saucers and cups and coffee spoons and put the sugar basin on the desk. When everything was ready and there was nothing left to do, he went to the window furthest from the desk and looked down at the Seine flowing imperturbably past the Île de la Cité as it had done a hundred or a hundred thousand years ago. He occasionally sensed that Knochen was looking at him, and he sometimes glanced at the SS major out of the corner of his eye. It seemed to take an age for the coffee to come bubbling up through the tube.

While Léon was pouring, Knochen took his boots off the desk, cupped his chin in his right hand and gazed at him. Then he said, 'Le Gall, I ought to feel sorry for you. It's always the best who are disobedient, that's apparent from even a cursory look back at history. It's disobedience that marks out the special from the ordinary, don't you agree? Unfortunately, though, we aren't living between the pages of a history book, we're living in the here and now, and present indications are that most of what will prove to be of historic importance is pretty banal. We aren't here to make history, we're here to get these god-damned index cards copied. That's why you're now going to obey me and make no more mistakes, and that goddamned lamp is going to remain on your desk, nowhere else. You won't move it so much as ten centimetres without asking my permission in advance, understand?'

'Yes.'

'It's a Siemens lamp, Le Gall, get used to it. It's staying exactly where it is and you'll use it. You'll turn it on every day when you arrive for work, and you'll turn it off before you go home. Understood? '

'Yes.'

'Good. And now sit down and drink a mocha with me.'

'If you wish.'

'Yes, I do wish it. I also wish you to drink mocha every day from now on. What on earth have you got against the stuff? Don't you like it?'

'It's excellent, I'm sure.'

'You're going to drink a lot more mocha in the immediate future, Le Gall, you've got some catching up to do. It isn't worth kicking against the pricks any more, by the way. The copies will soon be completed.'

The two men drank their mochas in silence. Then Knochen rose, nodded a curt farewell, and went out. Léon carried the cups over to the sink. On second thoughts, he threw the SS major's into the waste bin.

༅

For three days Léon wondered how to get rid of the mocha without having to drink it. He left the Italian mocha jug and his cup unwashed beside the Bunsen burner, so as to be able to prove that he'd already drunk his daily mocha. In reality, he continued to drink his woody-tasting wartime brew.

On the following Monday, when his weekly quarter-kilo of mocha arrived on his desk, he put it in his briefcase and took it home that evening.

'What's that?' asked Yvonne.

'German mocha. I told you about it.'

'Get rid of it.'

'Wouldn't you like to – '

'Get rid of it, I said. I don't want it in the house.'

'What should I do with the stuff?'

'Go to the Rue du Jour behind Les Halles. Ask at the Auberge du Beau Noir for Monsieur Renaud. He'll take you to a hatter in Avenue Voltaire who'll give you a good price for it.'

'What shall I do with the money?'

'We don't need it.'

'I'll take it to the lab.'

'Do something clever with it.'

'I'll think of something.'

'Don't tell me. Don't mention it to a soul. It's better nobody knows.'

ક્ષ

In exchange for his quarter-kilo of mocha Léon received a wad of banknotes almost equivalent to half his monthly salary. Because he went to the Avenue Voltaire every Monday from then on, and sometimes, in order to reduce the surplus in his cupboard, took along a couple of extra packets as well, it wasn't long before the lockable drawer in his desk contained a large sum of money.

Léon never counted the money. He never toyed with it or divided it up into batches, never kept accounts or checked that it was all there – he never even looked at it. He opened the drawer only once a week on his return from the Rue Saint-Denis. Having tossed the new banknotes in, he locked the drawer again and put the key in the bakelite tray containing his pencils and rubber, where, just because it was in plain view, he could be sure no one would notice it.

For a long time Léon had no idea what to do with the wealth Sturmbannführer Knochen was thrusting on him at gunpoint, so to speak. He only knew he wanted to spare himself the humiliation of profiting from it personally. He also realized that he must look for some way of sharing the money out, and that in this second year of the war there wasn't a single police officer in the Quai des Orfèvres who couldn't use a little windfall to buy some steak, a pair of children's shoes or a bottle of red wine on the black market.

The question was, how to distribute the money. If he openly went round the offices and handed it to his colleagues in person, Knochen would get wind of it and have him arrested for insubordination and attempted sabotage. And if he distributed it secretly by depositing it in his colleagues' overcoat pockets, intrays and desk drawers, the more dutiful of them would take the money to their superiors and call for an investigation into attempted bribery by some person or persons unknown.

So Léon decided against scattering the cash around and envisaged adopting a more specific approach. Working downstairs in the investigating magistrate's office was a clerk named Heintzer whose Alsatian law degree had been rendered worthless by the outcome of the First World War. He lived in a damp three-room flat behind the Bastille with his six children, his tubercular wife and his alcoholic sister Irmgard, who spoke no French and had turned up on his doorstep, unannounced, some years before. He also had to send money to his old father, who still resided with five sheep and three hens in the dilapidated little farmhouse between Osenbach and Wasserbourg that had been the family home for two centuries.

Heintzer walked with a stoop, his hair hung over his ears like dishevelled feathers, and his mouth odour could be detected at a range of several paces. To make matters worse, everyone in the Quai des Orfèvres called him 'the Boche' because he was tall and fair-haired and had never quite managed to lose his Alsatian accent. He had a spiteful boss named Lamouche who liked to tweak his off-white shirt collars and poke pencils through his threadbare sleeves in front of the assembled staff. Because the Boche endured all these things in dignified silence and never complained about his ulcer, carious teeth and slipped disc, the softer-hearted of the secretaries gave him sympathetic glances – not that they cared to venture too close to someone who seemed to possess a magnetic attraction for misfortune, poverty and disease.

One misty autumn evening, Léon followed the luckless Heintzer home in order to discover where he lived. Next morning he got out the typewriter and screwed a sheet of paper into it. His first step was to type an impressive letterheading larded with words like 'Ministry', 'Republic', 'Security', 'President', 'National', and 'France'. Then he wrote 'Lump-sum back payment of outstanding family allowance, February 1932-October 1941', inserted an astronomically large figure, and added the corresponding number of banknotes. He adorned the document with an illegibly baroque signature and wrote a non-existent sender's address on the back of the envelope to ensure that the Boche's inevitable letter of acknowledgement would not turn up in some genuine government office and give rise to puzzled frowns.

Léon allowed several days to elapse after making a special trip to the 16th Arrondissement to post the letter and forbade himself to indulge in any unjustified visits to the magistrate's secretariat. After a couple of weeks, however, when no rumours of a suspicious windfall had come to his ears, he went down to the second floor to see how Heintzer was faring. He sat on a bench in the passage, leafing through a file for camouflage, and when the man actually appeared he gave him a casual nod which Heintzer returned just as casually.

Léon was relieved to note that Heintzer obviously suspected nothing, but that his appearance had much improved. The smudges beneath his eyes were only pale blue, not dark green, his suit and shoes were new, his breath no longer smelt, and he walked erect like a young man, not bowed down with sorrow.

217

When Léon returned a few days later he heard him laughing heartily, exposing a mouthful of teeth which, though not all genuine, were dazzlingly white; and the last time he passed by a month later, the Boche was standing in the passage with a young blonde and holding her hand as she applied the end of her lighted cigarette to his.

Encouraged by his success, Léon got out his typewriter again. To the sad-faced telephonist in Vice he sent a tax refund, to a colleague in the photographic lab a lump-sum back payment for travelling expenses covering the previous five years. Madame Rossetos received a retroactive supplement to her widow's pension and some extra educational credit vouchers for her two fatherless daughters, and Aunt Simone in Caen was sent belated compensation for the refugees billeted on her in 1914–18. The waiter in the bistro around the corner received a windfall from a hitherto unknown uncle in America, and the woman at the news-stand in the Place Saint-Michel was reimbursed for rent charged in error.

Although this distribution process gave Léon pleasure, it was time-consuming, and besides, he was gradually running out of suitable recipients. Moreover, as time went by he began to feel that his arbitrary choices were unfair. Why should his favourites benefit from Sturmbannführer Knochen's mocha money to the exclusion of everyone else? Unable to see any other way of arriving at a fair selection, he decided to eliminate the arbitrary element altogether and leave it entirely to chance.

When work was over he took the Métro to the Gare du Nord and walked down the Rue de Maubeuge. Regardless of the address, he inserted a banknote in every accessible letter-box – sometimes a ten or a fifty but mostly a hundred-frank note. When he came to the Rue La Fayette he continued south down the Rue Montmartre, switching sides as the fancy took him, and inserted a banknote in every letterbox. At Les Halles he spent the remainder of the money on a chicken for himself and his family and took it home with him.

17

Then came the morning when Léon turned up for work and found no index cards lying on his desk – neither old and water-damaged nor new and virginal. He scanned the entire laboratory, then sat down and waited. When nothing happened he put some water on for coffee, went out into the passage and kept watch. When the water was boiling he made coffee and poured himself a cup, then sat down and waited some more.

After finishing his coffee he went out into the passage again. The door of the room immediately opposite was ajar. A colleague was leaning back in his chair with his hands clasped behind his head. Léon looked at him enquiringly. The man's lips twisted into a horizontal, mirthless grin. 'It's over, Le Gall,' he said. 'Over and done with.'

Léon nodded, turned on his heel and went back into the laboratory. To his surprise he felt no relief, just shame. He felt ashamed of himself and the whole of the Police Judiciaire, which would now have no further opportunity to lay aside the ignominious task that had been imposed on it.

Outwardly, Léon's routine regained a kind of normality. Sturmbannführer Knochen and his orderly no longer showed their faces and the coffee deliveries ceased. Although there were still plenty of banknotes in the drawer, Léon had lost his unremitting urge to distribute them. There was little actual laboratory work. Although substantially more people were dying unnatural deaths than during the strangely peaceful summer of 1940, most of the victims displayed bullet wounds rather than signs of poisoning.

Léon decided to resume work on the unofficial thesis he had discontinued eighteen months earlier, but he had to avoid riling Knochen. Before he produced any written work of his own, he would have to request the Sturmbannführer's formal permission and demonstrate that his research was innocuous. He felt ashamed of being pre-emptively subservient and even more ashamed of his inability to see any way of being less so.

❦

At the beginning of February 1942, Léon received an unexpected visit from Jules Caron, an accounts clerk who had never before been seen on the fourth floor. Caron had pock-marked cheeks and tortoiseshell glasses, a snub nose and a mouth like a surgical incision. Léon knew him by sight from sporadic encounters on the stairs. They would exchange perfunctory nods, as people from different departments tend to, but had never stopped and talked. And now Caron was standing in front of Léon's desk, rubbing the bridge of his nose like a schoolboy summoned to the headmaster's study.

'We've known each other for a long time, Le Gall.'

'Yes.'

'Not very well, though.'

'That's true.'

'What are you doing at the moment?'

'Some statistical work. Deaths by poisoning, 1930 to 1940.'

'I see. I've been here twelve years now. You?'

'Since September 1918. Nearly twenty-four.'

'Good for you.'

'Thanks.'

'Time flies.'

'It certainly does.'

'Mind if I shut the door?'

'Not at all.' There was some filter coffee left in the jug. Léon poured two cups.

'You must be surprised to see me here, considering we don't really know each other.'

'Work is work.'

'I'm not here officially. It's about, well…'

'I'm listening.'

'I wouldn't be here if I had the slightest prospect of…'

'Do go on.'

'I'm here because… Don't get me wrong, but people talk.'

'About me?'

'One hears things.'

'Like what?'

'Well, things. Look, Le Gall, I don't care what you get up to, I don't want to know. I'll make it short: Will you buy my boat?'

'Come again?'

'I own a boat not far from here. Nothing special, just a clinker-built cabin cruiser, seven-point-two metres long, three in the beam, twin bunks, twelve horse-power diesel engine. Eighteen years old but in good condition. It's moored in the Arsenal basin.' Caron looked round anxiously. 'Can I talk here? No one can overhear us, can they?'

'Don't worry.'

'You've got to help me, Le Gall. I have to disappear – into the unoccupied zone. By tonight, tomorrow morning at the latest.'

'Why?'

'Don't ask. The warning I received was quite explicit. I need some ready cash for myself and my family. For my parents-in-law too, if possible. Will you help me?'

'If I can.'

'They say you've got money.'

'Who's they?'

'Is it true?'

'How much do you need?'

'I'll sell you my cabin cruiser.'

'I don't want your cabin cruiser.'

'And I don't want charity.'

'How much?'

'Five thousand.'

'Will you keep your mouth shut?'

'Nobody here will ever see me again, my train leaves at half-past two.'

Léon took the key from the bakelite tray and opened the drawer, counted out five thousand francs and added another thousand. As he slid the wad of notes across the desk, Caron held out a key ring. 'The boat's name is *Fleur de Miel.* Pale-blue hull, white cabin, red-and-white checked curtains.'

'I don't want your boat.'

'It's got a diesel engine, a wood-burning stove and two bunks.'

'I don't want it.'

'And electric light. Take it as security and keep it in good condition for me.'

'Put that key away.'

'You must turn the engine over every couple of weeks or it'll deteriorate from disuse. If I'm still not back in two or three years' time you'll have to take the boat out of the water and repaint it. When the war's over I'll reclaim it and give you your money back.'

'Forget the money,' said Léon.

'In that case, forget the boat ever belonged to me.'

Caron got to his feet. He put the key on the desk and raised his hand in farewell.

જી

Léon put the key in the drawer with the money, locked it up and bent over his statistics again. After a few weeks, however, he took to standing at the window more and more often, watching the river traffic. Barges now glided along the Seine only rarely and in ones and twos, but he paid special attention whenever a cabin cruiser appeared. When he asked for Caron in the accounts department, he was told that the man and his entire family had disappeared without trace.

As time went by he thought more and more often of the boat with the red-and-white checked curtains and worried about the diesel engine. He thought of rusting shaft seals and corroding plugs, crumbling gaskets and obstructed valve springs. It also worried him that seagulls would encrust the boat with their droppings if no one looked after it. Tramps would break into the cabin and leave the door open; then wind and weather and schoolboys would complete the work of destruction. He also thought occasionally of Caron somewhere in the sunny south, homesick for the milky skies of Paris and hoping that Léon Le Gall was looking after his *Fleur de Miel*.

One tentative spring day at the end of the third winter of the war, Léon didn't go home for lunch but walked across the Île

Saint-Louis and the Pont de Sully to the Arsenal harbour. The brown waters of the basin were rippling in the spring breeze. Three winter-proofed *bateaux mouches* were moored to their bollards and two or three dozen cabin cruisers were rocking gently in the wind. Many were green and many red, some were pale-blue and several had red-and-white checked curtains, but only one was called *Fleur de Miel.*

Léon came to a halt on the quayside and studied the boat. It was covered with seagull droppings, the cockpit was full of dead leaves and the hull below the waterline furred with green waterweed, but the decking seemed to be in good order, the seams had been freshly caulked, and the paintwork was immaculate. The red-and-white checked curtains were neatly drawn and the padlock on the cabin door was intact.

The moment Léon took the key from his pocket, he felt *Fleur de Miel* become his. He had a boat again at last. He felt just as he'd felt back in Cherbourg with Patrice and Joël, when they hid the wreck in the bushes. How long ago was that – a quarter of a century? It surprised him that he'd never felt a desire for a boat of his own all those years. He had coveted a Renault Torpedo and a motorcycle, a country house beside the Loire, a Bréguet wristwatch, a billiard table and a Cartier lighter, but never another boat. And now, there it was.

He drew a deep breath and boarded the boat in one long stride. At that instant he knew for certain he would never relinquish it or share it with anyone. He would never welcome unwanted guests aboard – in fact he would never divulge the boat's existence to a living soul. He wouldn't even enlighten Yvonne, who had said she wanted nothing to do with his coffee and cash transactions, nor would this boat become a children's playground. It belonged to him alone, no one else.

Léon was in a solemn, elated mood as he made his way from the bow to the stern. The padlock sprang open with a faint click. The door stuck, being slightly warped, but it swung silently open on its well-oiled hinges when he gave it a vigorous push. The interior was pleasantly redolent of woodsmoke, wax-polished planks and pipe tobacco, perhaps also of coffee and red wine. Lying on its side in one corner of the cabin was a toy locomotive, and beside it a raffia basket containing a ball of wool transfixed by two wooden knitting needles. He decided to take the locomotive home for little Philippe and the knitting wool for Madame Rossetos. Van Gogh's *Sunflowers* hung between two portholes and there was a bookshelf holding two or three dozen books. Léon sat down in the worn leather armchair beside the stove and stretched his legs. He filled a pipe and lit it, then shut his eyes and expelled some little puffs of smoke as he listened to wavelets lapping against the hull.

My dear old Léon,

Are you still there? I'm still here, where else? I'm drowning in water – water from above, water from below, water from ahead and behind, water from the side. Water wells out of holes in the ground, trickles down walls, falls from the clouds, evaporates on the hot soil and returns to the cold sky, only to descend once more and beat a nerve-fraying staccato on the corrugated-iron roofs. Wherever there's room to breathe between downpours, the air is filled with such a stench of mould and mildew, you feel you want to lie down and die. I can't take a step outside without sinking ankle-deep in mud. The mud oozes up between my toes and insinuates itself beneath my nails. I've already got fungi and lichen growing on my scalp and am suffering from hallucinations about maggots and worms, and my feet have taken on a terracotta tinge from the red mud which no amount of vigorous scrubbing will get rid of. In a desperate attempt to protect myself from the everlasting mud, I recently dug out my nice Paris calfskin boots, which I stowed in a chest the day I arrived, only to find that they were thickly furred all over with snow-white mildew. It's time for me to return to the chilly north. Until that day comes I'll go barefoot.

You can't imagine how fatuous my daily routine here is. I may have head lice and broken fingernails, but I still play the dauntless office girl. I emerge from the building every morning, complete with portable typewriter, to find my personal black orderly waiting for me with my personal umbrella. Then I fall in behind my two superiors and their black orderlies and our personal escort, which consists of another twenty riflemen.

First we proceed to the watchtower that stands beside the railway line a stone's throw from our fortress. A soldier props a ladder against the tower and my boss climbs up it to the doorway, which is three metres from the ground, and checks to see if the seal is still intact. Meanwhile, another soldier puts up a folding table for me and holds a big umbrella over it, and when my boss is back on terra firma – in other words, has warm mud under his feet – I sit down at my machine and record the proceedings. Rain-bedraggled hyenas cower in the bush and watch us with their tongues lolling. Wet hyenas are an incredibly pathetic sight, believe me. They're the epitome of natural imperfection even when dry, but wet? They look simply heartbreaking.

As soon as I've completed my record of the proceedings we take ourselves off to the railway station, where our little train already has steam up. We board the first-class carriage reserved for us while the native soldiers squeeze into an open cattle wagon with the farmers making their daily trip to the market in Kayes, twelve kilometres downriver, with their vegetables and millet, hens and goats. Then the train gets under way and we trundle off, first across a stream, then through some hills and into the ravine that leads to the Kayes Plain.

Our carriage looks like something out of a Mickey Mouse cartoon and the locomotive was probably built by Boy Scouts. The railway is a narrow-gauge railway, and narrow-gauge railways resemble men with small penises: it's hard to take them seriously. You can tell yourself a hundred times that length and breadth don't matter, and that truly important qualities aren't a question of dimensions, but appearance does matter for all that. Certain things simply look better full-size than in miniature, don't you agree?

The station at Kayes is a doll's-house station with splendid signals, neat stretches of grass and tracks devoid of weeds. The farmers in the cattle wagon have to stay put with their hens and goats – such are the rules – until we have got out and are past the barrier. The station's shady interior is seething with people: naked children with swollen bellies, women with lifeless eyes and faces indelibly imprinted with the pain of their ritual mutilation, and their menfolk, who regard us with hopeless defiance, covert pride, or tail-wagging subservience.

Under their mute gaze we cross the street to the administrative building of the Chemins de Fer du Soudan Français, which rises above the dusty plain like some fairy-tale Mauretanian castle. Stored in its cellars – I can tell you this now because it really doesn't matter any more – are 180 tonnes of gold. We've deposited another 200 tonnes in the customs building down by the river, 120 tonnes in the district commander's cellars, and 80 tonnes in the magazine at the barracks. We check all the seals, inspect the sentries, and satisfy ourselves that none of our useless precious metal has been stolen. It takes two hours to complete the circuit, then we catch the midday train back to Medina.

We make an inventory every two months during the dry six months of the year. That takes us a full day for each location. When the seals have been removed and the doors opened, soldiers carry all the boxes outside and lay them down in rows of ten. Then my boss climbs on top of the first box and strides to the next, and the next, and the one after that, and so on, counting out loud: 'Two hundredweight!' – stride – 'Four hundredweight!' – stride – 'Six hundredweight!' – stride – 'Eight hundredweight!' Meanwhile, the office girl sits at her folding table ticking the boxes off, and when it's all over she types out a formal report. Finally, when all the boxes have been counted (they're still stencilled 'Explosives' for security reasons), they're replaced in the cellar and the doors are sealed, and we return to the officers' mess to recover from our day's exertions.

Now and then a plane lands on the airstrip and the pilot produces some bumf authorizing him to pick up two or three boxes. We don't ask questions, just unlock one of the cellars. At first these couriers came from Vichy, but for some time now they've been coming from London. We had to hand over the Belgians' gold a while back, to satisfy the Germans, also the gold belonging to the Poles. It'll be interesting to see if anyone gives it back to them when the war's over.

This is the third rainy season I've spent here. Time goes so quickly. Another three months and the world will dry up again. Then I'll be able to get out the decrepit man's bike I bought in the market at Kayes the year before last, which gives me an illusory feeling of freedom during the dry season. I visit the surrounding villages or pedal a few kilometres downstream to the power station at Félou and go to the rapids to watch wildlife with the Bonvin brothers, who perform their electrical engineering duties in monastic seclusion. They realized a long time ago that the local fauna are infinitely more interesting than their power station's tunnels, sluices and turbines. Once you've grasped the way that installation works, it's a very simple affair. The last time I visited them, I learned that the hyena's famous laugh is a submission ritual performed by low-ranking individuals begging for a share of the prey or for admission to the pack. You see? Laughter is the weapon of the powerless. The powerful don't laugh.

I've gone quite grey, by the way. When I arrived here three years ago I had a few white hairs; now I've only a few dark hairs left. I think I've lost a bit of weight as well, because I've got the legs and *breasts of a twelve-year-old. But I can also run and cycle like a twelve-year-old, and – yes, thanks for asking – I've still got all my own teeth.*

How often have you written to me since I've been here, Léon – ten times, a hundred times? No letter from you has ever reached me – I did warn you, didn't I? Nothing ever reaches us here. No pay, no instructions, no supplies or ammunition, no newspapers or clothing. From time to time, as I say, an airman drops in and tells us stuff we find hard to believe, and a few months ago the commandant ordered the arrest of three young men who appeared from nowhere, spoke very poor French, took a suspicious interest in our watchtower, and eventually turned out to be German. Apart from that, we're on our own – the world has forgotten us.

Conversely, we're starting to forget the world. After a while you get used to the heat and don't miss the winter any longer. You eat couscous as if it were pommes dauphinoises, and one night not long ago I had my first dream in Bambara, not French.

We don't get any first-hand news of the war out here. Baobabs are baobabs and cockroaches are cockroaches, rifles rust because they're never fired, and our soldiers die of typhus and malaria, not in combat. We might have lost all idea of why we're here at all if Galiani, our radio operator, hadn't concocted a short wave radio out of the cadavers of various electronic odds and ends. It enables us to pick up BBC London quite well.

Have I forgotten you? Well, yes, a bit – there's no point in being eaten up with longing day after day. But you're always with me, nothing changes that. It's strange: I've only vague memories of my father and mother and can hardly remember the names of my childhood companions, but you I can still see quite vividly.

When the wind blows through the trees I hear your voice

---

whispering nice things in my ear, and when the hippos in the Senegal River yawn I see the corners of your mouth, which always turn upwards even when you don't mean to smile at all. The sky has the blue of your eyes and the parched yellow grass is the colour of your hair. Now I'm getting lyrical again!

Love is an imposition, isn't it? Especially when it lasts a quarter of a century. I'd dearly like to know what it really is. A hormonal dysfunction for reproductive purposes, as biologists claim? Consolation for little girls who aren't allowed to marry their daddies? A raison d'être for non-believers? All of those things at once, perhaps. But more than that as well, I know.

While we're on the subject, I should tell you that, for well over a year now, Galiani the radio operator has been – for want of a better word – my lover. Does that make you laugh? Me too. It's like in the theatre, isn't it? If an Italian with a moustache appears in the first act, he has to kiss the young heroine in the third. Mind you, it's quite a while since I was a young heroine and Galiani isn't perfectly cast as a romantic heartbreaker, what with his eternal spitting, his bad language, his stubby limbs, and the curly black hair that escapes from under his uniform.

But he does have one outstanding feature: he's quite unlike you. Because he's childishly uncouth and leers at every skirt in sight, and because he pays women grotesque compliments and is forever swearing on his mother's grave although he has no idea where it is – that's precisely why he's right for me. He has to be different from you, understand?

It all began one night in the officers' mess smoking room, well over a year ago. I was suffering from a fit of the blues, as everyone does from time to time, and trying to conceal it from the others by cracking jokes and laughing uproariously. At some stage Giuliano Galiani got up and went over to the sideboard behind my chair to pour himself another glass of our home-brewed millet beer. In passing, he casually – half unconsciously and with no ulterior motive, so it seemed – put his hand on my shoulder in an instinctively sympathetic way. I was grateful to him for that.

After midnight, when everyone was asleep, I went to his room and got in beside him without a word. He said nothing and asked no questions, just made room for me as if it were something he'd long been expecting – as if he'd been used for years to my getting into bed with him. And then he took me as a man should, saying little but pleasurably and confidently, with gentle determination.

Galiani firmly and unerringly guides us to our destination every time. He makes no vows or proposals afterwards, but releases me and lets me sneak back to my room, and the next day he betrays no sign of what has happened. He never winks at me or waylays me, takes no liberties and doesn't pester me to pay him another visit. On the contrary, when we're with other people his manner towards me is markedly offhand, sometimes even distant. But, when I slip beneath his bedclothes a few days or weeks later, he welcomes me as if I'd never been away.

He's a gentleman in the outer skin of a roughneck, and I like that. There are enough of the opposite kind. It'll be over between us as soon as the war ends, of course, because I can't be doing with him in daylight. At night he's a wordly-wise, warm-hearted man, by day an orally fixated infant. Whenever he opens his mouth he brags about his wife's breasts – she's waiting for him somewhere near Nice – and blathers about Milan and Juventus, Bugattis, Ferraris and Maseratis, and betweentimes he complains that the government damned well owes him the Legion of Honour and a pension for life, and that he'll spend the money on a boat and go fishing off the Riviera every day.

It won't be too long before the war is over. Even out here in the bush we've heard of Stalingrad, and ever since the Allies landed in Morocco and Algeria, every sergeant, customs officer and petty criminal who comes our way claims to have been a hero of the Resistance. Before another few weeks or months are up, says our commandant, we'll be loading our boxes into the train and going home to Paris via Dakar and Marseille.

I know exactly what I'll do when I get out of the train at the Gare de Lyon: I'll take a taxi to the Rue des Écoles and ring your doorbell. And if you're still there – if you and your wife and children have all survived – I'll kiss each of you in turn. We'll rejoice that we're still alive, and then we'll go for a walk together – or have some cabbage soup, whichever. Nothing else will matter then, will it?

Be alive, Léon. Be happy and healthy and tenderly kissed. See you very soon!
    Yours, Louise

18

Léon now spent every lunch break on his boat in the Arsenal harbour – and sometimes the couple of hours between the end of work and suppertime as well. At lunchtime he would eat a ham sandwich in his cabin, then lie down on one of the bunks for half an hour. He would never have done that in the old days. As a boy he had found it faintly horrific when his father subsided on to the sofa like a dead man after lunch and instantly fell asleep with his mouth open and his eyes tight shut. Now he himself had reached the stage where a little siesta was indispensable. It gave him the energy to return to the laboratory and patiently endure the recurrent humiliations, rituals and spells of inactivity that life demanded of him.

Fleur de Miel remained his secret. He never spoke of it to anyone. No one at home missed him. Yvonne was too busy with the fight for survival and had neither the time nor energy nor desire to concern herself with the meaning of existence, affairs of the heart, or similar minutiae. She had long known about the boat, of course, because it was essential for safety's sake that she knew whether her husband was doing things on the side that might endanger the family. Because he wasn't, the boat didn't bother her. All she expected of Léon was that he help to feed and protect his family, neither more nor less. In return she granted him absolute freedom, demanded no emotional input from him, and refrained from troubling him with any of her own.

Léon appreciated this. A few years ago he had been saddened by Yvonne's sour, prematurely aged manner and missed the light-footed girl she used to be. He had occasionally longed for the return of the capricious diva, and sometimes even of the housewife tormented by doubts about herself and the meaning of existence; but now he felt only gratitude and respect for the selflessly pugnacious lioness Yvonne had become during the war years. To expect her, in addition, to sing coquettish songs and toy with the top button of her blouse would have been unfair in the extreme.

Yvonne and Léon had demonstrated long ago that they were a good, strong couple who had already weathered many a storm and would jointly confront any future threats as well. Their mutual trust and affection were so profound and strong, they could allow each other to go their own way in peace.

The children were equally uninterested in where Léon spent so many hours on his own. Apart from young Philippe, they were now of an age to be preoccupied with their own battles. All they expected of their father was that he hold the fort and supply the family with affection and money. They were also grateful to him for being a mild-mannered, amiable paterfamilias who seldom asked questions or demanded anything of them.

It should in fairness be said that Léon was able to afford his mildly paternal manner only because Yvonne's supervision of the four children was all the more rigorous. Not a minute of the day went by without her being apprised of their whereabouts, and she demanded to be fully informed about their doings, state of health and circle of friends.

Far from relaxing when another day fraught with peril had been successfully survived and the children were safely asleep in their beds, Yvonne kept Léon up until late at night. Obsessed with every conceivable form of potential threat, she spoke of fascistic schoolmasters and drunken SS men, of paedophiles on the loose, of car drivers running amuck and highly infectious microbes, of heat, rain and frost, of inflated food prices and the imponderables of the black market. She never tired of discussing possible escape routes through the forests, overland or by water. She even suggested retreating into the catacombs of Paris in the event that the Germans did, after all, unleash an apocalypse.

Yvonne was so taken up with her mission as a guardian angel, there was no room left inside her for anything else. She cultivated no friendships and kept no dream diary, wore no pink sunglasses and sang no more songs. Although still Léon's faithful companion, she had long ceased to be a wife, and she was so solicitous of her children that she showed them no affection.

The years of exertion and tension were written on her face. Her eyes were lashless and her cheeks gaunt, and the long neck that had once been so graceful was tensed up and threaded with veins and sinews. She had broad shoulders but no breasts, and the stomach below her ribs was hollow.

She offended the neighbours by passing them on the stairs without a word. She no longer wore make-up and was becoming steadily thinner because she forgot to eat. She kept two suitcases lying ready beside the front door at all times. These contained the bare essentials for an escape by the whole family, and she couldn't help checking, several times a day, to ensure that she really hadn't forgotten anything. It wasn't until she refused to take off her shoes so as to be ready to leave at a moment's notice, even in bed at night, that Léon gently called her to order and insisted that a minimum of the proprieties be observed for the children's sake.

The children themselves took a more realistic view of the dangers they faced every day. Being baptized Christians and the offspring of a police employee, they knew that they weren't typical German prey, and that the city's other potential threats tended to be fewer under the occupation than in peacetime. So they all devised their own ways of eluding their mother and taking the first steps along their own road to independence.

My Aunt Muriel, who died of cirrhosis of the liver in 1987, was then seven years old. She had freckles and wore pale-green ribbons in her chestnut-brown hair, and she liked to spend her Sundays and Wednesday half holidays in the concierge's lodge with Madame Rossetos, who dandled her on her lap for hours on end, fed her sweets, and told her eye-rollingly horrific tales of love, murder and the torments of hell. Madame Rossetos provided Muriel with the affection she didn't get from her mother, and the little girl consoled her for the perfidy of her daughters, who hadn't shown a sign of life since they left. Shortly before five p.m. Madame Rossetos always went to the dresser and poured herself a small glass of advocaat. And because Muriel was such a dear little girl, she got a thimbleful too. She didn't like it much at first, but she soon learnt to appreciate its effect.

My Uncle Robert, who later worked for a small employment agency in Lille, installed a rabbit hutch in the attic and spent his days gathering greenstuff from mossy gutters and overgrown backyards throughout the Latin Quarter to feed his rapidly multiplying livestock. He handled the slaughtering himself and delivered the carcasses to his customers oven-ready.

One rabbit a month he relinquished to his mother; the rest he sold on the black market. Robert died at the wheel of his Renault 16 one rainy morning in September 1992, when he lit a distracting cigarette on the Route Nationale between Chartres and Le Mans and aquaplaned off the road.

Thirteen-year-old Yves, who later became a doctor and still later abandoned medicine for theology, distressed his parents by volunteering for the Chantiers de la Jeunesse, Vichy's paramilitary youth movement. He was issued with a black uniform, combat boots and white spats, learned the Marshal's speeches by heart, and spent weeks marching through Fontainebleau Forest with rucksack, forage cap and hunting knife.

Nineteen-year-old Michel, who was to go down in history as the inventor of Renault's lockable filler cap, was waiting for a place at engineering school. He killed time by taking day-long walks through the city in search of some escape from the prison he felt his life to be. He nursed an unspoken contempt for his father's self-absorption and his mother's opportunistic fight for survival. Although he knew he lacked the makings of a martyr for a good cause, he had no wish to be a conformist. He had wanted to leave school a few months before matriculating because all the girls in his class – every last one – had opted to take German, not English, as their first foreign language. To dissuade his eldest son from dropping out, Léon for once brought paternal authority to bear. He initially tried to convince him of the value of a traditional education and pointed out that most of the boys in his class had entered for the English exam, and then, when these arguments failed, simply bribed him with 500 francs.

Born in the second year of the war, Philippe – my father – was still tied to his mother's apron strings except on Sunday afternoons, when Yvonne slept alone in the darkened bedroom and would tolerate no child near her. Then he went with Muriel to Madame Rossctos, sat on his sister's lap while she, in turn, sat on the concierge's, and listened to her gruesome stories. And because he was such a dear little boy and kept so nice and quiet, he was allowed a sip of Madame Rossetos' advocaat. Sophisticated but unable to cope with life and a lover of women but incapable of being faithful to them, Philippe was sentenced to solitude by his own charm and ultimately condemned to death by alcoholism.

⚘

Léon continued to live the life of a hermit. He went to work and fulfilled his paternal responsibilities; that apart, he took refuge in his floating hideaway. As luck would have it, Jules Caron had had a predilection for 19th-century Russian literature, so the bookshelf was filled with works by Tolstoy and Turgenev, Dostoievsky and Lermontov, Chekov, Gogol and Goncharov. Léon read them all while smoking a pipe and drinking red wine, which didn't stupefy him so much as induce an agreeable state of metaphysical well-being.

He divided his time between reading in a leisurely fashion and looking out of the porthole at the reflections on the surface of the basin, the seasonally changing colours of the plane trees, the passage of the stars, and the succession of rain, sunshine and fog, all of which were equally to his taste. Punctually at seven every evening he turned on the radio, put his ear to the loudspeaker, and, as if the announcer's voice were a delicacy not to be wasted, absorbed the news on the BBC. That was how he heard about Stalingrad and the landing at Anzio,

Operation Overlord and the night raids on Hamburg, Berlin and Dresden.

He was appalled to find that hatred had grown up inside him like a tree during the thousand days the occupation had lasted; now that tree was bearing poisonous fruit. He had never dreamt that he would rub his hands at the news that Charlottenburg had been gutted by fire and had never thought it possible that he would loudly rejoice at the death of 3000 women and children in a single night. It shocked him how ardently he hoped that the bombs would continue to rain down, night after night, until not a single German was left alive on God's good earth.

His hatred helped him to survive, but he also underwent some unsettling experiences. He once witnessed a scene that made him feel profoundly ashamed because it shook his hatred. One afternoon in the Métro he was sitting opposite a Wehrmacht soldier with a rifle slung over his shoulder. At Saint-Sulpice a young man with a yellow star on his overcoat got in. The soldier stood up and silently gestured to the Jew, who must have been about his own age, to take his seat. The Jew hesitated and looked round helplessly, then sat down on the vacant seat without a word and, probably in shame and despair, buried his face in his hands. The soldier turned away and stared at the blackness outside the window with a face like stone. Meanwhile, silence had descended on the carriage. The Jew was sitting immediately opposite Léon, so close that their knees were almost touching. Neither the soldier nor the Jew got out at the next station or the one after that. Their journey together seemed interminable. The Jew kept his hands over his face the whole time, the soldier stood stiffly beside him. The train stopped and started, stopped and started. At last came the station where the soldier turned on his heel and made his way out on to the platform. Silence persisted when the doors closed behind him. No one ventured to utter a word. The Jew kept his hands over his face. Léon could see that he was wearing a wedding ring, and that the corners of his eyes, most of which were obscured by his forefingers, were twitching.

ॐ

Summer 1944 was fine and warm – an invitation to bathe, but the beaches of Normandy and the Côte d'Azur were inaccessible because of the Allied invasion, so the inhabitants of Paris stayed at home and used the Seine as a lido. The fourth of August was the hottest day of the year so far. Asphalt melted, horses hung their heads, and anyone who couldn't avoid going out kept to the narrow strips of pavement shaded by buildings.

ॐ

One evening, when Léon was passing the entrance of the Musée Cluny on his way home after spending his usual couple of hours after work on the boat, a man was standing in the shadows beneath the archway with his flat cap pulled down low over his face. Scenting danger, Léon walked on faster and deliberately averted his gaze.

'Psst!' said the man.

Léon walked on.

'Fine evening, isn't it?'

Léon stepped off the pavement and prepared to turn down the Rue de la Sorbonne.

'Hey, stop!'

Léon walked on.

'Hands up! Don't move!'

Léon halted abruptly and raised his hands.

The man behind him laughed. 'Relax, Léon, I'm only joking.'

Hesitantly, Léon lowered his hands and turned round, then stepped back on to the pavement and scrutinized the man. He had clean-cut features and piercing eyes, and he looked vaguely familiar.

'I'm sorry, do we know each other?'

'I've brought your four hundred francs back.'

'My four hundred francs?'

'Eight hundred times fifty centimes, don't you remember? I wanted to get to Jaurès bus station and you helped me.'

'Martin?'

'Didn't recognize me, did you? Yes, I'm your personal tramp, the embodiment of your clear conscience.'

'How long is it, three years?'

'We guessed the war would last three or four years. Not bad, eh?'

'It isn't over yet.'

'But it soon will be. Let's walk on, I'll keep you company for a little way.'

The man looked ten years younger than he had the last time they met. His eyes were as clear as his complexion, he didn't smell of red wine, and he seemed to have lost all his body fat. Léon had noticeably aged in comparison, he had to admit, and his hours aboard the boat had probably left him smelling of red wine.

'How long have you been back in Paris?'

'A few days. It won't be long now, as you know.'

'I don't know a thing.'

'Of course you do, every child does. The Americans are already in Rouen, things are brewing up in Corsica, and we ourselves have five thousand men in the city.'

'Who's we?'

Martin pulled a piece of white cloth from his jacket pocket and held it up. It was an armband with the letters FFL stencilled on it in black.

'At last,' said Léon.

'The balloon could go up any time, possibly next week.'

'Just as long as the Germans don't do what they did in Warsaw.'

'We'll take care,' said Martin. 'But so should you, Léon.'

'Why?'

'The day of reckoning will soon be here. We plan to tweak a few people's ears.'

'Good for you.'

'It'll be summary justice, and we won't be squeamish. We won't be holding any coffee parties or discussion groups beforehand.'

'I see.'

'I'm not sure you do,' said Martin. 'You really ought to look out for yourself. People are talking about you, did you know?'

'No.'

'They're talking about your handouts of coffee from the SS. They're talking about your boat and your black market activities.'

'But I – '

'I know, but coffee's coffee and a boat's a boat. People are going to get it the neck for things like that in days to come, and there won't be time for any fine distinctions. Our comrades' blood is up, you've got to understand that.'

'So is mine, and you of all people should know – '

'Yes, but the others don't. They'll be deaf to any fine distinctions, as I say. In the days ahead they'll dispense rough justice and ask questions afterwards. That's why you must make yourself scarce for a week or two. Right away, until things simmer down. Then you can come back and explain about the coffee.'

'Where should I go?'

'South. It's summertime. Treat your family to a few weeks beside the sea.'

'The Côte d'Azur, you mean?'

'Well, no, not there. There'll be plenty going on down there in the next few days. I'd recommend the Atlantic coast, the Germans have already withdrawn from there. Biarritz or Cap Ferret or Lacanau – it's a question of taste.'

'And money.'

'Here are the four hundred francs you lent me.' Martin handed Léon a wad of banknotes. 'And this...' – he reached into his breast pocket and brought out another, considerably thicker wad – '...is what's left of the money in the drawer at your place of work.'

'How did you – '

'I got someone to fetch it while you were on your boat, I hope you don't mind. It'd be better if you didn't have to go back there again.'

'But – '

'Take it. The FFL is officially handing it over – as of now, it isn't Nazi cash any longer. We've put the key back in the bakelite tray. A bloody silly hiding place, if you don't mind my saying so.'

'Still, nobody found it.'

Martin smiled. 'We've been checking on the money for the past two years. It'll count in your favour that you didn't spend any on yourself.'

'There's the boat...'

'I know, Caron told me the whole story. That'll help too, but first you must disappear. You won't get your six thousand back, but you can keep the boat. Caron says he doesn't want it any more. It's yours now.'

'Really?'

'A boat's like a dog, he says. It can't keep changing owners.'

'Thanks.'

'Here are some railway tickets to Bordeaux – you must fend for yourselves after that. And here are two travel permits. One is for the Germans, the other for our people. You'd be wise not to get them mixed up.'

'I understand.'

'Don't come back before the twenty-sixth of September. The train to Bordeaux leaves at eight twenty-seven tomorrow morning. Trust me, Léon. Do as I say, and do it tomorrow, not the day after. Now go home and pack your bags.'

So saying, Martin crossed the street and disappeared beneath the trees in the Parc de Cluny. They had exchanged a farewell hug on the last occasion, Léon recalled. He wondered why they hadn't this time.

৪৯

On the day when the staff of the French capital's hospitals, the Banque de France and the Police Judiciaire joined the popular uprising and went on strike, Léon Le Gall, wearing an old-fashioned black bathing costume and shaded by a sailcloth awning, was lying in the sand dunes at Lacanau, 600 kilometres south-west of the Quai des Orfèvres. His wife was sitting beside him, straight as a ramrod, watching her four older children playing in the surf while little Philippe built a sandcastle at her feet.

The beach ran north to south for many kilometres and was deserted for as far as the eye could see. The dunes were surmounted by the bunkers of Hitler's Atlantic Wall. Gun barrels pointed ominously out to sea from their loopholes as if the Wehrmacht soldiers had merely gone to fetch some ammunition and would return to their posts at any moment.

Several times a day, Léon and the children walked along the shoreline to see if the waves had washed up any interesting odds and ends. Their finds included a leather ball, an intact kitchen chair, and a sail complete with mast and rigging. This they had converted into the awning at the foot of the sand dunes.

Punctually at midday every day, Yvonne gave the signal to leave. Then they all pulled on light summer clothes over their bathing costumes, trudged back across the dunes to the pinewoods, and rode their rented bicycles along the narrow concrete tracks the Germans had laid for the benefit of their dispatch riders. After lunch and a siesta at the *Hôtel de la Cigogne,* they returned to the beach. In the evenings an accordionist played for dancing in the village square. Wednesday was market day, and on Saturday night the football ground became an open-air cinema.

Léon found it happily but also bitterly ironical that he should be fated, for the second time in his life, to spend the closing stages of a world war at the seaside. Although he was thankful to have been able to bring his family to such an idyllic place of safety, he gathered from daily newspaper and radio reports that courageous men were making history elsewhere. With masochistic avidity, he registered the fact that at the moment when General Leclerc's tanks entered the Champs-Élysées he had been sitting at the breakfast table and dunking a second croissant in his *café au lait*; that he had eaten a spoonful of vanilla ice cream just as an SS detachment gunned down thirty-five young Frenchmen at the Carrefour des Cascades; that, when the FFL hoisted the tricolour on the Eiffel Tower for the first time, he had been busy whittling a miniature sailing boat for young Philippe; that, when General von Choltitz defied Hitler's express order to destroy Paris and surrendered the city to Leclerc intact and without a fight, he was having his afternoon rest; and that on the night the Luftwaffe launched its last air raid on the French capital and destroyed 600 buildings, he was sitting with Yvonne on the balcony of their hotel room, looking out over the silvery, shimmering sea beneath a star-spangled sky and drinking a bottle of Bordeaux. And after it a cognac. And another cognac. And, to round the evening off, a beer.

❦

News of the Wehrmacht's withdrawal from Paris reached the Le Gall family as they lounged beneath their home-made awning at a quarter past three in the afternoon. A horde of young people irrupted on to the beach from the north. Many were riding bicycles and others running alongside, and two boys on a tandem were towing trailer containing three girls. All were yelling and waving. Michel went to meet the newcomers.

After speaking to them he dived back under the awning and hugged his father and his siblings. Little Philippe and Muriel clamoured for an immediate return to Paris and Madame Rossetos' advocaat, but Yves wanted to stay in Lacanau until further notice because he had started a rabbit-breeding business in the hotel's backyard. Léon and Michel, who discussed the possibility of a precipitate return home, came to the conclusion that it would be too risky to go back before the 26th of September without any valid travel permits.

Meanwhile, Yvonne stood on the sidelines, looking out across the sea and rubbing her thin arms as if she were cold. 'We'll see,' she said. 'I won't believe it till de Gaulle speaks on the radio.'

'He was on the radio yesterday.'

'I want to hear him speaking from Paris, and the bells of Notre Dame must be ringing in the background to prove it. He'll do that if he's smart.'

'De Gaulle is smart,' said Léon. 'If you insist on proof, he'll supply it.'

'You think he knows me that well? We shall see.' Yvonne turned round and took her husband by the arm. 'Know what I want right now, Léon? A steak. A thick, bloody *steak au poivre* with *pommes frites*. And some Bordeaux to go with it – the good stuff. And goat's cheese and Roquefort to follow. And for dessert a *crème brûlée*.'

❧

The next day General de Gaulle really was smart enough to ensure that his radio address was accompanied by the bells of Notre Dame. When the bells and the general had fallen silent,

Yvonne went to the hotel kitchen and informed the chef that she wanted some wild boar pâté right away, followed by a *truite au bleu* with mushroom risotto and a main course of *boudin noir, pommes dauphinoises* and red cabbage, and for dessert a *crêpe Suzette* – oh yes, and a *coupe colonel* betweentimes. When the chef objected that it was half-past three in the afternoon for one thing, that the kitchen was closed for another, and that, thirdly, he had nothing she'd requested but the potatoes, Yvonne blithely told him, first, not to be a clock-watcher, secondly to open up the kitchen, and thirdly to get hold of all the necessary ingredients. Money was no object.

୨ଲ

From that moment on, food was Yvonne's sole interest. As soon as she opened her eyes in the morning she reached for the oatmeal biscuits of which she always kept a ready supply. At breakfast she drank *café au lait* by the potful and daubed whole baguettes with thick layers of butter and jam. Feeding the children, which had been her exclusive concern for years, she now left entirely to their father. When they departed for the beach she no longer worried about the dangers of the surf and the currents but casually left her brood to their own devices and took a preliminary walk to the pâtisserie to buy herself some Madeleines and apple turnovers. Soon after that it was time for an apéritif and some form of *amuse-bouche* before lunch.

Léon looked on in bewilderment as his wife devoted herself to gluttony and turned into a creature he had never, in all their twenty-two years of marriage, dreamt was slumbering inside her. The lizardlike indifference and emotional frigidity Yvonne now displayed was in utter contrast to all she had been hitherto. This gorging, grunting Moloch must have been lying in wait within the stern guardian angel she had been throughout the war years; and the guardian angel, in turn, had previously resided in the sexy diva, and the diva in the tormented housewife, and the housewife in the coquettish bride. Léon wondered what other surprising metamorphoses this woman would undergo.

Because she did nothing but eat and seldom moved, Yvonne quickly put on weight. Her eternally vigilant expression gave way to a look of smug contentment – sometimes, too, of weary satiety. The children eyed her with covert surprise and shunned her even more than usual. Within a few days her neck had filled out, her shoulders and hips lost their angularity, and her fingers and bosom swelled. Her blue eyes, which had always been alert and slightly prominent, sank ever deeper into the cushions of flesh surrounding their sockets. At the end of the first week in September, because her clothes were beginning to burst at the seams, she took the bus to Bordeaux and bought three comfortable, voluminous summer frocks. And on the night of 25 September, when she was packing her bags for the journey home, she left her tight old wartime clothes in the wardrobe, realizing that she would never again be able to wear them.

19

On 26 September 1944, when Léon Le Gall and his family returned to the Rue des Écoles, the rainy season on the Senegal River ended as if someone had turned off a tap. News of the liberation of Paris having spread like wildfire to the furthest corners of French Sudan, the main institutions of the colonial world awoke to new life as if by magic. Trains turned up once more by land and steamers by way of the Senegal River, the telephone worked again and newspapers arrived by post.

But the special train that was supposed to collect Louise Janvier and the gold did not come.

Because there are no more letters from Louise among my grandfather's papers, we cannot tell how she fared at this period. We may assume that she waited impatiently for the train, or at least for a summons from the Banque de France, probably while sitting on her ready-packed suitcase. It is quite possible that she had already given away her umbrella, revolver and spare mosquito net in expectation of leaving soon. It is also quite possible that she refrained for once from cutting her own hair and paid a visit to the hairdresser in Kayes one Sunday. It is further conceivable that, when the mud had dried up and the roads were passable once more, she cycled out to the power station at Félou to say goodbye to the Bonvin brothers. She may perhaps have gone for a last walk with them to the basin below the rapids where the hippos reared their young. It is also quite possible that, on the way back, she gave away her bicycle to a young schoolboy named Abdullay, the only one of the seven- to twelve-year-olds in his village to have achieved a hundred per cent attendance record.

I further imagine that every night she spent in Giuliano Galiani's bed must have felt is if it were the last.

But the special train still didn't come.

Now that the radio and telephone were back in commission, Galiani strutted around the streets at all times of the day and night, proclaiming the latest news. He announced the capture of Aachen by the US VII and IX Corps, the failure of the Germans' Ardennes offensive, the bombing of Hamburg's fuel dumps and the surrender of Hungary, and the longer his personal exile lasted, the bluer became the half Italian, half French oaths he levelled at that sonofabitch Maresciallo de Gaulle and those *cretini* at the Banque de France, who were taking their fucking time about extricating him and that fucking gold from the arsehole of the world. Galiani might have moderated his oaths a little, had he known that General de Gaulle and the Banque de France were leaving him to moulder in the bush only because German U-boats well supplied with fuel and torpedoes were still awaiting an opportunity to send him and the gold to the bottom of the sea.

In March 1945 the dry season ended and the heat and humidity returned. Galiani got out his umbrella and stomped, cursing, through the mud. He reported the liberation of Auschwitz and the destruction of Dresden, raised his arms to heaven in reproach and asked the vultures in the trees why in God's name they didn't let him go home at last. Louise sat on her suitcase and waited. Galiani reported the Yalta Conference and the storming of Hitler's bunker, the trial of Marshal Pétain and, finally, the bombing of Nagasaki.

But still the special train didn't come.

Then another year was over and the rain abruptly ceased once more. Louise had long ago resumed cutting her own hair, which grew appreciably faster in Africa than at home. The mud dried up, went hard and became threaded with a network of dark cracks. Galiani stowed his umbrella under his bed in the absolute certainty that not a drop of rain would fall in the next six months. On her day off Louise took the train to Kayes, where she bought a new mosquito net and a replacement for her old bicycle at the market.

And then the special train turned up at last.

Perhaps it arrived during the day, perhaps during the night. In the latter case, Louise would have seen the locomotive puffing smoke in front of the buffers a stone's throw from her window when she got up in the morning. We don't know how many goods wagons were hitched to it, or whether it took more than one trip to transport the gold back to Dakar. All one gathers from the records of the Banque de France is that 346.535 tonnes of bullion were loaded aboard the *Île de Cléron* and that the ship put to sea on 30 September 1945. If all went well and the autumn storms in the Atlantic weren't too violent, the *Île de Cléron* must have entered Toulon harbour around 12 October.

I picture Louise going down the gangway to the quayside and setting foot on French soil after five years' absence, sun-tanned and slim as a girl, though her hair was now grey. She would have kissed her companions of the last five years fare-well, possibly devoting a little more time to Radio Operator Galiani, whose wife was waiting for him beyond the customs post, than she did to the others. And because she was only carrying hand baggage and the rest had to wait for their cabin trunks, she walked off quickly in the knowledge that she would never see any of them again.

☙

It may have been late afternoon when she walked up the Avenue Henri Pastoureau to Toulon station, carrying her suitcase, perhaps stopping at a pâtisserie en route to buy her first chocolate éclair for a long time. She could then have caught the eight-thirty night train to Paris from Marseille Saint-Charles and arrived in the capital shortly before eight the following morning.

I don't believe Louise was standing impatiently at the open carriage door with her head out when the train pulled into the Gare de Lyon. I don't believe she crossed the concourse at the double, and I can't believe that she actually, as she had forecast in her last letter, jumped into a taxi and drove straight to the Rue des Écoles.

It think it far more probable that she sat quietly in her third-class compartment until all her fellow passengers had alighted, and that she then, slowly and carefully – almost hesitantly – got down on the platform, made her way across the concourse in the brightness of that fine autumn day, and walked out on to the cobblestones of the Boulevard Diderot, which already, as if there had never been a war, resounded to the roar of the buses, cars and lorries streaming past.

I picture her crossing the boulevard and walking straight on down the Rue de Lyon, amazed to see the buildings on either side so incomprehensibly unscathed. At the Bastille she sat down in a pavement café, ordered a *café au lait* and a croissant, picked up a newspaper, and cast a casual glance at the house-boats peacefully rocking in the breeze in the Arsenal harbour.

Then she strolled on through the cool morning air, carrying her little suitcase like a tourist. She went straight on down the Rue Saint-Antoine and the Rue de Rivoli, and after a while, as if by chance, she came to the headquarters of the Banque de France. She climbed the broad flight of steps to the entrance. The porter, a walrus-moustachioed man named Darnier, had either returned to the bank or had never been away. Louise gave him an airy wave and disappeared down the long, gloomy passage she had trodden a thousand times before, ready to report back for duty.

I picture her going to the Rue des Écoles a few days later, not before. I believe she began by moving into a hotel room provided by the bank as temporary accommodation, and that she first bought herself a new wardrobe, had a manicure, and got a dentist to fix the left upper molar that had been paining her for quite a while. Then she went to the hairdresser and had her hair cut. She didn't have it dyed, though, I'm sure of that.

I picture Louise timing her visit to the Rue des Écoles for late in the morning. She would have come by taxi, not yet having a car of her own. I picture Madame Rossetos pricking up her ears at the sound of a car door, then glancing at the mirror that gave her a periscopic view of the front door via two other mirrors. The concierge would then have heaved herself out of the armchair beside the stove and gone to do her duty as a watchdog.

'Who were you wanting?'
'The Le Galls, please.'
'What's it about?'

'The Le Galls do live here, don't they?'

'What's it about, please?'

'It's a personal visit.'

'Are they expecting you?'

'I'm afraid not.'

'Who shall I say it is?'

'Look – '

'Residents' rules state that strangers aren't to be admitted except by appointment.'

'Are the Le Galls still here?'

'I'm sorry.'

'I've just got back from Africa.'

'I can't make any exceptions for reasons of security, you must underst… From Africa, you say?'

'French Sudan.'

'Then you're…'

'Which floor, please?'

ঙ্গ

The door to the flat was ajar. Louise rang the bell.

'Who's there?

'Louise.'

'Who?'

'Louise.'

'WHO?'

'LOUISE JANVIER!'

'LITTLE LOUISE?'

'Yes.'

'Well I never!'

'Yes, it's me.'

'Come in. Straight down the passage. I'm in the living room.'

ꝏ

Louise pushed the door open and pulled it to behind her. A few more steps and she was in the living room she had so often seen through her binoculars. Yvonne was sitting in Léon's armchair by the window. Louise wouldn't have recognized her, but it couldn't be anyone else. She was wearing checked carpet slippers. Her thighs were bloated, her neck was encircled by a thick roll of fat, and her straggly hair was shoulder-length.

'Léon isn't here.'

'You're alone?'

'The children are at school.'

'All the better,' said Louise. 'It's you I came to see.'

'Sit down, then, So that's what you look like. Quite like the photo you sent from Africa.'

'I've gone grey.'

'Time flies. One always looks younger in photos than in real life.'

'It can't be helped.'

'You don't wear make-up.'

'Nor do you.'

'I haven't for a long time,' said Yvonne. 'I suppose I've put on a bit of weight lately, too.'

'How are you?'

'Oh, you know, what I like best is just sitting here beside the window, sunning myself like a pussycat. When I'm tired I go to sleep and when I'm hungry I eat. The truth is, I'm always tired and always hungry. Except when I'm asleep.'

'You never go out?'

'Not if I can avoid it. I've bustled around so much all these years, all I want to do now is sit in the sun. Nothing else matters. How are you doing?'

'I've sat in the sun so much these last few years…'

'And I enjoy eating. I starved myself for so long, I like to have a good tuck-in. I've got some raspberry gâteau and whipped cream here. Would you like some?'

❧

So the two women sat there in the autumn sunshine and ate raspberry gâteau together. They ate slowly and in silence, passing each other the sugar, whipped cream and paper napkins. One of them occasionally said something and the other listened, then they both fell silent again and smiled.

Louise offered to go to the kitchen and make some coffee, and Yvonne said that would be charming of her. Meantime, Yvonne fetched a bottle of Calvados and two glasses from the sideboard and cut another two big slices of raspberry gâteau. The clock on the sideboard was ticking. Eleven o'clock had already come and gone. The children would be home from school in an hour. The two women ate and drank in silence.

'And Léon?' Louise asked at last. 'Is he well?'

'Outrageously well,' said Yvonne. 'You'll see, he's hardly changed.'

'After all these years?'

'After all these decades. I don't know how they manage it, but these Le Gall men certainly are durable. Not even war leaves a mark on them. We women show signs of wear and our warranty runs out, but Léon? He's indestructible. Rustproof and easy to maintain, I always say. Like agricultural machinery.'

Louise laughed and Yvonne joined in.

'His hair's a bit thinner,' Yvonne went on, 'and his toenails have developed these funny ridges in the last few years. Know the ones I mean? Do other men get them too?'

'Most of them, after a certain age,' said Louise.

'And do they sigh when they get up in the mornings?'

'That too,' said Louise.

'He never sighed once upon a time, but he does now.'

'Does he still laugh?'

'Would you say he laughed a lot in the old days?'

'Not very loudly.'

'No, he tends to smile.'

'Especially when he thinks no one's looking.'

'You ought to pay him a visit, he'd like that.'

'You think so?'

'Definitely. Why not, after so many years?'

'When should I come?'

'Not here. Go to the Arsenal harbour, he keeps a boat there. It's a blue and white boat called *Fleur du Miel*. He flies the flag of Lower Normandy, overgrown schoolboy that he is. Two golden lions on a red background. You know, William the Conqueror and all that. Anyone would think he was getting ready to cross the Channel in his cabin cruiser and conquer perfidious Albion.'

20

Louise and Léon met at the Arsenal harbour very, very often in the years that followed. From Monday to Saturday they spent their lunch breaks together, likewise the time between the end of office hours and supper. Sunday was the only day they didn't see each other. When it rained they stayed inside the cabin; at other times they sat on the wooden bench seat in the stern or went for walks along the canal bank. She took his arm and he sniffed the scent of her sunlit hair, and they chatted casually together.

But it wasn't until the end of the third week that they drew the cabin curtains for the first time.

When winter arrived in November they lit the cast-iron stove, made coffee and fried eggs. They bought a gramophone and some records by Édith Piaf, later by Georges Brassens and Jacques Brel. They made friends with the other boat owners and got on to first-name terms with them. Sometimes they invited them over for drinks. If anyone asked how long they'd been married, they said nearly thirty years.

But always, at exactly quarter past seven every evening without exception, Louise returned to the flat in the Marais obtained for her by the Banque de France and Léon went home to the Rue des Écoles to have supper with Yvonne and the children. Afterwards he helped the younger ones with their homework, played cards with the older ones, and then retired to bed with Yvonne.

By continuing to live like this, the three of them made no sacrifices, practised no deceit and kept no guilty secrets from each other; they merely continued their previous lives in the only possible way. There could be no new life without the old one, they knew, and because nothing could alter that, no altercations or arguments about the rights and wrongs of the situation were necessary.

So they kept silent about these things. Louise's name was never uttered in the Rue des Écoles and the boat in the Arsenal harbour was never mentioned. Yvonne, who had no wish to disrupt her feline, armchair-bound contentment, refrained from any needlessly explicit allusions to the arrangement, which would only have led to undignified scenes, sham reconciliations and insincere vows of fidelity. She did not, however, insist on keeping up false appearances because she was at peace with herself and Léon and the life they had led. All she asked was that her dignity be respected and tactless behaviour avoided.

There could in any case be no question of keeping the arrangement secret once Madame Rossetos had put two and two together, kept her eyes and ears open, and deemed it her duty to inform all the neighbours of what went on in the Le Gall family.

Even the children were in the know, but because they too maintained a discreet silence and communicated at most by means of ironical sidelong glances and muttered remarks, Yvonne could continue to live in peace inside her own four walls, which she seldom left.

Then came the time when the children moved out one by

one. Because of his mediocre examination marks, Michel had vainly waited, term after term, for admission to engineering college. In the spring of 1947, when Renault opened a new factory, he took an assistant mechanic's job and moved into a furnished room at Issy-les-Moulineaux. Two years later his seventeen-year-old brother Yves joined the army and was posted to the Tchad Regiment. The same year, Madame Rossetos died in hospital after a short illness and her functions in the Rue des Écoles were taken over by a cleaning firm and an electric intercom system. In summer 1950, Robert also took leave of his parents and went to learn how to breed Charolais cattle at an agricultural college in Burgundy, and another two years later, when sixteen-year-old Muriel departed the Rue des Écoles to acquire a primary schoolteacher's diploma at a convent school near Chartres, Léon and Yvonne were left on their own with eleven-year-old Philippe, who was girlishly delicate.

Yvonne did not labour under her sudden solitude but accepted it as the natural course of events. All she wanted was sunshine and plenty of food and sleep.

For a few months in the mid-1950s she received visits from a Jehovah's Witness whose bloodthirsty tales of human depravity and retribution by a vengeful God amused her for a while. In winter 1958, when young Philippe went off to do his military service, she had a television set installed in the living room. Her favourite programmes were boxing matches and car racing.

One morning in May 1961, when running a flannel over her neck, she noticed a small, hard lump beneath her right ear. The lump grew bigger every day. Then another one developed beneath her left ear as well.

'They may go away by themselves,' she said when Léon wanted to call the doctor.

'Maybe, maybe not,' said Léon. 'But the doctor should definitely take a look at them.'

'No,' said Yvonne.

'Yes.'

'No.'

'They may be serious. You want to die of them?'

'Not necessarily,' said Yvonne. 'But if the Almighty wants me to go, I'll go.'

'The Almighty doesn't care whether you go or not, you silly thing. He's got plenty of other things on his plate.'

'There you are, then.'

'But *I* care, and I'm telling you they should be operated on.'

'Are you a doctor?'

'No, but I've got a pair of eyes in my head and a brain between my ears.'

'So have I,' said Yvonne. 'That's why I'm telling you to leave me alone. When I'm meant to go, I'll go.'

'Just like that?'

'Just like that.'

So the tumours in her neck continued to grow until they constricted her windpipe. After a few weeks came a night when her breathing was so bad she could hardly speak. She told Léon about her indiscretion with Raoul over thirty years earlier, and he took her in his arms and said it didn't matter any more. Then she fell asleep, or pretended to, and Léon fell asleep beside her.

⁂

On the first anniversary of Yvonne's funeral, Léon and Louise met at the Arsenal harbour at seven in the morning. It was a cool, fine day, and the sun had just risen above the buildings in the Boulevard de la Bastille. They were wearing their Sunday best although it was a Tuesday. A healthy, happy, good-looking couple, they were both sixty-two years old.

Louise had brought some bread, cheese and ham; Léon had come bearing bottled water, cider and red wine.

'You're sure the tub won't sink?' she asked.

'Positive,' he replied. 'I've scraped and repainted the hull every two years, the way Caron asked me to. The engine is in tip-top condition too.'

'Let's go, then. It's high time we did.'

They went aboard, stowed their supplies in the cabin, and started the engine. Then they cast off, put out into the Seine from the harbour basin, and headed downstream towards the sea.

THE END